the
Irish
Key

DAISY O'SHEA

the
Irish
Key

Bookouture

Published by Bookouture in 2024

An imprint of Storyfire Ltd.
Carmelite House
50 Victoria Embankment
London EC4Y 0DZ

www.bookouture.com

ISBN: 978-1-83525-078-5
eBook ISBN: 978-1-83525-077-8

1

GRACE

By the time we reach Holyhead, it's late in the afternoon. Three trains, countless miles we had no need to travel, and Olivia, though I love her with all my heart, is being more difficult than I expected, challenging my already fragile state of mind. She's bored but not interested in her toys; tired but won't sleep; hungry but won't eat the sandwiches I bought – not that I blame her. Sliced bread is a poor substitute for the crusty loaves fresh from the bakery in Cheltenham. I could have made sandwiches and brought a flask, but had been justifiably concerned about the amount I was carrying.

I'm exhausted but, thankfully, the eternal *'are we there yet?'* ceases as we arrive at the ferry terminal. The water is a swathe of grey, as is the sky in which seagulls are wheeling, screaming their endless cry of hunger. A faint breeze wafts a rejuvenating scent of salt towards us, lifting my flagging spirits.

'Are we going on that?' Olivia asks, looking at the ferry with interest.

'Yes, love. We're going to Ireland. That's where Great-Grandma comes from.'

And where Graham will never think of looking.

Graham has never shown much interest in my family's background, and for the first time, I'm grateful for that. When I was thinking of running, all sorts of unlikely options rattled around in my mind, including Australia – about as far away as we could get. And yet booking a ticket there would have left a trail for him to follow, and Ireland is right on our doorstep, unnoticed, almost invisible. How strange that I never considered it, until Grandma suggested it.

Olivia persists. 'But is that where the seaside is?'

'There are lots of seasides, everywhere. You know that – we've looked at the globe together.'

'Yes, but are we at the right seaside?'

'Not yet, love. We're going on the boat, and we'll stay in a hotel tonight, then we'll set off for the seaside in the morning.'

Her lips quiver. 'I'm tired. I want to go home.'

'I know you're tired, darling. I'm tired, too. But it will be lovely when we get there, won't it?'

'Will Daddy be there?'

'No, I told you, Daddy has to work. This is a holiday for just you and me.'

A holiday leading into a whole new life, I hope.

I sigh. I can't possibly explain this to Olivia, and just hope that my love for her will see us through what's going to be a traumatic awakening: that her father will no longer be part of our lives. But for now, I have to treat it as a holiday, while I gather my thoughts. Poor Olivia has never known anything except our big house, with her own bedroom filled with everything a loving mother – and her father's money but not attention – can provide. It's going to be a culture shock, for sure. But we will find a way through. We have to.

'I can ring him and let him know we got there safely,' she states.

'Okay. When we get to the hotel.'

I don't argue. It's a little lie for peace as I pay for two foot passengers on the *Leinster* to Dublin. We're directed almost immediately to the embarkation point, where I slump onto a wooden seat, shell-shocked with exhaustion. I'd worked out the timetable weeks ago, so that we'd be here pretty much on time, but with privatisation causing turmoil on the rail network, we'd missed a connection, and I'd almost broken down at that point, wondering why I ever thought I could do it. A British Rail ticket collector, who seemed to know absolutely everything, worked out a different route that would get us here on time, if we were lucky.

In hindsight, I realise how lucky we were.

In the passenger waiting area, I pull Olivia onto my lap and rock her, humming one of the little ditties she'd learned at school. She's bright-eyed and limp with tiredness. I brush back the fuzz of fair curls sticking to her forehead and whisper, 'Don't sleep yet, love. We're going on the boat now, and there's a bed on the boat for you.'

'I don't want to go on a boat. I want my own bed.'

'It's a holiday, love. We always sleep in different beds on holidays.'

'I don't want to.'

The whimper is punctuated by a wide yawn, and a few minutes later, thank goodness, the barrier across the foot-passenger gangplank is hauled back, and a man gestures for us to embark. I stand, but Olivia refuses to let go and be put down, clinging to me like a monkey. I'm wondering how on earth I'll manage to carry her, two cases and a rucksack, when a grizzled old gentleman in a tattered tweed jacket tips his hand to a flat cap and, with a thick Dublin accent, says, 'Girl, ye looks fair fraught, so ye do. Let an auld one give yous a lift?'

'I'm so sorry,' I say, utterly spaced out. 'Please leave it. It's too heavy. There's probably someone else...'

But everyone else is making their way onto the boat, passing by, eyes averted. Even the staff seem to be avoiding the problem.

I guess they don't get paid enough to care. But surely caring is something you do because you want to be kind?

'Sure, they're light as a feather,' he lies, heaving the cases and leading the way. 'I was over seeing my own family, you know? I've got five boys and two girls. Three boys in New York and two in Birmingham, and the girls safe at home with their weans. Seventeen grandchildren I have,' he gasps proudly, 'and two on the way.'

'That's wonderful,' I say, not really meaning it. I don't understand why it's perceived as an achievement for one man to father a whole tribe when the planet is so overpopulated. But the man is kind and is useful in more ways than one. He knows his way around the ferry and leads us straight to the cabins. Ours is cramped, with a salt-scoured window and two berths.

'Thank you so much,' I say to the old man, who is standing, head cocked, as if waiting for my story in return, 'but I think I'm going to have to lie-down with her.'

'Not a bother,' he responds, tipping his cap with two fingers. He backs out and closes the door behind him.

I slump onto the narrow bed with Olivia crooked into my body and hum a lullaby. She's asleep within minutes. I'm exhausted, too, mentally and physically. It takes me a while to settle, though. I'm almost surprised we got this far without Graham catching up with us. At every step along the way, I imagined him driving behind us, getting closer and closer. Perhaps he's even on the ferry, in the cabin next to us, watching for an opportunity to steal Olivia back. My breath quickens, and I make myself breathe slowly and evenly. I can't let my imagination override my determination. I'm not just saving myself; I'm saving my daughter, too.

I'm awakened by a klaxon belling through the tannoy system, warning us we're about to berth. I must have slept for the full four-hour crossing.

There's no time for washing, but I make sure Olivia does

her teeth, and I brush her hair. She's subdued, confused and glares at me with impotent accusation, having realised that this is no normal holiday. Graham organises everything with clockwork precision: trains arrive on time, providing first-class accommodation, and we're chauffeur-driven to hotels where porters carry our bags and there are real beds to sleep in.

I'll find a hotel for the night, because there's another hard day of travelling ahead of us. But everything will be fine when we get to the cottage. It'll be basic, Grandma had warned me. I'll actually have to draw water from the well! But if several generations of Grandpa's family managed to survive there, so will we. When I open the cabin door, I'm surprised to see my saviour of a few hours ago, waiting outside.

'Patrick, at your service, ma'am,' he says, with a flourish of his cap. 'Jest thought I'd give yous a hand with the bags.' He bends to address Olivia. 'And how's the pretty colleen? Better for a sleep, no doubt?'

'I'm not Colleen,' she states. 'I'm Olivia Adams, and my father is going to come and get me soon.'

I'm slightly shocked by her statement, which tells the whole story in a sentence. 'She's tired,' I counter. 'We're going to stay in my great-grandpa's cottage, for a holiday.'

I don't mention that Great-Grandpa won't be there, and I don't mention that I'm more than a little worried about how we'll be received. Though I'm Irish by descent, I don't sound like it. It bothers me that people can be hated for something they didn't have any say over, such as their accent, where they were born or who their parents are, but Olivia's present tone won't endear us to anyone at all.

He doesn't seem to take offence, though, and hefts the bags, despite my protest.

As we come out into the fresh air, I instantly feel that I'm in a foreign land. I glance around at the cranes, the warehouses and beyond, on a small rise, the rows of terraced houses and wonder why I feel this way, when the landscape is not so dissimilar to where I grew up, in Birmingham.

'Have you any idea where we'll find a taxi?' I ask.

He indicates with his chin and begins to walk. 'Where will yous be heading?'

'A hotel for tonight,' I said. 'We need to rest up while I find a way to get down south. We've never been to Ireland, so I haven't a clue.'

'Good hotel?' he asks with a crooked grin, probably having seen the Harrods logo on the cases.

'Not the Ritz,' I said dryly, 'but better than a boarding house.'

'The Gresham then.'

'Isn't that expensive?'

'They have basic rooms, too, and it's right in the centre. Ideal for yous, I'm after thinking. But look,' he adds. 'It's a few miles into the city. We can give yous a ride. Ye don't need a taxi.'

He puts the cases down and waves at someone in the distance. A young man, lean and fit, walks up to us, a smile of greeting on his face. He dumps a hand on Patrick's shoulder, casting a curious glance at myself and Olivia. 'How's yerself, Grandpa? All well over the water?'

'Good, good, good,' Patrick responds in a machine-gun spatter. 'This lass and the wean need a lift into the city.'

'I'm Grace,' I say, holding out my hand. 'And my daughter, Olivia.'

He squeezes my hand briefly and gives us a charming smile. 'Sure, grand. Follow me. The car's over the way.' He lifts the bags as though they weigh nothing and heads towards the car. I grab Olivia's hand and follow, bemused by the ease of this unexpected assistance.

As we walk, the old man provides a running commentary for his grandson on his family in England. They're all grand, so they are. Doing well. The men have jobs in the steelworks, but there are rumblings of closure; but, sure, won't God provide? The women are kept busy, sure they are, with the weans clamouring for food like a pack of puppies.

The young man stops at what used to be a Cortina. The word 'car' doesn't describe the remnants of the vehicle. It's a wreck on wheels, and I'm stunned it's on the road at all. Its orange paint blends down into rust and peters into holes through which the chassis is visible. The bonnet is tied down with baler twine, and the back windscreen is a spider's web of cracks, as though it had been hit with a brick. Maybe it had.

I don't know whether to laugh or refuse the lift, but out of politeness do neither. My cases are stowed in the boot, which is closed with a hefty slam as it doesn't seat well. My old saviour offers me the front seat, but I reach for the back door. 'I'd better sit with Olivia.' She wouldn't want to sit next to a stranger, kind or otherwise.

I try to open the door, but it's jammed. The grandson reaches past me and gives it a heave. It opens with a complaining squeal, and he gestures for us to enter, as though it's a grand carriage, adding, 'Mind the floor, why don't ye? It's a bit ropey.'

He gives the door a mighty slam behind us, making us wince. I grin at Olivia, and thankfully, she grins back. It's an adventure, after all.

'Daddy's got a Rolls-Royce,' she states as we pull smoothly away, the engine apparently in better condition than the rest of the car.

I want to shrink into the upholstery with embarrassment.

'Oh, has he, indeed?' Patrick responds, glancing over his shoulder. I hear the smile in his voice, though I can't see it.

'Yes, and it's silver, like the princess's dress. Sometimes he goes to work in it, and I go in it, too. But not often, 'cause Mummy drives me to school in the blue Volkswagen because it's a safe car.'

'And how old are ye, Olivia?'

He's remembered her name somehow.

'Six and three-quarters.'

'Six and three-quarters is a very fine age, to be sure.'

'And when I'm seven, I'm going to a big school, after the holidays.'

'Well, now. That will be exciting, eh? And what are you going to be when you grow up?'

'I don't know yet,' Olivia answers seriously. 'I like drawing. But maybe I'll work in Daddy's firm. Arthur is going to work there, only he doesn't want to. He wants to be a deep-sea diver.'

Deep-sea diver? Poor Arthur. I suspect that was a wildly inventive wish; anything but become his father's understudy in the world of commerce.

'Arthur?' Patrick queries, looking over his shoulder.

'My big brother,' Olivia says.

'By my husband's first marriage,' I feel obliged to inform them. 'He's a lot older than Olivia. He's just finished university.'

'Ah.' There's a wealth of understanding in the word. 'Did she die, Arthur's mother?'

'Yes, but, well, they'd been divorced for a while.'

I belatedly recall that divorce is illegal in Ireland.

The road into Dublin is quiet compared with what I'm used to, and several cars going in the opposite direction seem to be in much the same state as the one we're in. A couple of tractors, old and tattered, pass in the opposite direction, too, and there's even a donkey cart which I point out to Olivia, who stares in amazement. She's seen horses, of course, when Graham took us to the races in Cheltenham, but nothing like this.

We cross a bridge and are suddenly within the city environment, with its tall nineteenth-century buildings and rows of shops. The Gresham Hotel is a huge block of a building with what seems like a thousand windows. We pull in to the kerb, and Patrick's young driver gets out and heaves my bags from the boot. He insists on carrying them inside for us.

I lean down and thank Patrick for his kindness.

'Ah, not a bother, not a bother,' he mutters, as if doing someone a favour is simply part of life.

'It meant a lot to me,' I respond, and his dark, wrinkled skin seems to grow a shade darker. I don't want to embarrass him further, so I leave it there. I try to offer the young man money for the petrol, but he shrugs it aside with a grin. 'Glad to help. Sure, it wasn't out of my way at all. Have a good stay in Dublin, won't ye?'

And here we are, in Ireland.

I don't feel complacent, but the wide stretch of water between myself and Graham provides hope that the hounds chasing us will have lost the scent.

2

GRACE

The evening at the hotel in Dublin is a trial. Weary from travelling and confused, Olivia doesn't sleep when she needs to and has slept when she shouldn't, so dinner is an expensive disaster. Exhaustion has overtaken us both. It's a long evening as I try to settle her by reading several Beatrix Potter stories from the omnibus I didn't realise she'd packed. No wonder her bag was heavy. She doesn't settle, and finally, in desperation, I switch the television on. Not caring much about what we're watching, we drift through a sitcom I've never heard of and never want to see again. Olivia is drooping, so I doubt she'll remember any of it. I certainly won't.

When she eventually falls asleep, I collapse suddenly and explosively into silent sobs that well up from somewhere deep inside. I'm exhausted, not just by today but by several years of burying myself beneath the burden of a life I began to loathe. I really don't know if my tears are those of happiness because I've broken free of my disastrous marriage, or those of fear that Graham is hot on my heels, and that I haven't broken out from under his controlling influence, after all.

I think I cried myself out, as I wake in the morning filled

with new determination. By hook or by crook, we are going to forge a new life for ourselves. I know what I'm doing, but my poor daughter has been lifted from her safe home environment into an adventure that must seem more like a nightmare. One day she'll understand that I've done this for her.

I sign out of the hotel, pay with cash and take a taxi to the train station. I told Patrick that I wanted to look around Dublin, but now isn't a good time. Maybe when we're settled, and Olivia has come to terms with our new situation, we can come up for a weekend. Now, all I want to do is find my new home and settle in.

The trains here are as ragged as the ones at home. But I must stop calling England home; this is home now. We're lucky, as the train to Cork is only half an hour late and is half empty, so the four-hour journey isn't the trial I expected.

Olivia is passive but obviously confused. She's in foreign territory in more ways than one. She knows where Ireland is on the globe, because I showed her where her great-grandparents came from, so long ago it's ancient history to her. But actually being here, without Graham's authoritative presence, is probably more frightening to her than liberating. She's accepted that Daddy isn't coming to rescue her, not at this moment anyway, so she needs to stick to me even though I'm presently the bad witch in the story. She has no idea that this move has no end date, and I hope she doesn't start to hate me for it. One day I'll explain that it's *me* rescuing her from *him*. She has no idea what Graham had in store for her, and even in this day and age, the authority of a rich businessman would have overridden the objections of his token wife.

I didn't want to rip her from her home and her father, but the truth is, I'm afraid. Not just for her but for myself. Graham would have manipulated Olivia to suit his purpose, but me? If I don't behave as the dutiful and obedient wife, which is my role in his world, what would he do? I don't know, which is why my peace of mind rests with the fragile uncertainty of remaining undiscovered. He doesn't like his will crossed and won't tolerate being made a fool of. The first wife absconding had been embarrassing, but the second following suit definitely wouldn't fit his schedule.

We steam past rolling swathes of green fields, speckled with little rocky outcrops, but it's subtly different from England. The hedges are barren of trees, and the land is polka-dotted with isolated houses. At one point there are a few hazy mountains in the distance, hinting of something bigger and wilder than England's Lake District. We pass through a few towns, but the journey is mostly endless green. Not the forty shades, as suggested in the song, but the relentless sameness of a green desert.

It's mid-afternoon when we get to Cork, and although I was hoping we could carry on down into the west, I decide to stop over. I can't imagine trying to find the cottage in the encroaching evening; besides which, we'll need to buy bedding and other necessities. The cottage has been vacant for a long while, so it's certainly going to need a good clean, if nothing else. I'm desperately hoping it hasn't been occupied by squatters.

I find a taxi and ask for lodgings near enough to the bus station that we can walk there in the morning. We end up in yet another big, old hotel, and I pay a small fortune for the privilege of a night in a somewhat seedy bedroom. It's either that or get cheaper lodgings, further away, and have to pay another taxi to get us to the bus station, so we make do.

Tomorrow, I think, we'll be there, finally, in Roone Bay, so I can stop throwing money away. Despite my years with Graham, when money was there for the taking, I wasn't brought up to be extravagant. It's surprising how little you can live on if you do your own cooking and don't go trawling the shops from boredom, looking for things to buy.

That thought makes me smile, reminding me of a song Dad used to chant, when terminal illness and a hacking cough had deprived him of his job and his singing voice: *Busy doing nothing, working the whole day through, trying to find lots of things not to do...*

The next morning, as we approach the bus station, Olivia throws the mother of all tantrums. 'I want to go home,' she sobs in rising hysteria. 'I want my bedroom! I want my daddy!'

'We're nearly there,' I croon, trying to rock this child who has turned into a curve of steel anger. 'Come on, love. Just one more bus and we'll be there, in Grandpa's lovely old cottage. It's got a garden, and we can walk from there to the seaside once we've had a little rest.'

'I don't want Grandpa's cottage! I don't want to go to the seaside! *I want to GO HOME!*'

We're standing just outside the bus station. It's within reach but might as well be a million miles away. I can see the bus we're supposed to catch. I've dropped the cases, and I'm holding on to Olivia as she tries to pull away from me with relentless and mindless fury. Right in the centre of the city, the traffic is a constant stream, and if I let go now, she might run... my mind suggests indescribable scenarios.

Olivia's face is red with rage, smeared with snot. Tears are running down my own face, and I don't know what to do. I truly don't. I've never seen her lose control in this way before. She can be difficult – can't all children? But this is beyond me. I imagine everyone watching, wondering if I've kidnapped this child. Well, I suppose, in a way, I have.

I'm wishing I'd been brave enough to blow some of my cash on a car, but I thought we could manage without one, and I was too afraid of Graham finding us. I'd imagined us travelling in harmony, looking out over mystical Ireland together as we discussed our idyllic new life. And here I am, overwhelmed, at my wits' end, dazed by my inability to cope.

'Which bus are yous catching?' a voice asks, startling me. I focus on the man beside us – a bus driver, by his uniform. Far from expectation, his lips aren't curled in sarcasm; his face is creased with sympathy. 'The wean is overtired, so. Let's get you onto a bus, and mebiz she'll sleep a wee while, give you a break, eh?'

'Skibbereen,' I manage to sniffle as he picks up my bags. 'I need to go to the ticket office and pay.'

'Not a bother. You can pay the driver when you get there.'

I follow him to where three buses are lined up, ready to roll. Olivia has run out of steam and is now gasping and hiccupping her distress. I swipe the back of my hand across my own face. We must look a right pair. Tumbled and scruffy from two days of travelling, with matching tear-streaked cheeks.

The driver leads us to the bus and chats with my driver as they load the cases. The driver indicates for me to get on first. I feel guilty, jumping the queue, but no one complains. There's empathy in the gazes that graze mine – and a quiet acceptance that the driver had simply made the only decision he could in the circumstances.

Finally, we're on the bus. I haul Olivia onto my lap and hug her. 'I love you, darling,' I whisper. 'I'm doing this for both of us. You'll understand – one day.'

A few minutes later, after everyone else has climbed on and baggage has been stowed, the driver comes up the aisle and offers me a carrier bag.

'Lunch,' he says. 'I reckon you didn't manage to get something for the journey, eh? Hard to cope with a little one on your own? There's a packet of sweets in there, for the wean.' He winks. 'Sometimes you just need the right medicine.'

'Thank you,' I manage to say. Tears cloud my vision at this kindness, and I blink them back as I reach for my purse. 'Yes, I was going to get something, but, well, you know... What do I owe you?'

He pats my arm. 'No bother. Have a nice stay in Ireland.'

Stunned, I smile through my tears. 'I think I will, after all.'

How I'd misled myself, assuming the journey would be easy by public transport. Nothing about it was easy, at any stage, and I have been grateful, more than once, for the kindness of strangers.

3

GRACE

Squeezing Olivia's hand as the bus disappears up the road, I have the desperate urge to run after it and ask 'is he going back to Cork?'

Panic chokes me.

I've changed my mind. I don't want to be in this tiny backwater town in a foreign land. I want to be back in Cheltenham, in my nice warm house, where I can just turn on the television and disappear into myself and survive another day. Cold rushes through my head. *I'm so alone.* But if I go back now, Graham will make sure I never have the opportunity to leave again. Not with Olivia, at least. For a second, I think I'm going to pass out. But I can't, not here, out in the street, where people can see. And not in front of my daughter.

The trouble is, Olivia adores her father. She's too young to realise how manipulative he is, that his plans for her will override any plans she might want to make for her own future, as he has with Arthur. If Graham gets his hands on her now, I might never see her again. Is it more selfish to deprive a child of a mother or a father? As a mother, though, do I really have a choice?

Deep-seated unhappiness isn't just a temporary state of mind, Grace, my doctor had said. *It's a mental illness that leads to depression and suicidal thoughts. You really should get therapy before it gets that far.*

He didn't realise I was already there. When the thought of simply closing my eyes and not having to cope any longer became a driving need, it scared me. When I began to think that dying was an option I should explore, I knew I had to do something.

Olivia tugs at my hand. 'Mummy?'

Her face is still blotched from the morning's tantrum. She's staring at me, wondering why I'm standing there, not doing anything. But I'm numb, overwhelmed. I want to be a child again, to throw off this mantle of responsibility and have someone tell me what to do.

I force myself to slow my breathing. I take stock of my surroundings, ground myself. I'm standing on a pavement, our baggage by my feet. I need to act. We're in a small town called Skibbereen, in the south of Ireland, and seem to have been dropped, randomly, in a narrow street of shops where there's no bus stop or timetable. I have to find someone to ask. 'Yes,' I state, straining to sound positive and in control. 'Right. Let's find someone. We're nearly there, I promise.'

I'd been promising the same thing for two days now, but this time it's the truth. Maybe there's a hotel here where we can just rest. It's tempting, but we're so close. I want to land, finally, at our destination, which, as far as I know, is only ten miles or so away. I have a fragile hold on that need. Like needing a cup of tea and finding comfort in it for no logical reason at all.

I reach for our luggage and heave myself upright. It seems to have inexplicably gathered weight on the journey. 'Hold the strap,' I instruct, but Olivia's already doing it, used to the drill.

I'd considered buying new suitcases, with wheels, but I was afraid of Graham finding them. He didn't see the need for wheels, because there was always someone, at the click of his fingers – a taxi driver, a concierge – to perform the manual task of humping our stuff around.

Graham had bought this set of matching suitcases for our honeymoon in Venice, and I'd been so proud of them. Matching luggage! Transported into our hotel on a gilded trolley! I'd been so thrilled then, floating on air, living the dream. We were treated like royalty – and treated ourselves the same way. Anything we wanted was ours for the taking. The honeymoon suite, dinners beneath chandeliers, lunches in the sunshine beside the canals, and the leisurely drift on a gondola between the towering homes of a doomed city that still reeked of historic and bloody vendettas.

The decadence of it all was euphoric.

What a culture shock for a working-class girl! I really thought I'd landed on my feet. Everyone else thought so, too. I'm embarrassed to recall that even their jealousy was mildly enjoyable. And even now, several years later, when the honeymoon period has long dissolved into the reality of marriage to a man who controls every aspect of my life, they'd think me foolish for running. I mean, who would leave all that wealth? And to leave Graham, the Mr Darcy of Cheltenham; was I mad?

The shopfronts in Skibbereen are old-fashioned, with carved wooden frames and glass that distorts my reflection. A bell tinkles as we enter a small shop, which sells, alongside milk and groceries, a peculiar selection of other goods: vests, buttons, sewing thread and coal scuttles. A vast, old till hunkers on a worn wooden counter, behind which home-made shelves rise to the low ceiling. It's like going back to my childhood, when Mum, with her bulging shopping bags, would traipse from shop to shop, me trailing her as Olivia now trails me. I dump the cases, and one falls over. I'm too tired to stand it up again.

The woman behind the counter is hefty, unsmiling, a white

pinafore wrapped around her middle like a sheet, her greying hair pulled back into a tight bun at the nape of her neck. If she's curious about who we are, she doesn't show it. Meekly, I ask for a couple of rolls, some cheese and a bottle of milk to keep us going. I have enough to carry, and there will surely be shops in Roone Bay.

'And will that be all?' she asks, placing them on the counter, ringing the amount into the till.

Olivia's eyes widen as the figures ping up in the glass display and the cash drawer crashes out with a thud and a rattle that shakes the counter. I hand over a note and receive unfamiliar coinage in return.

'And, can you tell me, is there a bus to Roone Bay?' I ask diffidently. 'I can't seem to find a timetable anywhere.'

'Monday, today and Friday. Sure, you've missed it for today.'

My heart sinks. I don't want to wait here through Thursday – another day wasted – and pay for two more nights in a hotel when we're so close. 'Oh. Is there a taxi, perhaps?'

'You might be wanting to stay here. The West Cork Hotel is just around the corner. Litten's, in Roone Bay, is after closing for the winter and won't be open yet for a couple of months. The tourists don't usually arrive until July.'

She looks at me as though I'm one of them, but I'm too tired to explain. She stares for a moment, no doubt taking in my dishevelled appearance and shell-shocked silence, because she says, finally, 'Wait here. Sean just delivered my honey, and he's after having a sup in the bar before going home. I'll tell him to give you a lift over.'

I wonder whether Sean, whoever he is, will mind being given orders to provide transport to an absolute stranger; but maybe having a six-year-old child, out on her feet with exhaustion, will tip the scales. I'm too frazzled to argue.

She walks briskly out, leaving the shop unattended save for

the two of us. Anyone could walk in, I think, empty the cash register and walk out again in the time she's gone.

She's away so long I wonder if there's some kind of disagreement going on. I'm half temped to leave but feel obliged to keep an eye on the shop.

Eventually, she returns, followed by a sturdy young man, possibly in his early thirties, who could be a builder, by the state of his clothes. He's wearing a ripped jumper over a checked shirt, and jeans so well washed they've bleached to a pale grey. He has a home-knitted bobble hat pulled down to his eyebrows – knitted by his wife, I guess. But the eyes under the garish wool are grey and intelligent, and I realise he's assessing me with equal, and warm, interest.

He smells heavily of drink, and I wonder whether this is a good idea. 'I don't want to put you out,' I begin hesitantly, but he overrides my objection with quick understanding.

'No bother – I just had the one. I'm quite safe on the road, and the old jalopy doesn't do more than thirty. I was just leaving, anyway. Where are you heading?'

'My grandpa's cottage, in Roone Bay. He was Connor McCarthy.'

'The McCarthy place? Past the mill? At Goosheen?' He raises his eyebrows. 'I know the one. It needs a bit of doing up, I'd say, if you're going to live there.'

I nod, relieved. 'I thought as much, but we can make do.'

He considers me for a bit, then says, 'Well, you'd best see it for yourself before you decide.'

Decide what?

He hefts our two suitcases and walks out. There's little I can do other than utter a hasty thanks to the matronly woman who'd hoisted him out of the bar for me and follow, clutching the carrier bag with our food.

Sean leads us down the road, behind the shops, over a humped bridge, to a pickup truck parked by the side of a small stream. The truck – Ford, it says on the robust bonnet – is years old. The side is emblazoned with MacDarragh's Honey, Roone Bay. He throws our expensive bags into the open back, where they nestle into a bed of straw, then wrestles with the passenger door and hoists Olivia up into the middle of the cab. I heave myself up after her, and he slams the door hard behind us. I'm worried that he's been drinking, but he seems steady enough as he climbs in behind the wheel. I pull Olivia close as he presses a button and the engine roars loudly into life.

He casts a quick grin. 'Sorry about the ride. I was helping MacDarragh out, and it was easier to use his truck than unload mine. Besides which, honey has a habit of being sticky.'

His smile is infectious, and I find myself smiling back. It's probably the first time I've smiled at an inconsequential comment in months, and I relax a little.

We head west alongside a wide, shallow river on our left. It must be tidal, because there are broad swathes of mud either side of the water, well below the bank's overhang. In the centre of the river, small islands squat, proudly capped with grass crew cuts.

'Look – swans,' Olivia says, leaning over me and pointing.

I'm pleased she's behaving more like herself. Perhaps because she knows we really are on the last leg of the journey. I try to be enthusiastic. 'And ducks, and, oh look! A heron!'

The bird is stalking serenely along the water's edge, gazing almost absently into the speckled surface in a continuous search for food.

I find the river calming, but all too soon it and the road part ways; the river meandering towards the sea, the road climbing upwards between tiny fields, the neglected hedgerows of overgrown hawthorn sprinkled with a snow-storm of spring blossom. As we rise away from the river valley, in the distance I catch the hazy hint of layers of mountains, overshadowing each other. The land around us quickly becomes scrubby, springing with rocky outcrops to which rafts of yellow gorse cling. It's beautiful, in a wild and unmanageable way. I can't imagine how farmers make a living on this marginal land.

We pass a multitude of turnings leading to places with unfamiliar names: Aghadown, Skeaghanore, Ardralla, Morahan and even more outlandishly spelled names, the pronunciation of which I can only guess at.

'So, where have you come from?' Sean shouts over the engine noise. He's been silent so far, perhaps because of the engine noise, but perhaps out of consideration for me, understanding that I feel a little awkward, out of place.

'Cheltenham,' I say. There's no point lying – Olivia would only correct me. 'Have you been to England?'

'Nope. Never had a mind to.'

'So, you've lived here all your life?'

'Pretty much. I might visit the continent one of these days. Have you ever been over the water?'

'I've been to Italy. To Venice.'

He gives a low whistle. 'That must have been stunning.'

'It was,' I admit. 'We stayed at the Gritti Palace and did a tour of St Mark's Basilica. It was surreal. A once-in-a-lifetime event,' I add, seeing the surprise on his face. Even I don't know how much that honeymoon cost.

We pass a few isolated, grey farmsteads before he says, 'So, what brings you here, then? It's, like, the sublime to the ridiculous, isn't it?'

'Different universes, anyway,' I agree. 'My grandparents came from here. All four of them from Cork.'

He takes his eyes off the road for longer than I'm comfortable with and assesses me. 'Ah, so you're almost Irish, so. Coming to find your roots, eh?'

I laugh and nod. And somehow that thought settles in my mind. Maybe I am, after all.

'Not so far now,' he adds. 'Are you intending to stay in Ireland?'

'I don't know,' I say honestly, shooting a look at Olivia that, surprisingly, Sean seems to understand. There are so many things that might happen, actually settling out here for good is beginning to seem like an impossibility. I mean, I'm used to city life, with all its noise and bustle. Here, I could be on another continent, not just over the Irish Sea. I hadn't expected it all to seem so different and foreign.

We go over a rise, and there, as we tip over the summit, I gasp at the beauty before us, as Roaring Water Bay and the wider region of Carbery's Hundred Isles is revealed like an open map; the sparkling blue sea dotted with distant islands, contained within a protective circle of black, rocky shores. The few moored yachts scarcely move in the still water, and beyond that, more land. Is it an island or a spit of land wrapping around the bay? I knew, from reading, that the small bay here is sheltered, but I hadn't expected it to be quite so serene. No wonder Grandma looks back on this place with a touch of nostalgia, after moving to Birmingham. Suddenly, living here doesn't seem such a nightmare.

Then we descend, and the vista is gone.

Sean points to a sign for Roone Bay. 'You know what that means?'

'I didn't know it would mean anything. Isn't it just a name?'

'It means the bay of the red-haired boy.'

'They named the town after a boy?'

'Why not? I expect there's some fairy legend attached to it. My mother could tell you. I think it's kind of nice, though.'

He casts me a grin, which I faintly echo.

I'm exhausted, but he lifts my mood slightly. He really is attractive, in a wholesome, earthy kind of way, but I came here to escape, not get entangled in another relationship. Any parent will tell you, things are different when you have a child, because the child is part of that relationship, too. I didn't understand that until I had a child of my own.

As if he's read my mind, Sean nudges Olivia with his elbow and winks at her. 'And what do you think of Ireland?'

'I want to go home,' Olivia states, gazing out of the window, lost in her thoughts.

I exchange a smile with Sean. Not wanting the conversation to end, I ask, 'Do you speak Irish?'

He shakes his head. 'There aren't many left who have the Irish,' he says. 'But, sure, you don't need to be fluent to understand the things that matter.'

'That's sad.'

'It is. It was beaten out of us, but it's making a revival with some. It's being taught in schools again.'

'Perhaps I should try to learn it.'

Sean chuckles. 'You'd win a few brownie points. There are few enough who try, even those who have roots here.'

I hesitate to suggest that I have roots.

He adds, 'All the Americans who come looking for the past have rosy blinkers on, of course. They kind of forget the reason their forebears left is because it was a hard, cruel life.'

'That's rather cynical!'

'No, just realistic.' Sean catches my gaze over Olivia's head and grimaces. 'There's not a lot of romance in being hungry. I'm glad I wasn't around in those days. As a builder, I can make a good living now. People coming over from England and Germany, or wherever, mostly don't want the old cottages; they want new-builds with insulation and central heating. You might consider that yourself.'

There's an undertone to his words, but I don't get it until a few moments later. He slows down and turns left onto a rutted, unclassifiable lane, metalled in two thin strips either side of a ribbon of coarse grass.

'The town's on up there,' he says, pointing to the road we've just left, 'but the McCarthy place is here, down the butter road.'

The lane weaves between some dramatic outcrops then slips into a valley where a strange building is perched on a rocky lump. Presumably there's a waterway, because there's a water wheel hanging incongruously on the side. We swerve around a maze of small roads and up another hill. Here, Sean pulls in and wrenches on the handbrake alongside a grey, derelict building, which squats amidst a riot of weeds, sad and abandoned. I stare in disbelief then cast him a startled glance. 'This is Grandpa's house?'

'Yep, that's the McCarthy place.'

My heart drops. This is the cottage I'd been imagining us living in? I slip down and lift Olivia out. We're both exhausted beyond words, because it's taken two long, stressful days to get here, and I feel my resilience drain out of me. I must be all cried out, because the blanketing calm of shock settles on my shoulders.

Grandpa had just one tiny, treasured, black-and-white photograph of him with his father and brother, standing outside the cottage. I didn't even know Grandma had inherited the cottage until she offered it to me. *What with your circumstances*, she'd said, *and no one living in it, sure, it will be perfect.* I remember thinking, with a kind of wonder, that I would have a home of my own. Something that wasn't Graham's.

So, there you go, love, she'd said. *Start afresh. It'll be basic, of course, after what you've been used to these last few years.*

I had laughed through my tears, saying, *Oh, Gran, you're a treasure! Basic I can cope with. And if it needs a bit of TLC, it'll give me something to put my energies into, won't it? But what about you and Mum? Graham will come looking for us.*

Let him, she'd said grimly. *He'll get nothing from us.*

I recalled, then, the big, iron key she'd given me on my wedding day and finally realised what it was for. She'd known,

all along, that I'd one day want to run. I'd imagined putting it in
the lock, turning it and entering my own home.

Only there's no lock. There isn't even a door. I take the
photo out of my bag and compare it with what I'm looking at.
It's the right place, though it's hard to reconcile this with my
dreams and expectations.

It's the house all children draw. A window either side of the
front door, three above. The cottage faces the lane, set several
yards behind a low stone wall and has, apparently, a bit of land
behind it. There's a path leading directly down to the rocky
shore where Grandma used to collect mussels.

It had sounded idyllic. This is certainly the cottage, but
time and neglect have worn it to its bare bones. Ivy leaves have
gathered in a pile beside the front door, which is lying on its
side on the exposed stone floor. In the tiny entrance hallway, a
wind-scoured wooden staircase rises.

There's still glass in the upper windows, seated precariously
in rotted frames. There's a roof, but the slates are swollen with
age, disintegrating into layers that are being washed away,
judging by the dark stain around the house, and there's a
distinct hole in the middle of the front slope. A thick ivy stem
has clawed up the right wall and curled around the chimney, as
if seeking warmth. As I watch, a couple of jackdaws fly over,
argue hoarsely and disappear into the chimney pot.

'Is this Great-Grandpa's house?' Olivia asks in a small voice.
The incredulity on her face echoes my thoughts. 'Is this where
we're going to stay for our holiday?'

'I don't think we can stay here, love,' I admit, defeated at the
last hurdle. 'Let's just look inside – see what needs doing.'

I nearly laugh at my own words. What doesn't need doing?
It starts to rain, adding to our misery. Sean reaches into the back
of the truck and hauls a canvas sheet over our luggage.

We enter through the open doorway, my curiosity sand-
wiched between utter incredulity and despair. The larger room

has a big fireplace filled with a rusted range. There's a sink nestled into a home-made wooden cupboard. A couple of wooden chairs, once painted green, lie on the floor, amongst the debris of damp, rotting leaves. As I nudge one with my foot, a leg drops to the floor. I want to do the same – collapse in a confused heap. And if Olivia and Sean weren't with me, I might have done just that, but it was Gran who instilled in me the need to remain strong and impassive in the face of adversity: *If you need to cry, do it when no one's looking. Don't let people know when you're vulnerable.* So I take a deep breath and carry on.

The smaller room, with a rusted cast-iron fireplace and mantle set into the end wall, is devoid of furniture. Back in the entrance hall, I test the bottom stair with my weight. It seems to hold. There's a small landing at the top, where the stairs divide; two up to the right, into an empty bedroom, two left to a narrow landing, with one tiny bedroom above the front door and another above the main room. In this there's an ancient iron bedstead with a chain-link base. I feel a laugh bubbling up. 'All we need is a mattress, then we'll be fine,' I mutter then laugh dryly at my own joke.

Ivy has crept in through the open sash window, both sections of which have dropped to sill level, the remnants of its feathered cord still hanging. Daylight peeping through a hole in the roof exposes a circle of rotting floorboards. I suspect the floor is like blotting paper.

'Careful now,' Sean warns, his soft voice deepening with concern.

I glance behind and am surprised to see that Olivia has allowed him to grasp her hand. After all the warnings we gave her about being wary of strange men, she must instinctively know he's one of the good ones. As do I.

The small, middle bedroom seems solid underfoot. We walk to the window. Grandma's right about the view. Through the gloom, I can make out an expanse of wrinkled water. A low island with a lighthouse cuts into the horizon, and beyond that, I presume, lies the Atlantic Ocean. It's atmospheric, exactly as I'd romantically imagined it, portrayed through her nostalgic memories. It would be stunning in sunlight.

I know Grandma still sees it in her mind's eye as it had been when she was a child, but why had I supposed it would be anything but derelict? I'd imagined it exactly as she recalled it, because that was what I'd needed it to be. A bolthole, some- where we could just live, get by for a bit while I got my act together, while Graham got used to the fact that I'd left him. Even Mum had assumed it would be sitting here, empty, just waiting for a good spring clean.

The house, battered on a regular basis for over 150 years by squalls belting in off the Atlantic, isn't in need of renovation. It's in the process of sinking back into nature. I'm not even sure it's recoverable.

'The seaside is down there,' I tell Olivia, inconsequentially, as we both stare. It's a rocky shore, not the wide expanse of sand that Olivia had probably envisaged.

A wave of guilt washes over me. I shouldn't have brought her here.

But even as I'm agonising, I recall my own despair, much too deeply engrained to be called unhappiness. It's amazing I got through each day, like an automaton, smiling and talking on command, while my inner self was curled up, dying, in a fairy tale turned sour. I'd also had the growing feeling that Graham was looking at me strangely, as if wondering why he'd married me. He said he loves me, but I'm sure what we had wasn't love but a convenient tolerance. And my previous starry admiration now leaned more towards fear. If I try to divorce him legally, I don't know how he'll react, because I'd be awarded a portion of *his* wealth and custody of *his* child. But if I died, he could hang on to both. He's a cold man, businesslike in his dealings even with his family, and possessive. But murder? Would he? No, I told myself. Yes, I argued.

How lucky I was, people thought. How jealous they were of my clothes, my house, my lifestyle, while behind that facade I was like a child crying for my lost life: poor but surrounded by a strong working-class community spirit.

And here I am, in Ireland, the home of my kin, a stranger, without even a house to live in. Had I known what waited for me here, would I still have left?

'You'll be needing somewhere to stay then,' Sean says, a smile in his voice.

It's not a question. He knew I'd expected to stay here. I nod, unable to tackle the looming problem of the future. If we can't live here, rent-free, then what? Would it even be possible to find a job down here, at the back end of nowhere? I'm not destitute; in fact, I've got a tidy sum in the bank, but it's a finite amount, and already I've been shocked by how easily it slithered from the account over our two travelling days, what with public transport, the ferry, the hotels.

Despite the culture shock of our arrival, the sound and scent of the sea, the hungry call of a seagull, even the wild and isolated nature of the house, all lend fuel to my determination. I don't know what I'm going to do, but I refuse to turn tail and run home. I might not succeed here, but I'm damn well going to try. This tiny, tumbledown cottage speaks to me; of Grandpa's childhood, and the friends he and Grandma left behind. Despite her tales of tribulation and troubled history, I had the feeling she'd been happy.

I suddenly realise that I can't see Olivia. I panic and shout her name.

'It's okay – she's just gone around the back,' Sean says.

We find her in what had once been a garden, at the back of the house, bashing at gorse with a stick, heedless of the rain plastering her hair to her face. I should reprimand her for being destructive, but she's out in the fresh air, enjoying a freedom she's never known.

Hearing me, she stops, swivels guiltily and slips over on the wet grass. I freeze for a moment, expecting tears, but she just gets to her feet and looks down at her dirty hands and smears them on her slacks.

Something bursts inside me. I giggle then break out into a manic laugh. 'You're a right mess,' I say. 'We both need a good bath and brush-up, eh?'

After a confused moment, she laughs with me.

Did I teach her to be afraid of a bit of dirt? Was that my fault? Mum always said dirt was healthy. And Grandma, with her endless supply of proverbs, would say: *You have to eat a peck of dirt in your day*. It's only now I wonder how big a peck is.

Sean heaves a fallen branch away from the path. I envy him his easy strength, which is attractive in a healthy, rustic kind of way. Around his eyes, sun-darkened skin is already beginning to crinkle with crow's feet, as if he spends his time out of doors, squinting against the elements.

He gives a sympathetic smile. 'Let's see if we can find you somewhere to stay, eh? Things won't seem so bad when you've a drop of tea inside you.'

4

GRACE

In the truck again, Sean takes off his bobble hat and wipes his face with it. He points his thumb back to the ruin and grimaces. 'It's been a while empty. Since before my time. I'm sorry you had to come all the way here to find it like this. It must be a shock.'

I'm staring at the rain trickling down the window. Beyond it, the sea is gloomy. 'If you knew what it was like, why did you bring us here?'

I didn't mean to sound so snippy. He was asked to bring us here, and he did, as a favour. But why not just tell me, before we came this far?

'You needed to see it for yourself before making any decisions,' he says simply.

He's right. I did need to see it for myself. Having got all the way to Skibbereen then to turn back within seven miles of Roone Bay – I never would have forgiven myself. I sigh, thinking back on Grandpa's stories, but I can't put them into perspective.

I gaze around again and try to imagine him here as a child, and as a young man in love. If I watch quietly, maybe I'll see his echo peering eagerly down the lane – no, he called it a boreen – watching for his lover, my grandma, before he married her and carried her off from this remote and wild environment to the grime of an English industrial city. I expect they'd been as culture-shocked then as I feel now.

'So, what now?' I ask eventually, more of myself than anything. I'll work it out when my brain starts to function again. I give a rueful grimace, search in my handbag and pull out the tiny photo to show Sean. 'This is what I was looking for.'

Sean gives a quizzical glance. 'Ah. Well, I'd say you're mighty disappointed, so.'

'A tad,' I say dryly. 'Is there a B & B in Roone Bay?'

'There's Mrs O'Hara's. She has a room she lets in the summer. And if she hasn't the room spare, we can ask around. Don't worry, I won't leave you wanting for somewhere to stay while you decide what to do.'

'You're very kind.'

'Not a bother,' he mutters, embarrassed, no doubt, by the tears of gratitude welling in my eyes. 'So,' he says, 'you'll maybe do the old place up?'

'I was going to, but, well, I don't know if it's possible,' I admit. 'It looks as if it's gone past the point of renovation.'

'Oh, I've brought back worse places.'

'You have?' I'm surprised, then my enthusiasm drains again. 'At what cost?'

'We'll have to work it out. Don't look so glum. It's not the end of the world.'

'It feels like it today,' I say grimly. 'I had all these plans...' I stop myself from saying out loud that I imagined Olivia growing into this community, going to school here, as far from the influence of wealth and prestige as I could imagine. After all, she still thinks this is a holiday. 'My dad always said to get three quotes on a job,' I say then add hastily, 'Not just for the cost but to get opinions. He said you'd know who was being honest when two opinions matched.'

I sense Sean knows that wasn't what I was going to say, but he doesn't push me.

'Well, now, that might be right for England, but I don't think it will work here. But sure, it's worth a try if it makes you feel happier.'

I really don't know what he means. But the safety net of wealth I accumulated during the few years of my marriage is shrinking in the face of these unexpected obstacles. If I have to pay for lodgings as well as renovation work, what I thought would last for years will be gone in months. All my well-laid plans, it seems, have turned to beggar's wishes.

'So,' he adds, 'let's see if we can get you and your exhausted girleen somewhere to settle in and leave fussing about the future until tomorrow, eh? You never know – the sun might come out.'

I don't know how he does it, but I smile. 'You're right. I'm too tired to think. Dinner and sleep, and tomorrow maybe I'll have a brainwave, and all my problems will go away.'

'Hah, that's the spirit, girl. No point being down.'

He turns the vehicle around, backing into an open field.

'Where does that go?' I ask, indicating back up the lane.

'Oh, back to Ballydehob, eventually. But you wouldn't want to do that, not without a compass. There are more roads in West Cork than the rest of Ireland. You could take a wrong turn and never be found again.'

'That bad, eh?' I find myself smiling – again. But I do wonder what's going to happen now. I sigh, admitting, 'I'm a bit stumped. There was me thinking we'd just need to buy some essentials. You know, bedding and pans and whatever. I guess I was a bit naïve.'

He takes his eyes briefly from the road and casts me a rueful grimace of acknowledgement. I was painfully naïve, of course.

'A bit of adversity makes a person all the stronger,' he says. 'You wait and see. It will all work out in the end.'

Exactly what Grandma would have said! I wish I had his confidence, but years of being repressed have taken their toll.

The truck bounces over a pothole, and I grab the dashboard with one hand, Olivia with the other.

'Sorry,' he says and slows down a bit.

Back on the road we left earlier, he turns towards the town. I look back and, for a brief moment, glimpse the cottage that had lived on in Grandpa's memories. I'm glad Grandma didn't realise it was like this. And I'm glad Mum didn't have a clue what she was sending me to, either. We were all seeking a way for me to disappear, and the cottage had been the answer to our prayers. Until Grandpa died, and Grandma had rescued his box of yellowing papers from the attic, we had no idea she'd inherited it. Even then, we didn't know what to do about it.

'Why didn't you sell it?' Mum had queried.

Grandma had reminded her that there was no work in rural Ireland, and there were countless similar properties lying empty. It would mean making the trip over to sort it out, which might cost more than she'd get for the place. Then she'd shrugged and added, with a somewhat confused expression, that she had a strange feeling that one day it would be more than just an empty property, that it had a purpose and would become a beacon of light for someone in the future. Did she always mean me? Was that why she'd given me the key when I got married? I never thought of my grandmother being fey, but she was Irish, after all. And she had been quite upfront about her innate dislike for Graham.

I glimpse a small harbour to my left before we swing up into a street of tiny shopfronts. There are several shops and bars, a post office and, at the top of the hill, an impressive bank. Even in the midst of poverty, bankers remain unrelenting in their arrogance. But there's something vibrant and cheerful about the little town of Roone Bay. Unlike the outlying cottages, the shops are painted in outlandish colours, as if waving a flag to poverty instead of allowing it to bring them down.

We stop by a small shop. 'Wait here a moment. I'll see if Mrs O'Hara can take you in.'

Sean enters the shop, and we wait. My fatigue has been replaced by a kind of fatalism. Whatever's being discussed is somehow out of my control, as though I'm the child again. It feels comforting to be looked after, but in a kind of inclusive way, so different from Graham's authoritative decisions. Eventually, Sean comes out, followed by a tall, thin, dauntingly severe woman. I think of the schoolmarms of old, but her gaze falls on Olivia's cherubic face and golden curls, and softens fractionally. Sean opens the door, helps me down and dumps Olivia on the kerb beside me.

'Sean says you've need of a place,' Mrs O'Hara says. 'You can lodge here for a bit. I've guests booked for June, but that'll give you time to find somewhere while you decide what to do.'

'Are you sure? I don't want to put anyone out.'

She looks puzzled. 'Sure, and you'll not be putting anyone out of the house. Now, who do I call you?'

'I'm Grace. This is Olivia, my daughter.'

'Well, come on in, so, and I'll get you a cup of tea, and find a glass of milk for the wean. You look fairly done in, what with the travelling, and the girleen is out on her feet.'

I remember the milk and rolls I bought in Skibbereen and hold out the crumpled carrier bag like a peace offering. 'Waste not, want not,' I say.

I almost cringe at my own words. I thought I'd curtailed my tendency to repeat Grandma's pointless adages, but they'd filtered down through the family, to seep into my psyche.

Graham had hated it. *Don't be a parrot*, he would say when one slipped out. *Use your own words*. And I'd tried, because I thought he was right. But here and now, the woman before me nods, as though I've pleased her, and takes the bag from me.

Sean heaves the luggage out of the truck and brushes off strands of straw.

'Take them on up, Sean, lad,' Mrs O'Hara tells him, stepping back to hold the door. She says to Olivia, 'Well, Livvy, I expect ye'd like a nice bit of bread and jam, so?'

That must sound like party food to Olivia, and with a sunny smile, she gives a little skip and jump, saying, 'Yes, please.'

I breathe a sigh of relief that her manners have finally discovered their way home.

Sean disappears through the shop, behind the counter. Like the tiny shop in Skibbereen, it's cluttered, filled floor to ceiling with household goods. There's a fridge gurgling away in the corner, and on the counter there's a huge rectangular woven basket, with a few loaves of bread left. The floor is stacked with cardboard boxes, one of which is spilling out men's checked shirts, wrapped neatly in cellophane. High on the wall there's a woman's dusty hat, dating from at least thirty years ago. I seem to have stepped through a portal into another world, a past age.

'Come on through,' Mrs O'Hara calls over her shoulder, leading the way.

We're led through the shop, into an old-fashioned parlour, smaller and even more cluttered than the shop. There's a massive old sideboard taking up the width of one wall, an ancient range against another, its white enamel burned to an unhealthy yellow. A single, low windowsill is piled with newspapers. Two comfy chairs bookend the range; sitting on one is a ginger cat, curled into a furry cushion. The dark and stained carpet is worn to hessian between the shop door and the narrow entrance to a set of steep stairs, which Sean stomps up, heaving our cases one before him, one after.

A table sits squarely in the middle of the room, one of those with leaves that pull out to accommodate two more diners. Four wooden chairs are tucked neatly beneath. The sideboard is thick with photographs, the wall above dominated by a fading picture of a benevolent, bearded Jesus, blessing the house. I'm touched by nostalgia. Grandma has one much the same, a relic of her Catholic upbringing. She says she has no time for religion, *but, sure, it would be a sacrilege to throw it.*

Mrs O'Hara instructs Olivia, pointing. 'Mind the range, now, girleen. It's very hot.'

Olivia tentatively touches the cat, who opens one eye to assess her before yawning widely, displaying an impossibly large mouth with a fearsome set of canines. 'Can I stroke it?' she asks.

'Oh, aye, Jennie will be after liking a rub.'

'But don't put your face too close,' I murmur. I've always been wary of cats, a legacy from my mother, who's allergic to them. But Olivia has already kneeled, hugged her arms around the animal and placed her cheek on its fur. It erupts into a loud purr.

The boards above our heads creak, then Sean thunders back downstairs and tips two fingers to his imaginary cap. 'I'll be off now, missus.'

'Take a loaf to MacDarragh on your way through,' she says. 'They'll be after going stale. And tell him I'll take some honey for the shop; I've only the one jar left.'

'Will do. Take care now.'

'Sean,' I say. He stops and turns. 'Thank you.'

'Not a bother,' he says, adding cheekily, 'Couldn't leave a damsel stranded now, could I?'

I collapse into a chair, and Mrs O'Hara, who hasn't given me permission to call her anything else, flicks out a white damask cloth, which floats down to the table with a sigh. A big jar of blackcurrant jam is set beside a wooden breadboard. She bustles to the range, lifts an enormous kettle, fills a teapot and

covers it with a knitted cosy. All at once I feel that we've landed
and aren't floating alone any longer.

'Seat yourselves around,' she instructs, and it's easy enough
to just go with the flow.

The tea tastes as though it has been laced with tar, and a
white crusty loaf has been sawn into thick slices, slathered with
butter and jam. I haven't had high tea since I was a child, when
dinner time was at midday, complete with some kind of milk
pudding – creamed rice or semolina, with a knob of jam – or
steamed roly-poly pudding and custard; and we had bread and
butter and jam before bedtime.

While working, I'd learned to eat lunch on the hoof, and
dinner had become an evening meal. Puddings were reserved
for Sundays and special occasions, because by then we knew
they were bad for us; all that carbohydrate and sugar.

The bread and jam and even the damask cloth remind me
so much of Grandma, I feel tears of nostalgia rise. I swipe them
back discreetly, but Mrs O'Hara casts a look that says she hasn't
missed them and maybe puts it down to tiredness, or perhaps
my disappointment in the cottage. I don't doubt Sean gave her a
precis of my story.

After tea, I offer to help clear, but Mrs O'Hara looks almost
affronted. 'Get on with you!' she says. 'Now you're rested, take
the wean out for some fresh air, then get yourselves an early
night. You look fair wasted. Come in around the back – it's
never locked.'

We're shown up to a neat bedroom busy with floral wallpa-
per, a wooden wardrobe, two single beds and a kidney-shaped
dressing table with a mirror.

'I hope you don't mind sharing,' she says.

'It's perfect,' I say, meaning it. 'Olivia will be happier in the
same room with me, what with all the strangeness, and travelling and the like.'

'And because Daddy's not here to keep us safe,' Olivia adds. 'He's got to work.'

I'm slightly taken aback by this unexpected interpretation of our previous roles. Graham had never been one to comfort her through nightmares or read to her at night. Where did she get that from?

I didn't want to go out, but in fact, it does us both good. We amble down towards the sea, where there's a small harbour – no more than a wall, really – where boats can tie up. There's a hatch for selling fish and chips, presently closed. The smell of the fishing industry wafts towards us on a faint breeze, but it's not unpleasant; it's the scent of a seaside holiday: salt water, seaweed, rank fish, diesel.

The tide must be out, for there are a couple of boats several feet below the level of the wall, and to the left, on a slope of shore, a couple of wooden rowboats rest on stones slimy with green algae. Behind us are piles of fishing nets and baskets, presumably used for catching lobsters. Everything seems so much smaller here, from the roads to the houses to the boats. It's charming, quaint, and yet so real, I feel we've stepped accidentally into a different world.

The sun is sinking fast behind a bank of clouds rolling in from the west, and I shiver in the cooling breeze. Out in the bay, the sea has lifted, churning with relentless determination, chopped with whitecaps scratched up by the fitful breeze. I hear the distant plinking of halyards flapping against metal masts from the yachts moored in the bay.

To the left, against the black rock, I can just about make out Grandpa's cottage. I point it out to Olivia, who states firmly, 'It's not Great-Grandpa's cottage; it's ours.'

I grin at her, and she grins back as I say, 'I guess it is, at that. Lucky us!'

I wonder why Grandma never had the notion to come back to see it, or even to do it up and rent it out, now times were changing. Did she leave something behind in Roone Bay that she didn't want raked up, didn't want to remember? A faint wind chills my neck. What might have happened here to make her feel like that? What if she and Grandpa Connor had left Ireland for reasons they never shared with anyone?

A drift of rain begins to dust the air. What is it Grandma calls it? A soft day? But it's not soft; it's cold and unforgiving, like the grey sea that whispers before us.

In the misty distance, I make out the ridge of a peninsula. I think it's the Mizen, past which the *Titanic* steamed on its fatal voyage. I envisage the terror of its last moments as a cargo of desperate souls seeking a new life in America found a somewhat different destination. The ship broke its back, plummeting two miles to the floor of the Atlantic, leaving a flotsam of bodies bobbing on the icy surface. I glance up at the low cloud, trying to imagine two vertical miles but fail. It's too far to contemplate.

Olivia gives a wide yawn.

Back at Mrs O'Hara's, I settle her into the bed by the window and read to her. It doesn't take long for her eyes to droop. Within minutes, she's out to the world. I'm sure I'll do the same, but I lie awake, in this strange bed, in this strange land, my disorientation complete. Behind the curtains, there's no orange glow of streetlights, no noise of revellers coming home late, no distant rumble of traffic. The quiet is almost unnerving. I wonder if I'll get used to it.

I try to sleep, but I'm beset by anxiety, all the negativity of my actions rising to confront me with annoying repetition.

What have I done?

Why did I think I could get away with this?

Graham's probably on his way here, right now. He'll find us because he never allows himself to fail. Not at anything.

My mind races and churns as I recall the weeks of planning, the daily terror of exposure, believing that somehow Graham had become aware of my plans and was just waiting to see whether I really meant it before leaping out to stop me. There would be a little curl of mockery on his lips before he pastes the bland expression back in place and takes me to task. He's done it so many times before. He has a way of making me feel small, like a child who's been reprimanded for doing something utterly stupid, and by the end of his carefully modulated explanation, I truly believe I have, until I think it all through again, later, and realise how he's manipulated my thoughts, when it's too late to quibble. I've known for a long time that I actually didn't like my husband very much, but at this moment, I hate him with a vengeance. How dare he court my innocence then stamp my dreams underfoot, and try to change me from the girl I was into the kind of woman he thinks I should be. How dare he!

And he's been doing that to our daughter, only it was so subtle I didn't realise it was happening until I noticed she'd become strangely silent at mealtimes. I asked her if she were being bullied at school. No, she replied. Then I realised she wasn't being bullied at school. She was being bullied at home.

5

GRACE

I wake in Mrs O'Hara's tiny bedroom and shrug off the guilt of running. I'd like to say I slept well, but those ever-churning memories are exhausting. I rise, however, with a new determination. I've actually done it. Despite my fear, we made it! We really are here, in Ireland, and there's no going back.

I feel a little awkward walking down the stairs into Mrs O'Hara's living room, as though I'm invading her private space. But the little table is already loaded for breakfast, like any other B & B. Cereals and milk are there for the taking, and the butter and jam are surely intended for toast. There's a mat for the teapot, and the kettle is steaming quietly on the range.

I settle Olivia, who's excitedly lining up little individual boxes of cereal, ready to choose. After much deliberation, she takes Sugar Puffs, while I take Snap, Crackle and Pop, which I've loved since childhood; I haven't called them Rice Krispies for as long as I can remember. I don't usually eat cereals, but today I'm determined to enjoy a holiday mood, for a while, at least. Already the dream has cracked around the edges, and reality is seeping in. There are decisions to be made, but I'm not in the right headspace to confront them.

Mrs O'Hara bustles in from the back, busying herself with the teapot, and I say, 'Oh, sorry, we started... I hope that's all right?'

She smiles. 'Don't be worrying now, sure, you're grand. I have some toast browning under the grill. You'll be needing to get your strength back after the journey.'

'We were a bit frazzled,' I admit.

'So, you slept well?'

'Like a log,' I lie. 'It's very quiet here, compared to the city.'

'You're from London?'

'Birmingham, originally.'

Luckily, Olivia is reading from the cereal box, ignoring our dialogue, or she would have corrected me.

'So, Sean said you were looking at the McCarthy house? Will you be after buying it, I wonder?'

I smile inwardly at the open interrogation. I have the feeling that anything I say will be running around the town as fast as gossip has legs. But perhaps I shouldn't mind. Get things out in the open. I have nothing to hide. 'I own it, actually. My grandfather was born there.'

Mrs O'Hara pauses. 'Your grandfather?'

'Connor McCarthy. Did you know him?'

Her brows rise up into her hairline. 'You're Connor's grandchild? By all that's holy! I know he ran off, in the night, to marry young Caitlin O'Driscoll, who didn't have a penny to her name. My mother told me – it was a scandal, so it was. Her father was that angry, she being the last of his children. He thought she would be after marrying Ben Dowd, who has a biteen of a farm, and was looking for them to take care of him in his old age.' She shakes her head. 'So many of our young lost in those days.' She takes a deep breath and changes the subject. 'But you don't want to know all that bad news. So, you're half Irish, eh?'

'All four of my grandparents were Irish.'

'Then you're Irish, so you are. And the wean?'

'Well, she'd be half Irish. My husband is one hundred per cent English.'

I don't tell her that I've run from him. That's one bit of news I'd rather wasn't bandied about, divorce not being legal here, and even separation frowned upon.

'So, you're having a holiday with the wean, seeing where your folks came from?'

'That's about right.'

'So, I wonder where your husband is?'

I'm a bit taken aback at the forthright question, but she's standing there, waiting, as if it's the most normal thing to ask.

'He's working, so I thought we'd take a look at the cottage, maybe do it up. I didn't realise it would be so far gone.'

'It's in a bad way, sure enough. But you could do worse than put it all in the hands of young Sean. Maybe you're thinking of renting it out, as a holiday let?'

'Maybe,' I agree, pleased that she's given me a good excuse.

'Well, times are changing, sure enough. We get more visitors these days, and isn't Noel O'Donovan after coming back from America with his pot of gold and building a grand hotel in Roone Bay? That will change things here, for sure.'

She says that with a bemused air, and I think she's probably right about the changes that will follow. A big hotel will undoubtedly put Roone Bay on the map as a holiday destination. Ireland is clawing itself into the modern era, seeking new money, new investments. Nostalgia is being sold as merchandise, but in reality, no one wants to live the old way any more. They want what they see everyone else has already got. But it comes at a price. I wonder what this sleepy little town will be like, flooded with tourists.

Soon there will be no green left at all, I recall Dad grumbling, on one of our Sunday drives. *I'm glad I won't be here to see it.* I'd thought he'd meant in the misty future; I hadn't known he was dying at the time, and yet his words come back to me now, with force.

Those last few months had been dreadful. It wasn't until he was on his final sick leave that Mum told me he was dying. It changed everything. We spent time together, as a family, which had been rare before, with Mum driving the Morris Traveller out of the city so that Dad could breathe fresh air. He'd worked in the steelyards all his life, and the dust had filled his lungs, poisoned him. *Devil's luck*, he'd said, laughing it off with a shrug. I'd been little more than a child myself, engrossed in growing up, and hadn't realised his hacking cough was anything significant. I mean, he'd always coughed, hadn't he? I wish he and Mum had been honest, prepared me a little sooner. His death was a blow I can recall to this day, leaving a huge hole in my life that never seemed to quite heal.

It isn't surprising, therefore, that Mrs O'Hara views the new hotel with a vague sense that her era is coming to an end. Maybe I'll feel the same one day. But right now, the change in my circumstances is one I've chosen, so I'm buoyed by a peculiar sense of hope for the future, as well as a curiosity about my surroundings. My fears yesterday seem irrational. There's no way Graham is going to know we've come to Ireland. The tightness in my chest eases. *No way at all.*

When Mrs O'Hara bustles in to clear the table, I ask, 'Where's this new hotel? I might go and take a look.'

'Ah, sure, you can look, but it's not open yet. You'd walk the road back towards Ballydehob and see it on your left. It will have a fine view over the bay, of course. Noel says he'll bring rich Americans visiting, to see where their destitute ancestors came from.' She sighs. 'Maybe I shouldn't mind; it's done, so. And bringing money into the community is maybe a good thing, for the young anyway.'

She's right, in a way. But like all those in small communities, they see incomers as people with endless good luck and finances to fritter, not realising how lucky they are, themselves, to have ties to the land of their forebears and not be burdened with the stress of modern lives.

'Well, now, don't listen to an old woman rambling on. Have yourself a good breakfast, girl, then go out and get your bearings.'

Meanwhile, having shovelled her cereal in at breakneck speed, Olivia asks, 'Please may I leave the table?'

'You don't want toast?'

'No, thank you.' Olivia slips from the table, wriggles her way onto the cat's chair and heaves the amazingly compliant animal onto her lap.

'Ah, the precious,' Mrs O'Hara says softly. 'Be at home here, why don't ye? It's not a bother. Come and go as you please. Now, can I fetch you anything else?'

'We're fine, thank you. So, it's all right if we come back here during the day?'

She seems puzzled by the question. 'Well, sure, and why wouldn't ye?'

Breakfast over, we exit through the back door and step outside into the courtyard, with no real plans. 'Let's explore, shall we?'

'I want an ice cream. And a bucket and spade.' She glances at me slyly and belatedly adds, 'Please.'

I smile. Trust a six-year-old not to forget a promise.

Like me, rested and knowing there's to be no more travelling, she's in a better frame of mind this morning. The courtyard backs onto two tiny houses, a parking area and a building that might be a garage or storage. A tiny road leads us back into the main street, as we found last night.

It's a warm, sunny May day. Real holiday weather. I feel overdressed in my thick, knitted cardigan, but I wasn't expecting warmth after the miserable weather of the last two days. Perhaps it's a sign, I think hopefully. To the right, the row of shops rises gently towards the Allied Irish Bank building, which dominates the town.

We buy ice creams then amble down to the harbour, where we sit on the old stone sea wall, our feet dangling over the edge. The structure reaches out into a small quay. Rafted up against it, in twos, are half a dozen working fishing boats, their paint flaked, their names battered and tired. There's a drop of six foot or more below us, and to the left, a concrete slipway marches down into the water, for launching small craft. Beyond that, a small beach has been exposed, but this close to boats, I suspect it's not the cleanest place for children to play.

'Don't fall in,' I say as Olivia leans over to peer down into water that's slapping gently against the wall. The softly undulating surface has an oily sheen that catches the sun, and there's the usual debris bobbing in a scum of yellow foam. 'I don't fancy jumping in after you.'

Up on the hill, the cottage is clearly visible, and even from this distance, its empty windows stare sadly back at us, like a neglected child desperate for nurture. Olivia chomps the last of her cornet then wheedles, 'Can I get my bucket and spade now please, Mummy?'

I heave myself to my feet. 'Alrighty. Come on – let's get some sandwiches and lemonade, too, and then go and find a beach.'

Olivia leaps up, and I'm struck by her resilience. An ice cream by the sea, and those two awful days of travelling have instantly disappeared into the past. I wish I could have retained the ability to live for the moment, but life, and the responsibilities that come with it, have a way of filling my head with all the things that could go wrong instead of what's actually gone right.

The tiny row of shops will provide for all our needs, I realise. As well as the grocery store, there's a restaurant, a tourist centre, a bookshop, a post office, a café, a hardware store – a dying breed in England, these days – and a couple of clothes shops. Goods here are more expensive than I'm used to, but our needs seem to have diminished. There might be little choice, but compared to the overwhelming shopping centres in Birmingham and Cheltenham, the simplicity is refreshing.

We find a bucket and spade, and I buy a couple of large towels, which I hadn't had space for in the suitcases. I also buy myself a book to read and would have browsed longer, except Olivia is tugging at my arm, pleading, '*Muuum...*'

There's an impressive, tiny, abandoned hotel in the main street, dating back a hundred years or so. It's pretty, with three storeys, the top sporting a row of dormer windows, presumably to attic rooms. I wonder what kind of visitor it was built for. Who would have travelled to this tiny backwater fishing town? There have always been travellers, of course. Salesmen, and those enabled by wealth and itching to explore.

The peeling paint and bushes growing on the gutters lend an air of despair, as though the building knows that the new hotel on the hill will be its death knell. Of course, I could never voice such idiocies to Graham. I can hear his response. *Don't be daft, Grace. Buildings don't have feelings. It would probably cost more to renovate than you'd recoup. Best thing would be to pull it down and build apartments, make a nice little profit.*

His life is all about profit.

I wonder what the owners of this hotel think of Noel O'Donovan's posh new hotel up on the hill and the implications for the future.

We walk back towards what I now know is 'the butter road', where the mill is situated, and scramble down to a small beach that's mostly rock but with a narrow band of light shingle that can pass as sand for today.

I lay the towels down and lift my face to the sun.

Even though I'm filled with worry for the future, we made it here, and I must do what Mum told me: take one day at a time. She'd added, of course, that God will do the rest, but I'm afraid I don't have that faith. Though it would be all too easy to blame Him when it all goes wrong, we make our own decisions and create our own problems.

Later that day I write a letter to Mum, letting her know we've arrived safely. I don't tell her the true state of the cottage or the trauma of the journey. I just say we're in temporary accommodation while builders repair the roof.

6

GRACE

Olivia had chilled out massively yesterday, happy spuddling about in rock pools searching for minute creatures; filling her bucket with sand that won't make sand castles; dragging great strands of seaweed around, while singing tunelessly to some internal make-believe story I'm not privy to. I recall, just vaguely, doing these things myself, though the motivation somehow got left behind with childhood.

'I need to get another book to read,' I tell her after breakfast. 'Let's go to the shops first, then maybe we can walk down to the little harbour by the old church. Remember, we could see the ruins across the bay. There's a beach there, too.'

'Okay,' she says, skipping away to find her bucket and spade. I wonder if she'll be so compliant when she discovers it's a couple of miles to walk, looping around the coast, on the other side of Roone Bay. It occurs to me that I'm going to have to buy a car. If I'd done that before, we could have driven down here from Dublin. I was worried, though, about having to show my driving licence, which is in my married name, unlike my passport, which is still in my maiden name. I have no doubt that

Graham will search for me, but I have no intention of leaving a trail of breadcrumbs.

And, I muse, if I'd bought a car, I wouldn't have experienced the many kindnesses of the Irish: the man who helped with my luggage on the boat, the understanding bus driver, the lady in the shop in Skibbereen. Nor would I have met Sean or stayed with Mrs O'Hara.

Grandma would say: *Everything happens for a reason.* I don't believe in fate, but life has a way of modifying our decisions with a pinch of unforeseen spice. I like the random unplannedness of life. In that respect alone, Graham and I are total opposites. While I've taken massive leaps of faith in my life – granted, some of them haven't been such good choices – he plans things down to the nth degree and absolutely won't deviate from his own plan once it's been finalised. At first, I thought it made sense, now I'm sure it's a kind of narcissism; he's playing God within the confines of his own world.

As I'm buying another novel, I see a plan of Roone Bay on the post office notice board. The place we're going to is called Colla Pier, and is about two miles away. It will take nearly an hour to walk, at Olivia's pace, but we have nothing to hurry for, and this time I've come prepared, with rolls and cheese and apples and a bottle of orange Corona, which I pack into her rucksack.

At the top of the hill, the road follows the bay around, flattens and becomes easier to walk. The sky is blue, dotted with fluffy clouds. Seagulls wheel overhead, crying piteously, their bright-button eyes ever-seeking food. A small measure of peace eases into my soul. In someone's front garden, in the branches of a small hedge, there's a gathering of little yellow birds. 'Look,' I whisper to Olivia, holding her shoulders and turning her towards the fresh green beech leaves. 'Siskins. Aren't they pretty?'

She smiles, enjoying one of Ireland's exotic flashes of gold.

Then something spooks them, and they scatter with a flash of bright, fanned tails. The sight fills me with a sense of nostalgia for Dad, who had been passionate about wildlife in all forms.

We walk past the bank and take the road signposted Goleen. It's an easy walk, past a few weather-worn cottages set back from the narrow road. A few cars pass, the drivers acknowledging us with a casual lift of a finger from the steering wheel; a farmer, going the other way on a tractor, tips his cap at us with a big smile.

Olivia stares after him. 'Do you know that man?'

'No.'

'Then why did he wave at us?'

'He's just being polite.'

She chews that over a bit then states, 'We never do that at home.'

'No, but it's nice, friendly.'

'Am I allowed to wave back?'

'Absolutely.'

'Daddy wouldn't like that.'

'No, but I don't mind at all.'

'Okay,' she says, taking a little skip and jump. Maybe she's feeling the freedom of being out from under Graham's controlling influence, too. No, Daddy wouldn't like her waving at a man on a tractor, or anyone he felt was beneath us. I wonder how long it will take her to recover from the years of only doing what Graham liked her to do, of the fear of doing something wrong. More quickly than me, I imagine. I hope.

We pass a long, green field, and gradually the wall of St Mary's comes into view, behind which the open arches of the ruined church rise with awesome beauty. Set on the edge of the sea, it welcomes visitors with a palpable sense of history.

The only sure things in life are death and taxes, Grandma liked to say. *Sure, the dead won't harm you; it's the living who'll cause you the most grief.*

I think of her now. Had she wandered here, as a child? In a community ruled by the church, I suspect she had. The community, back then, would have been more afraid of the priests and the vengeance of God than the dead. I find it deeply sad that Grandma had been uplifted from this tight community and deposited in Birmingham, the city of steel and smoke. I wonder if she ever regretted meeting Grandpa and being stolen away to England. But no, she loved my grandpa until the day he died, though he'd shrunk into a thin shell of the man she'd married; while I regret ever crossing paths with Graham.

The only good thing to come out of that is Olivia.

I'm hoping I've removed her from his influence early enough. Time will tell. At least I'll provide her with an alternative environment, and she can make her own choices. People still talk about nature versus nurture, as though there's a choice, an internal argument raging. From everything I've seen, nature has the battle won, from birth, and no amount of nurture changes the basic nature of an individual. Arthur, Graham's son by his first marriage, is a prime example of my unvoiced theory. Even under Graham's manipulative thumb all his life, he manages to retain a sensitive nature, presumably a legacy from his mother.

Now, standing here in the sunshine, I look back on the mistake I made marrying Graham and see how easily I was led. Mum and Dad had been concerned enough to ask if I was sure I knew what I was doing. But what young person ever accepted being wrong? Grandma had been more blunt. She told me not to marry Graham, but I didn't listen. I thought I'd be happy. I mean, how could I have thought otherwise, courted lavishly by a man who looked and lived like a film star?

Olivia and I wander through the church's tall arches, which have stood firm, while around them the roof has fallen in and the walls have crumbled. Vast capping stones hang above us, concreted by no more than gravity and the skills of long-dead stonemasons. I suppose they will fall one day, but not, I hope, today.

Olivia skips and jumps from stone to stone, balancing, her arms out, then asks, 'Can we go to the seaside now?'

The joys of old architecture and history pass her by, but she's young yet. 'Yes, love. Give me five minutes.'

There are generations of families here, gathered in silent companionship, probably bedded more closely than they had been in life. I'm seeking Grandpa's ancestors. There are some prominent family names, on impressive monuments, but I don't find any McCarthys. I'll come back and browse the names on the stones another day. I've never thought much about geneal- ogy. It seemed so pointless, searching back through time to find one's ancestors, but here and now, I realise it's not about names and lists; it's about continuity. I don't want to remain forever a blow-in, a stranger, in this small community.

I want to belong.

With that thought, I know I'm going to blow everything I have on the cottage. This will be our home. I'm going to make it happen, and never mind getting other quotes – I feel instinc- tively that Sean is the man to do it.

Surprisingly, Olivia, far from complaining about the long walk, is skipping and singing, wrapped within her own little world. It strikes me that I've rarely seen her so carefree, and I feel guilty for having been so wrapped up in my own unhappi- ness that I missed how withdrawn Olivia had become. The thought chills me. I always wanted to be a good wife and a good mother, but perhaps being unhappy as a wife made me some- what lacking as a mother. If so, I'm sure I've done the right thing for both of us.

Eventually, the road turns steeply down to the sea, and we find ourselves by a small bay with a sturdy quay, against which a few boats are moored. The shore is shingle, lined with seaweed, scattered with a few smashed shells. I find a dry rock to sit on.

Olivia divests herself of her jeans and puts on the rubber flip-flops I'd bought in the post office for her, slipping them on with the satisfaction of knowing that her father wouldn't approve. When we stayed at a hotel in Mallorca last year, he'd told her, quite categorically, that we don't buy cheap junk like that. I'd smothered my amusement when, a couple of days later, his expensive brogues were ruined by sand and salt water.

'Shall we have our sandwiches before you get your hands mucky?' I suggest as my tummy gives a warning growl.

'Yes, please. I'm hungry.'

She perches on the rock beside me, and I spread the picnic on a towel. I break the rolls with my hands, spread a bit of melting butter in them with a bendy plastic knife and add a chunk of cheese. There's something very wholesome about eating with your fingers, out in the fresh air, and we both consume the basic fare with relish, washing it down with fizzy orange.

'Daddy says that's bad for my teeth,' Olivia informs me, wiping her mouth with the back of her hand.

'I know, but we'll brush them before bed.'

'And can I have another ice cream?'

'Do you see anywhere selling ice cream?'

She looks around the bay. It's devoid of anything remotely touristy. We're the only humans here, in fact. Then she's distracted by a pair of swans floating serenely towards us. I guess they, like the seagulls, aren't too proud to check us out for leftovers. It's a waste, but I break another roll and hand it over. 'See if the swans will come close.'

She gleefully breaks off small pieces and throws them into the water. The swans drift closer, gracefully dip their beaks and shake the salty soda bread in a flurry of droplets before swallowing. I lean back on my elbows, close my eyes and lift my face to the sun. The soft shushing of the sea, the calling of seagulls and the slapping of water against the concrete quay are mesmeric.

What a revelation it would be to Graham that I prefer this empty paradise, with its faintly chilly breeze, to the bustle of a foreign resort with white sand, wall-to-wall sunshine and ranks of bars and sun loungers.

'You're looking rather better than last time I saw you.'

Sean's voice startles me. I'd vaguely heard the rattle of shingle but had assumed it was Olivia, playing. Now, my eyes flit to where she's crouched by a rock pool, poking at something with the handle of the fishing net. Satisfied that she's safe, I turn to Sean, who looks incredibly wholesome and windblown. He's wearing those pants that have loops and pockets all over for tools. He must be having a break from work.

'I didn't mean to startle you,' he says. 'You looked so peaceful there, I almost walked away. May I sit down?'

'Please.' I smile and pat the rock enticingly. In all honesty, I'm glad to have the company, especially someone who exudes peace and contentment. 'Best seat in the theatre.'

He gazes around appreciatively and agrees. 'Sure, it doesn't get much better than this. But it's a good job I'm well-padded in the rear, eh?'

I giggle, probably for the first time in years, as he hands me a note, scribbled by hand in pencil on a page torn from a notebook. 'I took the liberty of checking out your cottage. I thought it might be helpful. So, here's the damage; it's only approximate, of course.'

I scan it and sigh with relief. The big things – the windows, the roof and the internal floor – won't cost as much as I'd imagined. I could easily have frittered that much in a year, to keep Graham happy. 'Can you do it for me? Would you?'

'Of course.'

'Do we need a contract?'

He raises an eyebrow. 'Darling girrul, this is West Cork. We don't do contracts. We spit and shake, maybe over a pint.'

My cheeks flush at the casual endearment, but he either

doesn't notice or doesn't mind. 'So' – I clear my throat and grin at him – 'when can you start?'

'Let's sort out the process, first. I'll explain what needs doing, in what order and why. And you can let me know if you agree with my suggestions or have any ideas of your own.'

I rather like the sense of inclusion. 'When could we do that?'

'Now, if it suits. It's best if we do it on site. I can drive you up there.' He points to a blue pickup truck behind us, on the harbour. It's rather newer and cleaner than MacDarragh's, and probably less sticky.

I glance at Olivia. 'We haven't been here long. I don't think she'll take kindly to being dragged away yet.'

'I've got a message to run, so I'll come back in an hour. She'll be bored by then, and the promise of an ice cream should seal the deal.'

I almost laugh. 'You must have children!'

'A nephew, four years old,' he says with pride. 'Starts school in September, but he can already read. Either that or he's got a really good memory!' He bounces to his feet. 'Right then. I'll be back in a bit, so.'

'Thank you. We'll be ready.'

Olivia is watching now, and as Sean leaves, he throws her a friendly wave, which she returns before shuffling her way back to me in her flip-flops, creating a double snail-trail of footprints. 'Why didn't Sean stay? He's nice.'

I explain our plan and suggest she goes to play for a while, and that we'll look out for his pickup together. While sitting in the sun, I reflect on the day we left home. There had been moments when I'd almost wanted to turn back, but I am pleased, now, that some tiny remnant of self that hadn't been eroded over the years had propelled me to take action.

7

GRACE, A FEW DAYS EARLIER

The morning we ran away started like every other morning over the last few years, but at the point of waking, I knew it wouldn't end that way. I lay still, feigning sleep. Surely the frantic beating of my heart must have been shaking the bed? But Graham slid out, trying not to wake me. A few years ago, I truly believed he did this for my sake. His soothing voice echoes from the early days of our marriage: *Poor sweetheart, so tired, looking after the baby, didn't have the heart to wake you...*

I soon realised my mistake. He likes to have his breakfast in the silence of his own company. Half a grapefruit, a bowl of cereal. One piece of toast. No more, no less. He's worried about the possibility of a midlife paunch, but it's unlikely to happen in the face of his rigid self-discipline. And while silently consuming, he'll be mentally reviewing his schedule and internally phrasing answers to questions that hadn't yet been voiced. He calls it business sense. I call it manipulation. As he owns the company, I suppose he feels he has the right to make everything go in the direction he intends, but managers, ostensibly hired to take some of the burden from his shoulders, soon discover that their role is to agree with him and filter his wisdom down through the ranks. Just as his wife does at home.

When I heard Graham's car purr quietly down the drive, I got up and showered, the water as hot as I could bear it, a flagellation that beat my skin red. I remember thinking: *Today will not be like any other day. Today is the day I do the unthinkable and leave my husband. Am I mad?*

Those people who climb mountains or jump out of planes with parachutes think they know the meaning of fear. They don't; they experience momentary adrenaline-flooded exhilaration, fuelled by the possibility of death. Real fear is an insidious parasite that sneaks unnoticed into the psyche, embedding itself deeply, feeding on your independent will and self-respect, until its host retreats into a quiet corner to watch the external body perform and function as required, just to stay alive.

Leaving him in that way was deceitful, cowardly. It felt like betrayal of the worst kind. Because I'd given no indication that I was unhappy, my sudden absence must have come as a shock, a kick in the teeth. But if I'd told him, leaving would no longer have been an option.

A sickening wave of fear had stolen my breath, making my head go cold. A panic attack imminent, I slumped to the bed, folded over, head to knees, counting breaths until my heart rate slowed. Yes, I was scared of him. I still am. Scared of his anger, his power over my life and scared of the deliberate revenge he might exact. I've seen him do it in business. When his autonomy is challenged, he reacts with calm intimidation, but when deliberately crossed, the thorn in his side is pulled out, neutralised and eradicated from his life.

I berated myself firmly with the truth: *Women are allowed to leave their husbands. This is the twentieth century. I shouldn't have stayed so long.* I should have told him a long time ago that this wasn't how I wanted to live my life. I should have told him how I felt. But centuries of female submission must be hardwired into my genes, because whenever I got the urge to speak, my throat closed. I couldn't tell him anything. I couldn't face the theatrics of his disappointment, which would wear me down until I retreated into abject submission. People think I'm strong, determined. They think I married Graham for his money, but I didn't. It was dumped in my lap, and I was too stunned to see it for what it was: a kidnapping of my soul.

Leaving wasn't easy. It's the hardest thing I've ever done. When I had Olivia, I felt as if my fate was sealed, but it was her, inadvertently, who spurred me into taking action. I wasn't strong enough to save myself, but I had to save my child.

I dressed in practical clothes, dried my hair, slapped colour onto my lips and went to wake Olivia. I shook her gently. My grandmother's phrase *she sleeps like the dead* filtered through my mind. It's not a phrase I like. It tempts fate. I don't know what I'd do if something happened to Olivia. I don't know how parents cope with the loss of a child; I truly don't. I'm so filled with love for this child of mine, it's almost too big a burden for one person to bear.

She woke up grumpy, as usual. I stroked the hair back from her forehead and watched the sleep-world drain from her features. What do six-year-olds dream of? Barbie dolls? Teddy-bear picnics, jelly and ice cream? I don't know; she can never remember the good dreams, just the nightmares, when she wakes screaming because there are monsters under the bed. Though I know from experience that monsters trawl the streets on two legs, wearing humanity as a disguise, but it's too early for me to drive the fairy tales from her mind. She knows not to talk to strangers, not to go in a car with someone she doesn't know, but God forbid she needs to learn the reason why, just yet.

As she awoke, it saddened me to see her pretty face tighten with the onset of the day. I thought maybe she was being bullied at school, but I didn't know for sure. Her teacher, not a mother herself, and surely too young to have all that responsibility, said she wasn't, that Olivia was sometimes volatile, getting angry or upset, crying for no reason, and her work wasn't as good as it should be; otherwise, everything was fine.

Everything was fine? I wondered whether the teacher was being sarcastic at my expense.

Her expression, not quite as hidden as she believed, suggested that it was my fault. After all, as a working woman, she no doubt believes that wealthy housewives are selfish, caring more about themselves than their children. But there are only two other people in our home life who could be slyly bullying Olivia: my husband or his son.

The other mothers used to glance at me with a level of curiosity when I dropped her off in the morning or collected her in the afternoon. I didn't doubt they were wondering what it's like to live in a house with seven bedrooms and a full-time housekeeper – I'm not allowed to call her a cleaning lady – and the weekly attendance of a gardener-handyman. But they couldn't know how utterly redundant I felt in my own home, like an ornament taken down and dusted off when required.

They also, no doubt, wondered why I hadn't sent Olivia to one of the many private schools around, when I can clearly afford to. Graham wanted to, of course. After all, Arthur had gone to boarding school from the age of seven, and it apparently made a man of him. Poor Arthur. I don't think he's happy, even now he's moved on. But university will be finished for him, soon, and while it removed him from Graham's overpowering, manipulative presence for a few years, he'll be expected to come back and pull his weight in the company.

When I told Graham I want to be a mother to my daughter, and boarding school at the age of seven kind of negated that notion, I'm sure he thought I was criticising him. Maybe, subconsciously, I was, but he graciously backed down from the discussion when I assured him that when she's old enough, we could check out schools together.

I should have known better.

A month ago, a letter had arrived in the post, in answer to the application I discovered he'd gone on and sent. I had never, until this time, touched Graham's post, but the school logo had been emblazoned on the envelope. Olivia was to start there in September. They were thrilled that he'd chosen their school and would care for her with dedication, etcetera. I destroyed the letter, rather than let him know I'd opened it. Let him think it had got lost in the post.

That had been the catalyst. I couldn't leave for me, but I could for my daughter. Olivia's seventh birthday was fast approaching, and if I didn't go then, it would be too late. In September, just a few months away, I would stand and wave her off to school, as expected, a smile on my lips, grief shuttered behind the required facade. And then I would have nothing, because Olivia would learn to hate me.

Graham remains firmly entrenched in the Victorian concept of children being taught to survive boarding school and that the man in a relationship owns everything, even his wife and children. At first, I thought he enjoyed giving me presents, to please me, but soon realised he was pleasing himself by giving. He enjoyed receiving gratitude. It stroked his ego, while I was slowly but surely being undermined as an individual.

That morning, Olivia stared up at me, half awake. I forced myself to smile brightly. 'How do you feel about a little adventure, darling?'

'What about school?'

'We're going to skip school, just this once,' I said, 'and go on an outing. Come on, jump up. You can choose what to wear. But it has to be something sensible because we're going on a train.'

She looked interested, surprised. 'Where? To the seaside?'

'To the sea,' I agreed, bending the truth a little. The long summer holidays weren't far distant, after all, and the weather had been kind.

She leaped into action, eyes sparkling. 'I'll get my bucket and spade. They're in the garage. And my swimsuit and armbands.'

'I don't think we can fit the bucket and spade in the suitcase, darling. We can buy some new ones when we get there.'

She inclined her head and narrowed her eyes. I saw the argument raging in her head: the ones she has, that she likes, or shop for new? I breathed softly with relief as she nodded, probably having reasoned that ending up with two of everything was quite a good deal.

While she dressed, I hurriedly packed a suitcase for her. Mine was ready and waiting in my side of our massive wardrobe. Graham never looks in there, but I was nearly wetting myself with fear the previous night, in case, for some crazy reason, he did. My packed case was shouting loudly, like a child playing a sneaky game of hide-and-seek: *I'm here, look harder, here I am!*

I hate dishonesty, but it was the only way I could do it, because I was too scared to do it openly. I was weak in the face of his immutable nature. If he argued, I would fold, like the wet blanket Arthur once told me I was. I was angry that my stepson could be so rude, but actually, he's right. I'm not strong enough to argue. Conflict makes me feel physically sick so is best avoided.

I wanted to be honest with Olivia, too, but I envisaged her shock at the realisation that we weren't going to come home again. I used to think the expression on her face when he came home each night was hero worship, but later I realised it was fear. Like me, she was afraid of doing something wrong. Graham is massively sure of himself. Even I'm stunned by his charisma every time I see him. Tall and cleanly handsome, with hair that's tipping towards silver, he's moved into middle age with the confidence that comes of absolute self-belief. And he intended to pack his daughter off to boarding school, just a month before her seventh birthday? She might have learned to hate him, as I think Arthur does, but it's more likely Graham would let her believe that it was my decision.

I glanced around her pretty pale-blue room, the carpet cushioned by felt underlay, the tall windows swagged and draped with net curtains and night-blue velour, and the princess canopy over the bed. It's the room of a spoiled child, but how could I not spoil her when I had the money? I gave her the things I'd only been able to dream of as a child. A self-defeating exercise, as it turns out.

'Let's have some T-shirts and jeans and hoodies?' I suggested. 'It can get chilly by the sea. And put on your trainers for the journey.'

'I need Jemima.'

'Okay, darling,' I agreed and stuffed the duck, her comforter, down the side of the case.

'No, I want to carry her,' she demanded.

It wasn't her fault. I woke her up with 'surprise!', and if she's anything like me, surprises are shocks, best avoided. Panic bubbled away beneath my calm exterior; the mask I'd donned daily for several years had become like a second skin. What if Graham had forgotten something and came back? He never did, of course, but what if...

I suggested, 'Well, let's take your school rucksack, then you can carry her on your back with some books to read on the train?'

'Okay,' she agreed, as Jemima, and her precious Game Boy, went in. I also suggested a colouring book, her pencil case and her skipping rope. This new fad for staring into a tiny screen and playing pointless games is something I don't really get. But Graham loves technology. It's his business, after all, and once he'd given it to her, overruling my uninformed argument, taking it away would have made me the bad parent.

Discussing anything with Graham, I discovered early in our marriage, was a painful experience. It always ended up with him saying: *There, see, sweetie? I knew you'd agree with me in the end.* So I learned to outwardly agree to things I didn't really agree with, simply to keep the peace. But isn't that how it starts? The loss of self. Just keeping the peace. Being Adam's rib, formed solely to be his companion and to bear his children. I learned to save my tears for when I was alone, and eventually my 'self' disappeared behind the stage curtain, and my fairy-tale marriage became a play I acted out, day after day.

In hindsight, I suspect I was deeply, blindly flattered, more in love with the fairy-tale castle than the prince. But who better to deceive us than ourselves? I enjoyed the change in attitudes towards me at work – Graham owned it, after all – and was thrilled by my upward shunt into moneyed circles. It was my childhood dream realised: marry Prince Charming, live happily ever after. I bought shoes whenever I wanted, without having to polish over the scrapes and have them re-heeled. I wore a ring made of real gold, set with a real, somewhat large, diamond. If I didn't quite love him, I'm sure I believed it would happen. How could it not, when I was so lucky? It took a couple of years for me to realise what an idiot I'd been, and by then Olivia was on the way. All I can thank God for is that, unlike women in past eras, I could stop more children from arriving, because each child would have added a bar to this self-made prison.

Mum, seeing the pain behind the make-up, had begged me, several times, to leave Graham and come back home, but I was too afraid of losing Olivia. Mum assured me that the child is always awarded to the mother, but Graham had the money, the lawyers. And he was possessive about his toys, even the ones he didn't really want.

When we were packed and ready, the need to leave became

urgent. I had passports and money, and anything I'd forgotten could stay forgotten. I loaded the Volkswagen and drove away, almost sure I was going to see Graham's Silver Shadow gliding towards us. Nothing, he once admitted, with a grin I then thought innocently ingenuous, ever surpassed the thrill of driving the best car ever made.

The further I drove from home, the more my resolution strengthened. I should have done this sooner. The trouble was, I hadn't known where to go. Mum's would be the first place he'd look, and I couldn't go to some women's shelter; I'd feel like a fraud amongst all those women desperate to escape poverty and domestic violence. It was Grandma who provided me with an escape route: the cottage Connor had left behind in Ireland, all those years ago, which we'd all kind of forgotten about.

I parked the car in the long-stay at the Cheltenham bus depot. I was sad to have to abandon my car, but it was necessary to stall the chase until I was safely out of reach. It would be easy to trace. When they find it, they'll assume I've gone somewhere by bus. I don't know who 'they' are, but I don't doubt Graham will search discreetly rather than go to the police. He never was one to air his dirty linen in public.

Several streets away from the depot, lugging the two unexpectedly heavy cases, with Olivia hanging on my arm, I flagged down a taxi to take us to a mainline station in Birmingham.

'Where ya goin'?' the cabbie asked chattily as he pulled away.

'London,' I said.

'The seaside,' Olivia said at the same time.

The cabbie caught my eye in the mirror. 'Brighton,' I lied quickly, my tone suggesting that I didn't want to engage in conversation.

Olivia was kicking her feet to some internal song as she stared out of the window. She went along with everything, unquestioningly, to start with, because that's what children do.

We train them to accept that adults have the situation in hand, that they know what they're doing, even when it's absolutely not true.

My stomach was churning, but I'd put a little planning into this escape. I left a note on the kitchen counter to say I'd taken Olivia shopping in London for the day, and we might stay over. In the meantime, the housekeeper would get on with her job, pleased to be alone in the house.

Graham would eventually begin to wonder. And when I didn't come home the next day, he'd probably make some phone calls to find out if I'd booked a hotel or stayed with one of his friends. He wouldn't call the police. Not because of the twenty-four-hour rule, but because he wouldn't want to embarrass himself; especially when he discovered our cases gone, along with Jemima, which would be the clincher. Only then would he realise I'd left him and taken *his* daughter with me.

We changed trains three times. Each time, I made Olivia stand by our luggage, just out of sight of the ticket booth as I bought the tickets with cash. I wanted my trail to vanish. A tall woman with Harrods bags and a pretty girl of about six? No, we haven't seen her.

Finally, the train arrived that would take us on to Holyhead. Gone are the days of secluded compartments with doors that lead out onto a corridor. As a child, I used to like those, because sometimes, if it wasn't busy, the family could take over a whole compartment, and I could lower the window by unhooking the leather tab from its eyelet. I used to smell the coal smoke, and put my hand out and feel the weight of air as we rushed onward to our annual holiday destination, invariably Weston-super-Mare, all the way down in Somerset.

We ended up in a large, dirty, open carriage that smelled of sweat and cigarettes. I put the big case in the rack at the end of the carriage and heaved the smaller one onto a rack above my head. I checked the upholstery for sticky substances and chewing gum before ushering Olivia into the window seat. Then I leaned back and closed my eyes.

Surprisingly, I found myself fighting back tears of loss: for my car, my nice home and even for Graham, before the rose-tinted spectacles had tarnished.

8

GRACE

The beep of a horn startles me back to the present. For a second, my heart beats out in panic, thinking Graham has found us and has come to haul us back to Cheltenham, then my eyes focus on Sean's truck. I take a few slow breaths and call Olivia, but she's already running back to me. I shiver slightly in a rising breeze. The water in the bay has turned an iron grey. Clouds have gathered while I've been reminiscing, and a spit of rain drifts across the beach. I hurriedly dry Olivia off and throw our stuff in the rucksack as she wriggles back into her clothes.

'Timed that right,' Sean says, opening the door and lifting Olivia in. 'I think you would have been in for a soaking. There's no shelter out this way, and you know we get four seasons in a day and never a winter.'

I'd heard Grandma say that about Ireland, and it seemed so peculiarly *Irish*; if there isn't a winter, there are only three seasons, after all. But, she said, there's no one can make Irish jokes better than the Irish.

There are only two seats in the front of the truck, but they're obviously built for men, so Olivia is squeezed in between Sean and me. She's wary of men, on the whole, but doesn't seem worried.

Sean winks down at her, his face creased into a grin, and says solemnly, 'If you see a guard, duck.'

She blinks, not understanding. I explain that a guard is an Irish policeman, and he's not talking about the bird. Meantime, I hope we don't pass any. Being fined wouldn't be an auspicious start to my stay in Ireland.

It takes a couple of minutes to drive back down into Roone Bay, through the town. He stops by a small garage, where he leaps out and comes back with three Walls' choc ices. I'd forgotten what he'd said about ice creams. He thrusts them at me with a grin, saying, 'Don't let them melt,' and drives on up to the cottage, Olivia bouncing on the seat with anticipation.

The cottage doesn't look any better in the cold light of knowledge, but at least it's not a shock. Sean jumps out and hustles us in through the empty doorway, where we rip the papers off the ice creams. Sean's is demolished in half a dozen bites, while he scans the building with a calm and obviously experienced gaze, which diffuses my own trepidation slightly. His relaxed manner is in total opposition to how Graham would have been, faced with the same situation. His rigid disapproval would have radiated visibly, and his staccato utterances would have been wrapped around self-congratulation as he mentally managed each individual problem.

I stand where the front door should be and try to envisage living here, staring out on a daily basis over Roone Bay quay. It sounds quite romantic, watching the storms flail the shore, the fishing fleet plying its business, the summer sailors mooring in the bay... but these wrecked walls make it seem like some kind of distant, elusive dream. I usher Olivia before me into the little living room and stand just within the gaping window frame.

In the bay, the blue sky has been obliterated by low cloud

rolling in from the mercury-coloured sea. Quite a different story from the morning's casual walk down to the beach.

I collect the ice cream wrappers, screw them up together and stuff them in the rucksack. I wipe Olivia's face and hands with the towel, and rub at the smear of chocolate gloop down her front. 'Well, at least you got some in your mouth,' I say, laughing so that she doesn't think I'm cross. Graham would have been; he expects us both to set an example, all the time.

I suddenly realise I'm spending far too much energy on wondering how Graham would behave in any situation. I must push him to the back of my mind. I'm here; he's not. Sean's physical presence is as solid as the rock this house is built on, so I don't need to know what Graham would do.

'Okay, so,' Sean states, and we follow him around like a trail of cygnets as he points out what's necessary and in what order. His enthusiasm is infectious as he discusses possibilities and skates over obstacles as if they aren't there. He makes me imagine this room painted in a cheerful colour, with curtains and a carpet, and us luxuriating before a log fire.

'Not turf?' I joke.

'Oh, it's still available, and the scent does lend a certain ambience, but I'd suggest a log-burning stove, in fact. More heat more quickly, far more efficient and less of a fire risk. Okay, let's take a look out the back.'

The back door, straight off the main room and kitchen, is made of vertical planks of wood on the outside, nailed to horizontal planks on the inside, and one diagonal to stop it sagging. Though still resting on its hinges and one simple, metal latch, the wood has rotted off about nine inches from the slab of slate beneath. He heaves open the protesting back door and steps out. 'We'll go around the side, so. I'll show you where I'll put the septic tank.'

The back of the cottage opens directly onto a field that rises towards a rocky ridge. It's been grazed closely – by sheep, presumably. It's bound by a ragged complement of unkempt hedges and bits of wire, and the back garden has the remnants of a drystone wall. The stones have long been dislodged by roots and gorse and animals, and there's no gate. If I want a garden, I realise, looking back at the house, I'm going to have to put up some kind of barrier. Somehow a boundary would make me feel safer, too. It's all so barren and exposed.

To the left, Sean points to a small building made of concrete blocks. 'That's the well. Mulcahy built the blockhouse around it, for the electric pump that feeds water into the animal troughs.'

'I thought there was no electricity?'

He grins. 'Sure, it's only for the pump, and that's robbed off the house below. Don't tell them, eh? Electric Ireland will need to run a proper supply through.'

He takes my arm to turn me, and a jolt of warmth shudders through me at the unexpected intimacy.

'Here, we'll build a new kitchen and bathroom,' he's saying. 'Those are the two rooms you really want to have neat and modern. We can put in a pump and filter to bring in water from the well.' His eyes crinkle in amusement. 'No need to go carrying buckets like your grandma did.'

It all seems frighteningly complicated. 'Perhaps,' I suggest diffidently, 'I'd be better off buying a little town house?'

He shakes his head. 'For the same money, you could buy a town house and move in straight away, but you'd probably be buying a bundle of problems. Damp rot, woodworm, a new range, a new roof, heating, insulation – and they'd trickle in one at a time, and you with no money to spare. At least here you'd be starting fresh. You'll know exactly what you've got, and how long it will last. Not to mention the fifteen-acre field.'

'Fifteen acres?' I repeat blankly.

He nods. 'I've been talking around. Mulcahy has worked that land on charity for his whole life, but everyone knows it belongs to the cottage. There's not a lot of money to be made out of it, of course, but he can't really grumble at paying a bit of rent after all this time, eh?'

Grandma never said anything about that. She did say Grandpa's father kept a donkey and chickens, and reared a pig and a cow for meat. But *fifteen acres!* And although I haven't a clue what kind of rent it could generate, it means I won't be entirely dependent on my savings.

'Now, for upstairs…'

Sean leads the way, and we huddle on the little landing while he explains that having the bathroom downstairs means we could keep all three upstairs rooms as bedrooms. One each for myself and Olivia, and a spare. Sean seems to be more excited about the project than I am, but he makes it all sound possible. Maybe we will one day live here, after all.

He thumps down the stairs and out of the front door, and waves an arm to encompass the front of the house. 'These old places can be gloomy, even in summer. If it were mine, I'd build a sun room on the front, too. Like half a greenhouse. It would help to keep the weather off the building, keep it a bit warmer, and you could enjoy the view, even in bad weather.'

'Something for the future,' I say. It's a rather attractive idea. 'It all depends on the cost of the renovations and whether I can find a job.'

He pauses, raising an eyebrow. 'A job?'

I flush. 'I have money, but if I'm going to spend it all on the house…'

'Ah,' he says. There's a wealth of understanding behind the word. I hope my finite resources don't go into public record. 'Well, it's not as bad as it seems. You'll see. Things have a way of working out.'

To my shock, he puts an arm around my shoulders, gives me a quick hug and has let go before I can even think of reacting. He has all the sensitivity I'd wished Graham had, to understand my fears without me having to voice them. I find him very easy to be with. He's nice and kind of *ordinary* somehow. I'm wondering if he's married and what he's like as a husband. Caring, I imagine, and considerate.

I glance at the lowering sky. 'It looks as if the heavens are going to open.'

'Sure, it's just a bit of wet. It'll pass soon enough, and you can get warm and dry in Mrs O'Hara's; she has the range fired. I called to find out where you were, earlier. June will no doubt bring a few more dry days, but maybe bring a raincoat with you when you go walking? You know why Ireland's so green? It's the wet, of course!'

'I'll remember that for next time,' I agree, smiling.

As the rain starts with a vengeance, I accept his offer of a lift into town rather than risk a drenching, and we run out to his truck, laughing. As he suggested, the squall is brief; in five minutes it's gone, and rays of sun are shooting through the gaps in heavy black clouds which are just waiting for their turn.

I realise now how basic life must have been when Grandpa was growing up here. The home was simply an enclosed space, with no frills. No bathroom, no running water, no curtains, dressing tables, fridges, cookers, washing machines... Any furniture required was made by hand. Water was lugged from the well, daily. Candles or oil lamps provided light in the evenings – if they could be afforded. Fires were lit from scavenged wood or cut turf, and were used for cooking food and providing warmth at the same time. Sheets, Grandma told me, had been made from flour sacks sewn together, and mattresses had been filled with straw.

When I said to Grandma I could cope with 'basic', I really had no idea what that meant. How conditions have changed!

That evening, we sit in Mrs O'Hara's living room, listening to the rain hammering at the windows. I packed cagoules, but I think I might need to invest in some more substantial rainwear if this drenching downpour is usual. Ireland is notoriously wet, but the speed at which the weather changes is alarming. It's because we're by the south coast, Sean told me. Atlantic squalls rip through and are gone just as quickly. We'll get used to it, apparently.

Later that night, I sit and write another letter to Mum, telling her about the builder picking us up from the beach and about the changing weather. I give a positive take to Sean fixing up the house for us and don't mention the true state of the place. I'll break the rest of the news when I have a clearer picture, myself, of what the future holds. I tell her about the journey south from Dublin and make it sound amusing. Maybe one day I'll look back and remember it that way. But as I'm slipping into sleep, the past catches up with me.

9

GRACE, ONE YEAR EARLIER

After the dreadful photo exhibition, I shocked myself with the realisation that I was mulling over *how* to leave Graham. There was no *if* any longer. I needed to leave, for my own sanity. After all, why was I not happy? I had everything, didn't I? If anyone had asked, I would have said Graham had done nothing more awful than simply be himself: overbearing, arrogant, master of his domain, and always totally and utterly in control of everything – including Olivia and me.

But, in fact, it wasn't long before I realised that I didn't know Graham at all, that I was wary of crossing his will, even in tiny ways. Then Margery Mannings sowed bigger doubts in my mind, but I chose not to believe her sly gossip. Also, having a child added a new dimension to any decisions I might make regarding my own happiness. I thought that staying with Graham was best for Olivia. She needed a stable home, and I truly thought I could sacrifice my happiness for her. But that kind of unhappiness can only be contained for so long. For a long time, I didn't tell anyone quite how miserable I was, either. If I'd unpacked my unhappiness and shared it, I would never get it back in the box, but Grandma guessed and wormed the story from me.

Graham and I had been at an art presentation when Margery chose to confide in me. I arrived as one person and left as another. Her snippet of gossip sank into my subconscious and bred there, out of sight for several years, though I wasn't aware of it at the time. And the moment I knew I had to leave, for my own sanity, I realised I was actually frightened of Graham.

It said in the exhibition brochure that Graham was kindly sponsoring the event, avoiding the underlying truth that he only considered money well spent if it gave him kudos in some way. The whole superficial pretentiousness of the opening night made me wonder how I'd ever thought I could fit in. The exhibition of stark monochrome photography wasn't beautiful. Shocking, as advertised, but also shockingly unpleasant, which I hadn't expected. I should have, as it was clearly labelled erotic. *Erotic* used to mean a suggestive impression of desire beneath something beautiful, but now the word is used to encompass blatant pornography. What a waste of a lovely word.

I wandered past this wall of larger-than-life obscenity, but my eyes migrated to the salacious expressions the other guests were trying to disguise behind intelligent dialogue.

I had a glass of champagne in my hand – my second, actually, as I'd downed the first in hefty gulps. When opportunity arose, I slipped out of the group I was with and found a small seat by an angular alcove. I was lost in inner contemplation when a voice stated, 'You aren't enjoying the exhibition.'

There was a young man standing beside me. His thin legs were encased in tight leather trousers that were too revealing. I looked up past the blatant bulge of his crotch, unfortunately at my eye level. He had a strongly defined face, all bones and

angles and brooding self-awareness, framed by a tangle of dark
hair. His eyes were darkly hooded, lending a sardonic hint to a
supercilious expression, undoubtedly practised in front of a
mirror. Instinctively, I knew this was the photographer.

'Exhibition is certainly the right word. I'm not enthralled,' I
admitted; an understatement. Such obsession with sex defines
humans as the most confused species on the planet.

'But the images are good, don't you think?'

'I'm sure the photography is professional.'

'They've been described as groundbreaking.' He sounded
peeved, like a child whose coveted new toy has just been dissed
by a peer.

'I'm sure they have,' I responded cynically. 'Art critics love
the sound of their own ambiguity. I find those images unpleas-
antly intimate. I like my art to be somewhat less, ah, revealing.'

'Art is supposed to create an emotional response in the
viewer.' His voice was cold, his lip curled in a sneer. He clearly
felt I was incapable of understanding.

I wanted to tell him to go away, shave and grow up but said
lightly, 'Art is an ill-defined word, these days. I know what
people do, but I don't want it thrust in my face.'

'You're just a prude.'

I gave a hiccup of genuine amusement. That was nothing if
not rude, but honesty begets honesty. 'You might be a good
photographer, but this...' I wave my hand behind me. 'This isn't
so much insulting to intelligence as childish. Maybe one day
you'll realise that the need to shock betrays immaturity.'

I wondered whether he was going to stamp his foot and
have a tantrum. Instead, he swivelled on the heel of a black
leather boot encrusted with silver studs, and stalked away to
engage with those who better understood his talent.

'Well, you really know how to make friends,' an amused
voice said. 'Do you mind?'

Margery, the wife of one of Graham's banker friends, seated

herself beside me without waiting for my response. She was one of the in-crowd: manicured, polished and painted. She must have been stunning when she was younger. I didn't think we'd connected in any way, so I was a bit surprised at being singled out.

'I take it you're not enthralled, either?'

'No.' I turned to survey the small murmuring groups surrounding each image. 'They're all trying to sound clever, but look at their faces. Someone has finally given them permission to walk through a forbidden door.'

She smiled and settled back. 'I agree. I was also enjoying the freedom to indulge, but seeing you here, alone, was an opportunity I've been hoping to get for a while. It's no concern of mine as to why you married Graham, of course.'

'What on earth do you mean?'

'Well, like me, you clambered out of the gutter and won the jackpot, and I don't blame you for that. We only get one shot at this life, and standing by your principles doesn't provide some of the more material benefits.'

She glanced over at her own husband as she said this. He was florid with good living and not at all attractive. *Did she marry him simply for a better life? Is that what she thinks I did?*

'It wasn't like that at all!'

'No?' Her smile was slightly cynical, and I felt my cheeks grow warm. I wondered if I'd said that a bit too loudly, too quickly. I was aware of the rumour that I'd married Graham for his money, but jealousy provides a solid platform for such gossip. I'm sure his peers saw me as the token young wife, brought in to provide home comforts. There's truth in that, too. He was lonely; he admitted as much, after we were married. He also admitted that he found me immensely attractive, the moment he saw me during my job interview – one of the reasons he hired me in the first place. He thought I'd be flattered, but I found it rather unnerving, as though I'd unwittingly interviewed for a very different kind of position.

'Well, dear,' Margery continued, 'that's not really what I wanted to say. I just think you should know quite whom you've married. I suspect no one has had the courage to tell you what everyone else knows.'

She waited a moment, as if giving me a chance to say *stop,* or to get up and walk away, but I didn't. Curiosity is a powerful incentive. And if people were gossiping about me, I wanted to know what they were saying.

She took my silence as permission to continue. 'Did Graham tell you how Cynthia died?'

She was referring to his first wife. 'Of course.'

'I suspect he left out the bit where the Spanish cops arrested him for her murder?'

'What?' Her words sent an involuntary shiver of apprehension through me before I laughed it off. 'Well, obviously he didn't, or he'd be in prison, wouldn't he?'

'There are those who think he should be.' Her eyes flicked briefly over to where her husband was now engaged in dialogue with Graham. They weren't looking at the images, so I suspected they were talking business.

As if reading my mind, she said, 'It always comes down to finance, don't you think? Everyone knows Graham married a wealthy woman, but what isn't generally known is that he didn't get his hands on her fortune until after she died. Cynthia was wise to gold diggers. When they married, she kept the majority of her wealth in a separate account. She invested a substantial sum in Graham's business, of course, but when she died, he got the rest. A considerable sum. I know that because Frank dealt with the transfer of the funds from her private account into his, after probate.'

I tried to sound cold. 'Your point being?'

Her smile was feline. 'I liked Cynthia. I was sad when she

died. She'd already left Graham for another man; a widower
with three children of his own. Then she asked for a divorce.
Bang. There goes the fortune, along with his wife. Then, before
things were finalised, she very conveniently died, in a somewhat
bizarre accident abroad, at which point Graham inherited
everything because they were still legally married.'

'A coincidence, surely!'

She patted my hand and stood up. 'It might have just been
lucky for Graham, but the police must have suspected otherwise.' She shrugged. 'I'm surprised you didn't learn this sooner,
but I don't have a vested interest in keeping you in the dark, like
the rest of his satellites.' She bent over and whispered, 'I meant
it for the best. Now, take that look off your face, or tell Graham
it's because you find the images offensive. They're on their way
over.'

When I told all this to Grandma, she said I wasn't put on this
planet to keep Graham happy at the expense of my own life,
that I should think of myself, too, but I didn't know what to do.
If I'd told Graham I was unhappy, he would have bought me
something expensive, as if that solved the problem. Because he
was content with the way things were, he wouldn't see the
truth. And if I told him I was going to leave, he would have
immediately put everything in place to secure his own interests,
assessing my value in terms of an asset or a liability. And worst
of all, he would have made sure I couldn't take Olivia with me.

Graham's power lay not in understanding anyone else's
point of view but in subverting it. He might even have suggested
a marriage counsellor. The way I saw it, though, was that a
marriage moderated by a third party would be a compromise. I
didn't want my life to be a compromise. I didn't want to give it
another shot, to put myself back on the rails and then have to go
through it all again when it didn't work out. Once I'd made the

decision, I knew it had to be a clean and absolute break, because Graham was as inflexible as the tide.

Domestic revelations are never sudden events. They creep up sneakily, and that apparent epiphany is simply the moment when the pieces of the puzzle come together, and the incomplete picture pops into focus.

10

GRACE

The next morning there's a letter from Mum waiting beside my plate at breakfast. I eagerly rip the envelope open and scan the contents. After telling me that she's well, and pleased that I arrived safely – she'd been worried! – she said that Graham had, indeed, gone there looking for me, the day after my flight, and she'd told him, in no uncertain terms, that I'd left him. And when he asked where I'd gone, she said she wasn't going to tell him, and that I was somewhere he wouldn't find me. Apparently, he'd thought about this for a moment then concluded that I must be having some kind of midlife crisis, and that he'd discuss it with me when I came home.

It was typical of him to believe I hadn't really left but was just making some kind of statement, and would come crawling back apologetically in the end. I wondered if I should send him a letter and mentally began writing it: *I'm sorry I left you in that way, but...*

I laugh out loud. Begin with an apology? Absolutely not! No. When I can write a letter that's about Olivia and me, not him, then I will write it.

I have no idea whether there are any opportunities in Roone Bay for typing and PA skills, and have a suspicion that available work is networked to friends and family. But I have to try. I draft a notice – *Seeking Employment* – and place it in the post office. I itemise my secretarial and typing skills, and my history of work, without specifying the companies. If someone asks for references, that could be a problem. And if it doesn't generate any interest, I might have to put an advertisement in the local newspaper.

I wonder at my own hopefulness. How can I get a job at all, when I have Olivia? But she'll start school in September, and we can surely survive until then. There's a small school here – quaint, with just two classrooms – which I intend to visit, but not yet. She hasn't realised this is any more than a holiday, and the moment we visit a school, my dastardly plan will be clear. I only hope we'll have moved into our renovated house by the time school starts.

I made an appointment at the bank to open an account, and walked up briskly at the appointed time. Mrs O'Hara was kind enough to let me leave Olivia with her for an hour.

Mr Briggs, the manager himself, sees me in his plush office. As is our bank manager in Cheltenham, he's self-important and plump with good living. 'Mrs McCarthy?' he says, almost as a query. I'm startled for a moment, having forgotten I'd given him my maiden name. 'Please, take a seat.'

And that's where his affability ends. He pompously talks down to me as if I'm being interviewed for a job. Presumably used to being treated with almost subservient respect, he queries me unashamedly. Why have I moved here? Where is my husband? Can he not come in and sign his name to the account?

I conceal my fury and remind him that I have the legal right to open an account in my name and use my own money how I see fit, without asking a husband for permission. How dare he suggest I need a man to vouch for me? I ask. Does he want my business, or shall I take it elsewhere?

I don't raise my voice, but I doubt any woman has ever spoken to him like this before; he's a demigod in his narrow world. I inform him I intend to renovate my inherited cottage, and the sum I'll immediately transfer into the account from my English bank is required to reimburse Sean Murphy for the building materials. The assumption is, of course, that it will be a second home, a holiday cottage.

He slams his hand on a brass bell, the kind once fashionable on the reception desks of hotels.

A young man in an impeccable suit and tie immediately answers the door, as if he's been lurking outside. 'Sir?'

Mr Briggs glances up then looks down at me over his triple chins as he opens a ledger, the actions dismissing me in more ways than one. 'Mr O'Rahilly will oblige with the account and the transfer. Good day, *Miss* McCarthy.'

'Yes, sir,' Mr O'Rahilly responds.

Annoyed, but vaguely amused, I'm shown into a less grand office, where the paperwork is competently and quickly completed. 'When will the money arrive from England?' I ask.

'It will take about two weeks to clear.'

I refrain from asking if it's brought over in person, by horse-drawn carriage. I rise and take my leave, realising that I've scuppered any chance of employment in the one establishment in Roone Bay where my experience would be useful. But in any event, I wouldn't want to work in this stifling, cumbersome remnant of a past era.

It seems that being single with a child or divorced with a child equally undermines the fabric of Irish society, which is clinging precariously to the old order. But other things are changing here, so no doubt that will, in due course.

When I was young and naïve, I used to think that if a marriage was bad, a woman should just up and leave. The world wars and the suffragettes' fight for equality changed the social landscape forever, didn't they? So why don't women just leave unhappy relationships?

I learned, of course.

Having a child changes everything. And sometimes it's *better the devil you know than the one you don't*, one of Grandma's endless stock of platitudes. But what would she know? She married the love of her life, went to England with him, and lived her life poor in wealth but rich in happiness. I don't recall Grandma ever being unhappy, her only regret being having just the one child, my mother. She said she'd once thought she'd have a houseful. Now, I wonder if the fates weren't being kind in providing just the one! Her endless optimism is a character trait, I guess, but it's also a kind of blessing. Without aspirations of grandeur, perhaps happiness is easier to achieve.

I wish I'd known that when I met Graham.

Having clawed myself from a life of permanently counting pennies to one of comparative luxury, for a while I truly believed I was lucky, even though my good fortune came with strings and obligations. But my luck became a cloak I had to wear day in, day out. Because Graham's wife, an expression of his power and wealth, had to be perfect. She was an object in his empire, not so much revered and cherished as owned.

His wealth was his, not mine.

I take a deep breath. I mustn't dwell on this. I've escaped. I own a house we'll be able to live in one day. This community I've dropped into will eventually accept me; and if not me, it will accept my daughter. That's my goal, and my goal must become my strength.

. . .

Two weeks pass with strange speed. Some days it rains, and the temperature plummets. On those days we sit in the parlour reading or playing board games. Sometimes the sun comes out, and it's surprisingly warm, so we walk into the town or down to the beach. I don't know when Olivia stopped asking when was Daddy coming, but I feel lighter with that possibility sinking into the distance with every passing day. I have the feeling she's relaxing, too, becoming the carefree six-year-old she's supposed to be.

May has slipped into the middle of June and two things have changed. Firstly, Mrs O'Hara tells me that her first booked visitors will arrive soon, so I'll need to find somewhere else to stay. Secondly, I'm informed by the bank that my money has arrived, so I phone Sean's mother, as instructed, from Mrs O'Hara's telephone, to pass on the message. Sean rings back that evening, and I hold the phone tight to my ear as if it will bring us closer together.

'I've been pushing to finish my last job,' he says, 'so that I can get going all the sooner on yours. That is, I assume the job's mine? Didn't you get a couple more quotes?'

'I tried,' I tell him, 'but the people I spoke to just looked at me strangely and said, *Isn't that Sean's job?*'

He laughs. 'That's the way it is here. Mind you, I did warn everyone that I'd scupper their boats if they stole my work. So, will I order the materials?'

'Please.'

'And I'll meet you on site soon?'

'That would be good,' I agree.

An awkward silence follows, before he says, 'Right. Fine. We'll do that then. See you soon.'

'See you soon.'

I experience a little thrill of anticipation as I put the phone down. I thought something had clicked between us as he was walking me around Grandpa's cottage, discussing what he planned to do, and I wonder if he felt it, too. It's strange that so soon after leaving a bad relationship, I'm contemplating another, but maybe the fates are pushing me, after all, because it feels absolutely right.

11

GRACE

A few days later, I'm quite surprised to arrive back at Mrs O'Hara's to be presented with a letter, addressed to me by hand. There's no stamp, no postmark, and for a moment I assume it's from the bank then realise that if it were, it would have been typed.

Mrs O'Hara can't contain herself. 'It's from himself at the Big House,' she informs me in tones of almost religious reverence.

'Who?'

'Noel O'Donovan!'

I must still have a look of confusion on my face, so she elaborates. 'Roone Manor, behind the new hotel. Jane Weddows brought the letter down. She's his housekeeper now. Her father used to drive the trains, before the rail shut down, back in the forties it was. What with her husband dying of the cancer, her only daughter running off to England, and no boys to support her, she had to go out working again.'

Oh, goodness. What on earth does the man from the Big House, who came back from America with his pot of gold, want with me?

My stomach drops. *Perhaps he knows Graham!*

I take the letter and go on up to my room. Mrs O'Hara's curiosity follows me up the stairs, but I need to satisfy mine in private.

'What is it, Mummy?' Olivia asks. 'Is it from Daddy?'

'No, love,' I tell her. 'It's from the man who's building the big hotel up on the hill.'

'Oh,' she says, unimpressed, and throws herself down on the bed to read her new book.

The notepaper is thick bond with an embossed heading detailing Noel's name, address and telephone number. The handwriting, which I recognise as old copperplate, is that of someone who can no longer quite control the pen. Age, or some kind of disabling condition, maybe. The note is brief and to the point, written with old-fashioned courtesy.

Dear Mrs McCarthy

Regarding your search for suitable employment, I would be pleased if you would attend me at Roone House on Tuesday morning, at 10 a.m. If this is not convenient, please call Mrs Weddows at this number to rearrange. I have a proposition for you, which, of course, you are quite at liberty to refuse should it not be of interest. I look forward to meeting with you.

Yours,

Noel O'Donovan

I'm curious, of course. Who wouldn't be? I'm guessing that a boy who sloped off to America to find a fortune, and actually came back with one, is something of a novelty in Ireland, especially in a small town like Roone Bay. So many emigrants simply disappeared, or remained disappointed, particularly in a time notorious for postscripts to job advertisements reading: *Irish and Blacks Need Not Apply*.

I've noticed that Noel O'Donovan's name is spoken with awe, tinted, perhaps, with a little envy. Certainly, he has celebrity status in this small community, though whether the older generation will appreciate the kind of changes he's bringing to the town is anyone's guess at this time. I'm assuming that the man who owns a mansion and a hotel under construction might well need some sort of secretarial or administrative support, especially in the light of failing physical abilities.

If so, this isn't just interesting; it could be a lifesaver.

I write my acceptance letter and decide to deliver it by hand. I admit to wanting a peek at the one-time Roone Manor, now renovated and demoted to Roone House, or 'the Big House', by the locals.

The weather has turned mild, and we're dressed informally, ready for the beach, as we walk up the steep slope past the new hotel, which, I've learned, is to have the highly original name of Roone Bay Hotel. I'd vaguely supposed it might be called Roone Manor Hotel or something with a little more flair.

With the functional concrete blocks partially smoothed over with render and the three steep, pointed gables at the front cleared of scaffolding, a little charm is visible. Maybe it won't be such an eyesore, after all. I wave at the guys on the scaffolding, and they wave back as we head on up the small lane to the Big House beyond.

'Daddy said people who do building are too stupid to do anything better,' Olivia says.

Goodness. Did Graham really tell her something so horrible? I say in reproof, 'You shouldn't judge people before you know them. Sean does building, and he's not stupid, is he?'

'No. He's nice.'

'I'm sure the men working on the hotel are nice, too. Some people enjoy doing that kind of work, being outside, creating something with their hands. Just because they're doing building work doesn't mean they're stupid. Daddy isn't always right.'

She thinks about this strange possibility then adds, 'Well, being builders is better than being scrounging freeloaders anyway.'

I don't reprimand her; she doesn't know the meaning of the words. I can only suppose she's parroting Graham's philosophical outlook on life; he who was born to inherit the status of employer rather than employee, just two generations removed from the man who built the business from the ground up. How easily Graham became arrogant, taking his wealth for granted.

I suspect Graham's grandfather must have been fairly ruthless, to build a successful business from almost nothing; Graham's father had been blunt and arrogant, trampling on everyone to take the business to the next level, and Graham had wrapped the mantle of authority around himself as if born to royalty. I'm wondering just how self-important this Noel character is going to be, coming from nothing to the kind of wealth a poor Irishman couldn't even conceive of, even fifty years ago. I hope I don't dislike him!

I stop for a moment and look back down the hill.

The new hotel is going to have an amazing view of the bay. It will sell itself on that, if nothing else. In this land of windswept coastlines, a warm hotel room with a view is going to prove a haven to Americans seeking the false romance of their forebears, with no intention of experiencing the hardships they had endured.

I turn back to the lane. Hand in hand, Olivia and I walk around the corner to be confronted with what I can only describe as a stately home. I stop short, in awe. It's magnificent, settled comfortably into the renovated landscaped garden as if it's been pushed up out of the rock, dragging ivy with it. I'm impressed with the building itself, and the social history behind its construction, more than its commercial value.

Built of warm brickwork, the tall windows gaze out at the view over a young lacework of Virginia creeper that's climbing the walls. There's stone balustrading in front of the house, and a raft of wide steps leading up to an impressive front door. From the side, a lower level is visible. I recall seeing such a house, once before, while on an outing with my parents. The family and guests, the guide informed us, enter on the floor where dining rooms and ballrooms are situated, while the lower storey is used by staff for laundry, kitchens and all other functional activities.

This isn't a National Heritage house that one pays to look around but is owned by one very rich individual. I'm brought back to the realisation that I'm a mere pawn in this game of life, and that whoever owns this monolith, in fact, holds the lives and livelihoods of many people in his hands. I wonder what he did in America that earned such wealth.

Even Olivia seems to be struck dumb, though it doesn't last long. 'Who lives here?' she demands, wide-eyed. 'Is it the king?'

'Ireland doesn't have a king, love,' I tell her. 'It's owned by a man called Mr O'Donovan. He sent me the letter, remember, and I'm just bringing up my reply to post.'

I wasn't quite sure where to post it, though, and feeling like we're trespassing, I lead Olivia up to the massive front door. There's no letter box, which doesn't surprise me but leaves me feeling rather silly, with the letter in my hand and no clear idea of where to put it.

As we descend back to the gravel drive, which circles around a small pond with a fountain, a man walks around the side of the house, pushing a wheelbarrow containing a shovel and some shears. He isn't so young, I think, from the deep crevices that line his face, but his stance is upright, and the eyes which assess me are a clear, twinkling blue. 'Can I help you?'

His Irish accent has been softened in some indefinable way.

'I, ah, was looking for a letter box,' I admit. 'Noel

O'Donovan sent me a letter, and as I was in the town, it seemed the obvious thing to bring the reply myself.'

He points back down the road. 'At the end of the drive, there's a box. It's green. Maybe a little disguised by ivy.'

'Oh,' I say, disconcerted. 'I didn't see it.'

'No matter – I'll take it,' he says, and I can do little but hand it to him. I hope it doesn't end up in the compost. He tips his hand to a flat cap before trundling on.

We head back down the lane. The letter box is exactly where the gardener said it would be, and if I hadn't been so entranced by the house, and wondering about its owner, I would have seen it.

12

GRACE

The next few days pass slowly, with nothing to do but walk through the small town, take Olivia to the beach and read. This really does feel like an interlude in life, but it's strangely uncommercial, this lack of things to do – there's no cinema or entertainment venue of any kind. I do wonder, for the first time, whether I can live here, whether it's the right place for us.

When the day of my interview dawns, I'm in a more positive frame of mind than I've been for many years. I'm determined that if I don't like the work, or don't like this rich Mr O'Donovan, then I won't work for him.

I wonder whether to take Olivia with me to the meeting then decide I will. After all, whatever he's proposing, he needs to understand my circumstances, and Olivia is, without a doubt, the driving factor in my life at this moment. I might have stayed with Graham, for her sake, had I not discovered that letter from the school. Being spurred to leave, though, made me rediscover myself and all the reasons why I should have left sooner. There's only one reason I didn't: I didn't know how to be a single mother without an income. I have a fleeting, horrific vision of an alternative me sitting at home, alone, with a huge glass of wine in my hand, trying to understand why being a pampered ornament in a rich man's home isn't actually enough.

On the whole, I'm feeling a little less frazzled now. The break, despite the setbacks, has done me good. I feel more like my younger self, the one who thought gaining a job in the office of a factory was a huge career move. I guess it was, in a way. But life hands out some strange chances, and we don't always make the best of choices.

I hold Olivia's hand as we walk up the steep drive, past the mammoth new hotel.

There it is. Roone House, once a bastion of power, owned by the local lord who held sway over everyone he looked down upon. Noel, once chattel to the lord of the manor, has raised a defiant fist at the injustices of the past by dwelling in it. No wonder the local community talks of him with a kind of awe. I'd been amazed at the house when I saw it previously, but now I take a more evaluated perusal. The mansion has been so largely renovated, it seems too pristine and new. It will take years for the stone to mellow, to attain that aged look of a stately home, but it's obvious he's expended effort into trying to recreate it as it had once been.

Olivia, skipping and chanting, takes it in her stride, as if we visit mansions every day. I find this slightly amusing. Does she think she belongs in this higher echelon of society, or is she simply being a child, immersed in her own world?

We tread up the wide stone steps to the entrance and use the big knocker to announce our presence. Behind me, I hear a throat being cleared. I turn. It's the gardener we saw before, wiping his hands on his trousers. His smile is infectious, and I smile back.

'Good morning. I'm here to see Noel O'Donovan.'

He beckons for us to come back down. He holds his hand out as I approach, and we clasp, briefly. 'Sorry about the dirt.

But it's good, clean, dirt, eh? I'm Noel. You must be Grace. And this' – he bends down – 'must be Olivia.'

'I'm Olivia Adams,' she says, in her best posh voice, and holds her hand out regally.

He takes it, encloses it in both his hands. 'What a polite little lady you are, to be sure,' he says. She beams at him. 'Shall we go in and find some orange juice? And, you know, Auntie Jane might just have made some fresh soda bread. Nothing quite like it. Hot, with lashings of butter, eh?'

'That sounds wonderful, thank you,' I answer for her.

I've met some of Graham's friends, and not one of them has clambered up through the social ranks without dragging the weight of an ego along for the ride, so I'm immediately relieved to find that Noel, who I'd previously taken for a gardener, is down to earth, ordinary.

'This way,' he says to Olivia, still holding her hand.

I've taught her to be wary of strangers, but somehow Noel doesn't feel like a stranger; he feels like someone I've known all my life. Olivia must sense this, too, as she happily skips along beside him.

We walk along a small path of herringboned red bricks, which runs along the side of the house. At the back, we come to a small, shaded, south-facing garden. It's exceedingly green, the rampant vegetation lending an underlying sense of something magical. I can imagine children making dens in the under-growth. Mature trees rise in the distance, but nearer the house are flowering shrubs and young ornamental maples, inter-spersed with rampant rhododendrons.

'It's stunning!' I exclaim.

'I had to argue with my landscape gardener,' Noel admits. 'He was all for native trees, a sentiment I admire, but I wanted something pretty and exotic. The farm I grew up on just had a few scrubby trees and no flowers, except for primroses in the spring.' He adds, with a twinkle in his eye, 'One of the benefits of being wealthy is that I always have the last say.'

'I think I would have done the same.'

His lopsided grin is both an apology and a lack of one; that of a child caught out being naughty but with the underlying suggestion that he'd do it again, given the chance. I remind myself that he was born poor so maybe hasn't lost sight of his roots. However, whatever he wants from me, I suspect it will be to his advantage, not mine.

The scent of baking wafts out as he opens a small door and indicates for us to precede him. 'Please.'

We enter straight into what was probably once a working kitchen for a large house, and which has been renovated into a functional, modern kitchen-diner. There's a huge range at one end and an impressive array of copper pots hanging above it, for decoration, presumably, rather than for use.

He introduces us. 'Grace, Olivia – my housekeeper, Jane Weddows. I'm just popping out to the mudroom to change my shoes. Do start without me.'

Mrs Weddows is a tall, thin woman around the same age as my mother, or a little older. She wears a nylon housecoat, buttoned up the front, which adds to the impression of height.

Her somewhat daunting severity is cracked by a broad, welcoming smile. 'Well, now,' she says. 'Sure, you must be Connor's granddaughter. Why else would you be owning the house?'

I sense the question behind the statement and smile with a nod.

'Sit yourselves down, now.' She flaps a hand towards a pine table already neatly laid out with cutlery and pretty, fluted bone china. 'I've made soda bread and some fruit scones, so you can take your choice.'

'Thank you, that's very kind. Did you know my grandparents then?'

'Not well. I was young when Connor stole Caitlin off to England – in the night it was, such a shock. I just have a picture in my head is all. Such a handsome couple they were, I remember. It was so sad, but it was all her father's doing, I guess, pushing her to marry a man she didn't love. But there were so many leaving, and few enough who came back.' She shakes her head, adding, 'And so many dead; it wasn't unusual for young women to die in labour.' She crossed herself absently. 'Noel only left for America after his wife, Sinéad, died in childbirth. Times were hard back then.'

'You're talking about me?' Noel asks, coming back in, wearing slippers.

'About my grandfather, mostly,' I say, seeing Jane look guilty.

'He was my best friend, you know, through school, though he never did learn to read well. There was a time he was going to come to America with me, but things didn't go that way. Is he well?'

'I'm sorry, my grandfather died ten years ago. I thought maybe you knew that.'

Noel was still for a moment then said, 'No. I'm sorry to hear it. I would like to have talked to him again, but it's not to be. Ah, the scones have arrived!'

A rich scent steams through a stripey linen tea towel on the plate Jane has placed on the table. She whips the cloth off like a magician, revealing golden-crusted scones and a fresh loaf. My mouth waters.

'You know, of course, that you have family here?' Jane says. 'I don't know what they'd be now; some kind of cousins from Connor's sisters. They'll be wanting to meet you, I'm sure.'

I'm startled by this revelation. I don't recall Grandpa speaking about his family. 'It hadn't occurred to me that I'd have relatives. I wonder if they know I'm here?'

Noel smiles. 'News is like the rain here. It falls on everyone.

I don't doubt they'll have heard. But, what, three generations gone? We'll have to write a family tree for you to get to grips with who's who. But for now, let's tuck in, shall we?'

He pushes Olivia's chair in, cuts a scone in half for her and tells her to mind, as it's hot. I love his interaction with my daughter and think he would have made someone a superb grandfather.

Jane lowers a large teapot onto the table and a glass of juice for Olivia, and asks, 'Will that be all?'

'That's lovely, thanks, Jane.'

Dismissed, she leaves us, and I'm subtly reminded of her status here, as Noel's employee.

Noel pours and asks me about my life in England. He includes Olivia, for which I'm grateful. The Victorian tenet of children being seen and not heard is still convenient for Graham, who could have learned so much by listening to his children.

I give as little away as I can about my reason for being here without Graham, and Olivia backs me up by saying it's just a holiday, explaining that we have a big house at home which is much nicer.

Eventually, Noel goes to the door and calls, 'Jane? Will you care for Olivia for a while?'

'Sure, I'll mind the precious,' she says as she bustles back in, holding out her hand to Olivia. 'Shall I show you Maggie, the parrot, while your mam is talking to Mr O'Donovan?'

She couldn't have said anything better.

'My friend Julia's got a parrot,' Olivia informs her with relish, reaching out her own hand. 'It's green, and it can say bad words.'

'Oh dear,' Jane says, winking at me as she leads her away. 'We'll have to see if Maggie knows any then. But, sure, we won't repeat them, will we?'

Olivia giggles and shakes her head.

Noel leads me up a wide concrete staircase with no banisters. The walls are painted pale apple green. 'It's extra wide, because they used to be rushing up and down here with food for the family,' he says.

'There isn't a dumb waiter?'

'Not at all. And they were big, heavy platters, no doubt. It would probably break all the health and safety rules these days.'

We come out into a corridor and from there enter an impressive dining room. 'I use this when I have guests,' he says, waving a hand dismissively. 'But really, it's a barn. Let's go through to my study.'

I'm itching to ask a load of questions, like why did he choose to buy this place and do it up, how much did it cost, did he have to get planning permission... but I manage to hold my tongue.

He holds open another solid, heavy door, and we enter a room which, though the high ceiling provides the impression of space, is fairly compact. One part is set up as a modern office, but to one side there are a couple of small, comfortable chairs set by a low table. He indicates for me to seat myself, but I'm drawn to the tall window.

'Oh!' I exclaim as the town is set out before me, like a child's toy town, curving around the bay. Beyond it, the wider vista of Roaring Water Bay reaches out into the Atlantic, the Fastnet Rock lighthouse clearly visible in the far distance.

'Yes, the view is stunning, isn't it? That rather explains why Roone built it here, and why I was attracted to it in the first place. The hotel, below, has much the same view. I think that's what will sell it to our American relatives.' He adds, somewhat cynically, 'They want to view their past through rose-coloured spectacles.'

I flash him a smile. 'Don't we all? When Mum said the cottage was lying empty, I had no idea how basic it was, or what a state it would be in. It must have been a grim existence; no running water or electricity, and just a hearth fire for heat.'

'It was a hard life, sure, but sometimes the simple life has a lot going for it,' Noel says softly.

'Well, I guess our expectations have changed. I want piped water, electricity and a bathroom, at least. And my builder suggested I should have a conservatory on the front, too.'

'I heard you'd employed Sean Murphy.'

'Goodness, there are no secrets here, are there?'

Noel dryly disagrees. 'Oh, there are plenty of secrets, all right! Tell me, what do you think of Sean?'

I feel my cheeks grow warm. 'He's nice. He seems sincere. And kind.'

Noel smiles, as if catching a meaning beyond my words. 'He is. You could have done worse. So, what's your story, Grace? I get the feeling that you've run from something unpleasant.'

I turn from the window and seat myself, somewhat primly. 'I don't mean to be rude, but my personal circumstances aren't open for discussion. I'm here because you invited me, apparently to make some kind of offer of employment?' I flush, recalling that when someone says *I don't mean to be rude, but*, they carry on to be exactly that.

There's a slight pause, and he says, 'You're absolutely right. But maybe if I tell you my story, you might tell me a little of yours in time. If you want to, of course.'

I give a rueful smile. 'I'm a little sensitive at the moment. But maybe, in time...'

He clears his throat. 'Right. I'm thinking of writing my memoir. Quite who for, I'm not sure. I never had any children. After Sinéad died giving birth, I didn't marry again.'

'You must have loved her very much.'

'It was a long time ago now.'

'But weren't you lonely?'

I think, for a moment, that I've crossed an invisible line, but Noel gives a faintly cynical smile. 'Sometimes. But it wasn't for want of interest. I had several offers, of course, once I became wealthy.'

'Wealth comes with conditions, doesn't it?' I say this softly, and his eyes flit to mine in unspoken agreement. We each have our secrets.

'So,' he begins. 'To the business in hand. I've had a somewhat interesting life. Well, it might be of interest to some, I don't know. Maybe it's hubris. But I had the sudden urge to get a few things down in writing before it's too late. I always thought I was fairly literate, but it's not as easy as it seems.'

He waves a hand towards piles of papers on the desk. 'My notes. I need someone who can organise it, type it up and fill in the gaps. I'm open to being interrogated. Do you think you could do that?'

'Most of my work has been secretarial. I've never worked on a memoir, but I don't see that it would be beyond me. Do you intend to publish?'

'Maybe. That I haven't decided. There are too many names.' He gives a small sigh. 'That's why it's so difficult. Should I be honest and hurt some people? Should I put different names in, to keep people's anonymity? Should some things not be said at all? You see my predicament. Of course, it could be published posthumously. But I'm not ready to give up the ghost just yet,' he adds with a smile.

'You don't have to publish. If you wrote it, it would be an interesting document for people to discover in the future.'

'Absolutely. Maybe it should be sealed until fifty years after my death, when all the people I mention will have passed, too. A record, for posterity, perhaps. So, here it is. You're probably wondering why you and not someone I know?'

'That had crossed my mind,' I reply with a smile.

'The truth is, I didn't want to employ someone local, because family connections are strong here. There are too many people involved, and not everything I want to say will be welcomed in the cold light of day.'

'Perhaps you should stick to the American part of your story?'

'I did think I'd start with that, to get the juices flowing, but a person doesn't come from nowhere. I am who I am because of my history: my parents, my peers, their stories...' His eyes are distant again, lost in some memory. 'And I didn't get where I am by always being nice. I'd like you to know that about me before we go any further. I think this will be a cathartic exercise for me. A confessional. Maybe when it's written I'll ceremoniously burn it.'

I don't know what to say to that, because I'm not sure whether he's joking.

'So, what do you think?' he says.

I feel my cheeks burn. 'Ah, we haven't discussed remuneration. And there's my daughter to consider.'

'Neither will give you cause to worry.'

'And you know I've never been involved in this kind of project.'

'You were honest about that. But you can type, and I'm a great believer in first impressions. I like you, and your daughter, and feel instinctively that I can trust you.'

'I feel that way, too.' I'd come here almost determined to dislike Noel but find myself inexplicably drawn to him.

'And you would stay to see the project through?'

'I'm not intending to leave. I'd like to make my home here, if it works out. In the meantime, I'll have to find accommodation. Mrs O'Hara has let the room out for the summer, so I'll need to rent somewhere until the cottage is liveable.'

He waves an expansive hand. 'I live in this mausoleum alone. There's rather a lot of empty space. It would be nice to have a child about the place. What do you say?'

'Goodness! That's... well... that's very kind of you. Thank you. But I'll need to find someone to look after Olivia.'

'I'll get Jane on to it. If there's a body in Roone Bay she doesn't know, I'll eat my hat. So?'

Relief trickles over me, and I smile. 'I can't think of anything I'd like more.'

'Right. Move in, have yourselves a holiday, and we can start when you're settled. Come on upstairs – I'll show you your rooms.'

13

GRACE

It's as if my prayers have been answered. Several days later, our cases, slightly sticky with MacDarragh's honey, are loaded into Noel's huge maroon Rover, a classic tank compared to the Minis and Fords I was used to seeing buzzing around the streets of Cheltenham. Mrs O'Hara isn't upset that we're leaving but is intimidated by Noel's presence in her tiny home. Olivia, of course, takes it in her stride. When I told her we were going to live in the Big House while our cottage was being renovated, she said, 'Can we stay there instead of moving to Grandpa's cottage?'

'It's just for a while,' I stress.

Noel glances over at me as we drive away and says, 'This will be all over Roone Bay in an instant. I hope you can cope with a bit of tittle-tattle. It will be interesting to see what stories get invented. No doubt Jane will update me in due course.'

'I've worked in offices,' I remind him, adding jokingly, 'I doubt whether the good inhabitants of Roone Bay can come anywhere near the creative imaginations of bored secretaries!'

As we near the hotel-in-progress, he stops and peruses the building. 'It's monstrous, isn't it? But it will blend in, eventually. I have no doubt it'll become a landmark, pointed out with pride. The idea was to make it look Victorian rather than modern. Olde worlde charm, eh? That will help to sell it, and we can liven up the advertising with some grim images of the past.'

'The famine?'

'And the *Titanic*. People do love a nice disaster to get their teeth into.'

His wry humour continues as he indicates his building project. 'Whenever I come back, I like to stop and assess the progress on my hotel. It does tend to instigate a brief flurry of activity from the builders, one of whom is your Sean, incidentally.'

My Sean? Something flutters in my stomach. *I've only just met the man!*

He puts the car back into gear, and it purrs quietly to his own impressive front door. 'Talk of the devil...'

Sean is waiting for us. He nods a greeting then opens the boot and hauls out our cases, which now have a battered appearance. 'Jane said you were just picking up your lodgers. Where do you want these, Noel?'

'Upstairs, second on the right,' Noel says. 'Thank you.'

Sean kicks off plaster-encrusted boots and holds the door open, giving Olivia a little bow and a flourish as she races past. 'My lady,' he says. He winks at me, and I can't help chuckling. I don't think I've smiled or laughed so much in years. The weight on my soul eases a little, allowing me to breathe more freely.

When Sean trots back downstairs, Noel says, with a smile, 'Sean, I think your work at the hotel is done for now. It strikes me that Grace's needs are more urgent than mine right now.'

'Great!' he responds. 'That was actually what I was about to suggest. The materials have been delivered. I'm on my way up now to check everything. It'll be good to get going.' He turns to me. 'Perhaps I'll see you later?'

'We'll pop up tomorrow afternoon, once we're settled in,' I suggest.

Noel interrupts. 'Why don't you come and join us for dinner tomorrow, Sean? Then you can tell us both what's going on in your life.'

The one almost unconditional commitment to our new circumstances is to have dinner with Noel every evening, promptly at six.

Sean raises one brow, pauses then grins. 'Why not? As long as you don't mind my working clothes.'

'Not at all.'

With that, Sean tips his imaginary cap and leaves.

I wonder at myself, blushing like a schoolgirl on a first date as I follow Olivia upstairs. My immediate concerns abated, I now have some breathing space and can think of the future. We have accommodation – and my goodness, what accommodation! Like a five-star hotel without the relentless smiles of ingratiating staff. And a wage! Noel's memoirs could either be incredibly interesting, incredibly boring and self-obsessed, or a little of both, but it's work I don't mind doing. And, meanwhile, Sean will be creating a home for us out of my wreck. I don't know how we'll afford to live here in the long run, but my immediate problems have been resolved in a totally unexpected way.

Jane, as I'm to call Mrs Weddows, has prepared two lovely bedrooms for us. They might have been created for visiting dignitaries, and even Olivia is stunned by the quiet aura of not just wealth but taste. The mansion, Noel informs me later, was an ivy-covered ruin when he bought it, on a whim. It had been abandoned during the famine, burned out during the fight for independence then scoured by rain, and robbed by locals of windows and lintels and doors for their own dwellings.

During the interview, I'd noticed two photographs, identically framed, on his office wall: one of Roone Manor in its previous, ruined state, and another as it is now. Had I not known, I might have supposed they'd been hung in the wrong order. There's a hint of sadness about the ruin, not just as a remnant of past glory but the magical manifestation of a fairy tale, in which years passed before the prince rode by searching for his lost love...

Noel's interior designers, it turns out, visited other properties of the same era, analysed photographs and oil paintings, and delivered a package that emulated the past so meticulously that it would take an expert to determine it was a reconstruction. The results of his labour of love are stunning, but thankfully backed by modern standards of living. Olivia and I have a bathroom to ourselves!

I spend the next day unpacking, washing and ironing our meagre wardrobe, and shopping in Roone Bay for toiletries and other essentials. Later, in the afternoon, I bundle us into our inadequate waterproofs, and we walk up to Grandpa's cottage. I know my quickened footsteps have more to do with seeing Sean than the building. He smiles a welcome from the gaping doorway, which reaches into my heart. I have the strangest feeling that I'd like to come home to this house and find him always here.

He beckons us into the small living room, saying, 'I've made a start, see?'

We brush shoulders as we pass, and I shiver; I wonder if he feels the same electrical buzz at the contact. After my disastrous relationship with Graham, I thought it would be a long time before I'd be ready to contemplate another relationship, to trust someone enough to let them in. But I know Sean is inherently good. I feel I've known him forever.

.   .   .

In the tiny living room, the remains of the cast-iron fireplace have been levered out, creating a pile of rusting iron, mortar and stones. 'I was after putting a brush up the chimney, seeing if it was clear to be lined,' Sean explains. 'Aside from evicting a few birds, we're fine. I can bump some liner in there fairly quickly and backfill it with lime plaster.'

'But surely the roof needs doing first?'

'There's method in my madness,' he says, making me smile. 'If I backfill with dry plaster around the liner, and stop rain from going into the chimney, it will start to draw some of the wet out of the walls as it sets. Now, I'll just explain about the walls...'

As I turn, I catch a brief glint in the pile of debris and fish out a little circle of metal. 'Something to do with plumbing?' I wonder.

Sean grins. 'No plumbing was ever in this house!'

No, of course. He follows me outside, where I find a puddle of water and swill it.

'It looks like a ring,' he comments.

I agree. The edges are worn smooth. I put my finger into it, but it's far too big. 'A man's ring. It isn't gold; maybe brass. It must have been wedged between the stones, and dislodged when you pulled the fireplace out.'

'Let's have a look?' He holds it up to the light. 'There's something scratched inside. M? No, N, I think. It's pretty crude. Then a – oh, that must be a heart! – and a C. N and C, that's it.'

'That's strange. Connor, maybe, but he ran off with Caitlin, so it can't be her. Maybe he had a previous lover?'

'It's a mystery, sure enough,' he says, handing it back.

He takes a glance at the sky. 'It looks as if the heavens are going to open. We should get back to the Big House. There's not much else to see, really.'

'You have soot on your face,' I comment, smiling.

'I'll have a brief wash-up in the mudroom. Noel isn't one to worry about the state of my clothes.' He reaches out and taps the end of my nose with a sooty finger. 'And you might want a wash, too.'

I laugh.

'Ha, that's better. You need to laugh more often. It must all seem a bit dire at the moment, but just you wait. A week or so and you'll see some big changes. Don't you worry about the future now. We have it sorted!'

'Thank you. You're very kind.'

He grabs my hand, briefly, and squeezes it. My cheeks grow warm, and I find myself hoping he's going to kiss me, but when he steps back and says, 'Not a bother,' I realise Olivia is watching us. He waves us out to his truck. 'Quick, now!'

On the way home, I clutch the brass ring in my pocket. From the little I know of Grandpa's childhood, it doesn't sound likely that his father would have worn jewellery. When I see Grandma, I'll ask if she knows anything about it; it might have a story to tell. At the least, she might know where it came from.

Thinking about Grandma brings a pang of homesickness. I want to see Mum and Grandma, but I don't know when that might happen. I can't go back to Birmingham, not even for a visit. I wouldn't put it past Graham to have someone watching her house, waiting for us to turn up. I'm hoping I've cut the ties so cleanly he'll have no idea where to look for us, but he didn't get where he is by being stupid. He might have little empathy, but he has a quick mind, and sooner or later, I'm afraid he's going to solve the puzzle of where we are. Strangely, the thought doesn't scare me as much as it once might have. I don't feel alone here. All the people I've met are seeing me as an individual, not as Graham's other half.

Back at the Big House, I take Olivia straight upstairs to get clean, while Sean disappears, presumably to the mudroom, to wash. It seems he knows his way around.

When we come down to the dining room, Noel is already

there, in quiet conversation with Sean, which stops abruptly as we enter the room. Noel ushers us to our seats, and soon the conversation takes up again, and I realise they're discussing the new hotel and the ramifications it has for Roone Bay. That suits me. I told Noel I didn't want to talk about my own situation, but shortly he overcomes that obstacle with uncontested simplicity: he talks to Olivia, and I can't stop her from chattering. We're being not-so-subtly interrogated, as every so often I feel obliged to step in and amend something she says. I catch Sean glancing at me with a sympathetic grin and realise he's fully aware of Noel's subterfuge.

I'm a little concerned, but Noel isn't the kind of person to tattle – to use his own expression – or try to discover who Olivia's 'daddy' is, in the mistaken belief that he can fix something I truly don't want fixed. Leaving Graham was the hardest thing I've ever done, but my determination not to return Olivia to him is absolute.

Noel asks Olivia about my Grandpa Connor, but he died before Olivia was born, and Grandma is just Great-Grandma; ancient and nameless. I think children tend to accept grandparents as distant, rather strange beings, possibly sent from another planet rather than a different era.

Noel asks me how I came to be a secretary, and I find myself truly wishing to unload. 'I didn't want to end up working in a factory,' I explain. 'I wanted a career, and at school, people from our background didn't have careers; they had jobs. This was Birmingham, not Cheltenham. It thrived on industry. My request for careers advice was met with a kind of stunned incredulity.' I smile at the recollection. 'Eventually, I was taken into a small office and informed, by the deputy head teacher, that as I was fairly literate, he supposed I could perhaps apply for teacher training, or become a nurse or a secretary. I genuinely thought those were my only options.'

I glance at Noel. I think he's surprised at my revelations. I grimace. 'I know, it's just a few years ago, but it sounds kind of last century, doesn't it? Anyway, I didn't want to be a teacher, but I thought I could learn to type. It took me a couple of years to realise how badly I'd put myself down, and that typing just leads to a different kind of low-paid job. There's a glass ceiling in the office environment, especially for women.'

'No one can put you down without your consent,' Noel quotes with somewhat self-righteous complacency.

'They can, and it hurts,' I respond acerbically.

Sean says nothing and drops his eyes to his plate.

'Determination doesn't always bring success, especially if the people around you are determined to keep you in your place. I wanted to at least become more than a shop assistant, though. Dad got me an interview for my first job, in the foundry where he worked. If he hadn't, who knows where I would be today. Getting on in life is often down to a little help from a friend.'

Noel's expression becomes pensive. 'I suppose it is,' he says, and I'm left wondering what jump-started his own rise to success. No doubt I'll find out in time.

We've been eating between sentences, but Olivia is now quietly shuffling the overcooked, over-salted cabbage around, as if hoping it will magically disappear. Jane might be an excellent pastry cook, but her dinners are somewhat lacking in imagination. Either that, or Noel simply chooses to eat the food of his childhood.

'You can leave that if you like, darling,' I say. 'Perhaps you could slip to the kitchen, see if Auntie Jane needs some help with pudding?'

She skips out happily. I haven't seen her so relaxed for a long time.

Noel's eyes follow her, his enjoyment obvious. He seems to have taken to her; and vice versa, I think with amusement. But Noel's fascination with Olivia might well run its course. We're ships in his night and will sail on by. I hope Olivia isn't hurt when he doesn't need us any more.

Noel pushes his own plate aside and leans back, saying, 'Go on, go on. You got your first job in your father's place of work. Did he work in the offices?'

'No, he was a labourer in the foundry. Immigrants made up a lot of the workforce in the steelworks. My dad was the offspring of an Irish immigrant, like my mother. He was a furnace worker, and he died of emphysema a few years back.'

'I'm sorry for your loss,' Noel says.

I curl my lip. 'The industry kills them all in the end, one way or another. Accidents, breathing in the dust. But they're up in arms about the steelworks being closed down, because there's no other work. Gran says the poor live between the devil and the deep blue sea. That's why I was determined not to be poor, to live on more than just subsistence wages.'

'But did you like the work?' Sean asks.

He's obviously interested in my background, too, though he's kept quiet so far. Noel said that writing his memoir was a cathartic exercise, and maybe I feel the same way, as my past pours out of me. 'It was okay. There was a camaraderie in the typing pool, but it was still a dirty environment; even in the offices, the dust got in your pores. I stayed there for a year then hunted for a better job, in the city. I got a job with a firm of accountants. I didn't particularly enjoy typing up reams of accounts, but I was better paid, which is the whole point of working, after all. Then, one day, it all changed.'

I wonder if I'm boring them, but Noel nods encouragingly.

'One of the girls, Sorcha, over from Dublin, was ambitious. She was pretty and vibrant, and I was a little envious of her, to be honest. I never had that kind of self-confidence or drive. She was determined to go places – and let us all know it. In the newspaper, she showed us a job that she'd applied for. *Personal Assistant to the Director. Must be smart, literate, well-spoken and conversant in all secretarial skills.* Sorcha was funny, too, and could put on a rich Belfast accent: *Jaysus, Mary and Joseph. Will yous jest look at the salary? And Cheltenham, too! I'd sell me granny to live there, so I would! I might get to marry a duke or something.*

Sean's eyes twinkle as I attempt to imitate her exaggerated accent.

'Well, we all giggled at the concept of her meeting a duke, never mind marrying one. I guess we were little more than children with romantic ideas. But it's true that Cheltenham, with its racecourse and top-hat types, is a far cry from Birmingham's factories.'

'So you applied, too?' Noel asks.

I take a breath, remembering the moment the course of my life changed. 'I wasn't going to, but that evening, I was standing at the sink with Mum, drying the dishes, and I told her about Sorcha. She said, *Well, you're as good as she is.* I said that I didn't think I should, because it wouldn't be fair to Sorcha.'

Noel raises an eyebrow.

'Yes, I really was that silly, but Mum put me straight. *It's a job application*, she said. *You wouldn't be stealing anything from her. And if nothing comes of it, well, so be it.* If she hadn't pushed me, maybe I wouldn't have applied.'

And the course of my history would have changed.

'I'm glad you did,' Sean states, casting me a sidelong glance.

I nod. 'I was quite shocked when I received a letter offering me an interview. I was too embarrassed to tell the girls in work, especially Sorcha. Mum, Grandma and I were prancing about like schoolgirls – you should have seen us! They fussed over me, bought me new clothes, and I had my hair done.' I pause, remembering. 'You'd think I was visiting the queen; we were so excited.'

Noel and Sean both smile.

'On the day of the interview, I saw this tall, smart stranger in the mirror, one who looked the part – externally, at least – and I felt so special. Anyway, the interview was daunting. I kept wishing I hadn't applied. I wanted to run out, to say it was all a big mistake, I didn't want the job anyway, sorry for wasting your time. The man who interviewed me was Graham. He was tall, handsome and utterly charming. After the interview, he thanked me for coming, and I thought that was that.'

The door barges open, interrupting my monologue. Olivia holds it open for Jane, who places a steaming bowl of rice pudding on the table.

'Oh!' I exclaim. 'My favourite. It would be in the oven for hours, and Mum would put a knob of jam on top when it was served out.'

'Ta-da!' Olivia says, bringing a jar of jam from behind her back.

I feel a belt of nostalgia as I tuck in. The pudding is demolished in record time, and Olivia is allowed to leave the table, to play for an hour before bedtime. Jane brings in a pot of tea and clears the dishes, saying, 'I'll just wash these up and be off home, Noel, if that's all?'

'Thank you, Jane. Yes, that's fine. See you tomorrow then.' He takes charge of the teapot and pours, saying to me, 'So, you got the job.'

'I was sure I hadn't, but a week later I got a letter. Mum and I were in the kitchen, and I opened it, expecting the standard rejection, you know, but I was offered the job. We were all gobsmacked.'

'Gobsmacked?' Sean repeats, shaking his head, chuckling.

I flush faintly but grin.

'Go on,' Noel says.

'That's it, really. I was to start a month later, when I'd worked out my notice. That was when Mum realised I'd be leaving home.'

'Ah, yes. It's a life-changer, isn't it?'

I change the subject and glance at Sean. 'Oh, when Sean was pulling out the old fireplace up at Grandpa Connor's cottage, this fell out.' I hold out the ring, which I've cleaned. The engravings inside are unmistakeable.

Noel reaches out and takes it. He stares at the ring, frozen in contemplation.

'I thought the C might be for Connor,' I say. 'But I don't know about the N. So maybe it belonged to someone else?'

For a moment I think he's going to slip it onto his finger, but he places it carefully back on the table and shakes his head. 'A mystery,' he says, but I'm almost sure I catch recognition in his eyes.

Sean rises and says, 'Well, I'd best get on. Thank you for the dinner, Noel.'

'I'll see you out,' I say quickly, flushing slightly.

At the door, we're on our own, and a tendril of warmth steals into me. *Will he kiss me?* But I'm quite pleased that Sean pecks me circumspectly on the forehead. It's a gentle goodbye that speaks loud and clear of his interest.

'See you soon, Grace. You sound sad about your life, but don't be. It gave you Olivia and brought you both here. Maybe it was a plan, all along.'

14

GRACE

It rains torrentially for a couple of days, and we largely confine ourselves to the house, with small forays into the garden when patches of light break through the lowering sky, like promises snatched back before we can fully grasp them. For now, Olivia seems to have accepted the strangeness of this holiday. Maybe she is, even if she doesn't realise it, pleased to be given time to just be herself and not worry about looking nice, keeping clean or being put down by Graham's insidiously undermining comments when things aren't exactly as he likes them.

Noel, it turns out, has three dogs. Apparently, they chose him, turning up at the door over the years, starving and bedraggled. They sometimes sit with him in his office, or spread out by the fire in the evenings when he's reading the newspaper, but during the day, they largely inhabit a mudroom off the kitchen, and can enjoy the freedom of the garden and the forestry beyond.

Animals have never been a part of our lives, but as with the parrot and Mrs O'Hara's cat, Olivia is drawn to them. They make a strange pack, ranging from a boldly marked white-and-black Jack Russell, through a shaggy golden collie, to a mixed-breed brindle Irish wolfhound, whose shoulders reach my hips. I've heard some horror stories about dogs and children, but Noel says she's safe with them. She certainly doesn't seem scared of them, or wary in the way I am. Imagination lends depth to my fears; I see every possible danger, while Olivia just lives for the moment and the pleasures of experience.

Noel seems to have an affinity with Lanky, the wolfhound, who pads quietly to him and pushes her nose under his hand, seeking comfort or giving it – I'm not sure which. They all seem to have taken to Olivia, which is useful, because I can tell her to go and play, and she runs off happily, inserting herself into the pack like an adopted puppy. They run out exuberantly and disappear through the overgrown shrubbery, the wolfhound blending quietly into the landscape, while the other two invest in some game that involves a lot of running in circles, sniffing and digging, their barking echoing back briefly, before sinking under the weight of the moisture-laden air. And all of them seem to mind Olivia, coming back to her time and again, to find out why she isn't keeping up.

Watching her try to catch them – quite unsuccessfully, of course – or throw a ball, and watching their antics as the Jack Russell and the collie charge off after it, is quite amusing. I never really thought about dogs before, but they have quite unique characters. The Jack Russell runs like mad, his little legs pounding, but doesn't always find the ball. The collie uses her nose to sniff it out, and is, more often than not, the one who drops it in front of Olivia, inviting her to throw again. The wolfhound watches, lying alert and regal as a sphynx, her eyes following every movement, as if wondering what all the bother is about.

I mention this to Noel, and he gives me an amused glance. 'She's a real dote,' he says. 'But watch her chase a deer, or kill a hare, and you'll see a different creature. That's what those long legs and big teeth were bred for.'

Jane, it turns out, has endless patience on these rain-soaked days, encouraging Olivia to help with the baking and even peel potatoes. I've never been able to get Olivia interested in cooking, but there's something comfortable about this big, old kitchen, with the heat radiating from the range, and its immediate access to the wild garden.

On a day when the rain has briefly abated, Jane shoos me out of the kitchen, telling me she'll keep an ear peeled. I must take some time for myself, for sure, isn't the wean happy enough getting dirty? She'll come to no harm and knows not to leave the garden. I take myself out for a walk, relishing the fresh, cool air. I stop to look over the bay, watching the dark clouds gathering in.

It's nearly a week after moving in, and I'm wondering when and how we're going to start work. I haven't heard about anyone being approached to look after Olivia and wonder if Noel's forgotten his promise. I'm vaguely worried that we've moved in under false pretences, and that I won't be up to the job Noel wants me to do. He wants a ghostwriter, and my experience to date is rooted in business language. But time will tell, if only we could get going.

A few huge, heavy raindrops warn me those dark clouds are ready to burst again, and I dash back to the house.

Later, we're all in the kitchen, listening to the rain, when Sean walks past the window and raps the kitchen door with his knuckles, before entering. He's followed by a girl I'd place at fifteen or sixteen. The epitome of an Irish colleen, with her porcelain-white skin, dainty features and blue eyes, I'm startled by her stunning looks. She has a thick mass of brown hair so dark it's almost black, gathered carelessly into an elastic band. A brief flash of worry surprises me, but her wide, inclusive smile, like the sun blasting out from behind dark clouds, lets me know she's unaffected by her own beauty.

'Finola!' Jane exclaims and gives her a brief, floury hug.

Noel rises to give her a brief hug, too. I raise my eyebrows slightly, amused, and Noel answers the unspoken question. 'It's the summer break – exams are over. She'll be earning a bit of pocket money, looking after Olivia in the afternoons, while we do a bit of work. If you approve, that is,' he adds as an afterthought.

He taps Finola lightly on the back. 'Take Olivia out, while the rain is resting, and give the dogs a run, eh? See if it's going to work out for you both.'

Finola gives Olivia a massive smile and holds out her hand, asking, 'Shall we go and find the donkeys?'

Olivia's eyes widen. 'Donkeys? Oh, yes please!'

The question must be sitting plainly on my face. Noel laughs. 'This is Ireland! Everyone has a donkey.'

I flush slightly, and Jane intervenes with a spiky rebuke. 'Not everyone has twenty and is daft enough to take in every donkey that comes trotting by with a hard-luck story!'

'Eighteen,' Noel corrects, shrugging off her comment with his rueful grin. 'It's hard for people to send them to the factory because they can't afford to keep them any longer. Times are changing. Everyone wants a car. It's sad, so it is.'

'Great, soft eejit,' Jane mutters and snatches her oven gloves from a peg.

'I'll be off then,' Sean says.

'You will not!' Jane snaps. 'Not when I have fresh scones cooked!'

'Ah, twist my arm, why don't you, auntie,' Sean says.

'Auntie?' I query, amused.

'Well, kind of. It's complicated.' As he seats himself comfortably at the table, I sense he's done this many times before. He winks at me. 'It's Tuesday. She always makes scones on a Tuesday.'

'And Wednesday and Thursday and Friday,' I whisper back.

Jane puts her hands on her hips. 'Don't think I can't hear you! There's butter in the dish. Now, don't burn yourself, you greedy great ox,' Jane mutters as Sean grabs for a steaming hot scone, but I see her smile as she turns away.

'You'll need to watch your weight, my girrul, if you're going to live here any while,' he says to me.

'I'd be gone sooner if you were up at the house, getting on with the building,' I jest. It's strange that I can indulge in repartee with people I've only known a short while. Had I dared make such a comment to Graham, he would have answered it in all seriousness, with that miffed expression I know so well.

'So,' Noel queries, 'how is the work coming along?'

'So-so,' he says complacently. 'You can't hurry these things, you know.'

'I know all too well,' Noel says, plucking a scone from the tray and dropping it hastily on a plate. 'It took seven years to get this house renovated, and that's with me handing out bonuses left, right and centre.'

'I don't think my cottage is quite in the same league,' I say diffidently. 'And I certainly hope it's not going to take seven years.'

'No,' Noel agrees. 'But there are times I miss the simplicity of my family home.'

'Where was that?' I ask.

'Up the hill, behind us. I can show you where it was; it's gone now.'

'Oh, that's sad.'

He glances up at me for a second then says, 'Yes, it is.'

After a brief chat about the weather, and people I know

nothing about, Sean rises. 'I should be getting on. Thanks for the scones, auntie.'

She pecks him on the cheek. 'Off with ye!'

Sean looks at me. 'See me out, Grace?'

'Sure.'

There's a faint spit in the air, and a chill wind as we round the corner of the house. I shiver. 'I hope Olivia is all right. They've been a long time.'

He puts his arm around me and gives me a hug. 'Well, put your mind at rest. Finola might be young, but she's sound. That's what I wanted to say. She's a good sort. And so are you. You did a brave thing, you know.'

'I don't know what you mean.'

'Leaving your husband.' He smiles. 'Don't go denying it, because that will upset my romancing.'

My face must be on fire. 'Romancing?'

'Come, sweetheart. Don't tell me I'm wrong?'

I think my expression must say everything, because he nods, adding, 'Just so you know, we have your back. All of us. He won't be after taking Olivia from you.'

'Oh,' I say inadequately. I wasn't aware that I'd told anyone anything that could lead to that conclusion, but maybe, in hindsight, it's obvious.

'Now, I need to get back to work. I have a house to renovate.' He nods, waves and is gone.

I stand in the drizzle for a moment and watch the sea before going inside. I feel safer than I had half an hour ago. How did he do that?

Noel is standing by the range, waiting for me. He indicates the door to the stairs. 'Olivia will be fine. Finola is fierce good with children; she has a bundle of brothers and sisters, so don't worry. Let them get to know each other, so? Can I show you what we'll be doing?'

I follow him up to his study, through a far door, and into

another room, where there's a large table cluttered with piles of paper, and an office desk dominated by a large, black typewriter.

'I made a start,' he says, 'but I got a bit daunted... What's wrong?'

I point to the typewriter. 'Am I supposed to use that?'

He looks confused. 'It works – I tried it out. I got a new ribbon, because the old one had gone dry.'

'Ah! I'm used to an electric typewriter,' I tell him. 'One with a correcting ribbon.'

He thinks about that for a bit then says, 'Right. I don't know what the difference is, but I'll make sure you get one. Meanwhile' – he waves a hand, encompassing the paperwork – 'maybe check out my notes, those there, see if you can make sense of them?'

'That'll be fine.'

As I briefly scan them, I realise the scope of this project, and a vague sense of panic descends. Can I actually do this? He's written things as they've come into his mind. Some events are duplicated, and some start with a clear, firm hand before descending into a barely legible scrawl, as tiredness obviously overtook his determination to get to the finish line.

There's no shape, no order to his scribblings, and within an hour I'm as unsure as he is as to how to move forward. It seems that my first objective must be to type the events on separate sheets and create some kind of basic timeline. The best way of doing this might be to create a card index so that they can be shuffled into some kind of date order before we begin to compile the actual book.

I explain this to Noel, and his eyes brighten at the thought of someone taking this burden from him. 'I didn't think of a card index. How clever! You see, that's why I need someone like you. Not just to type but to provide common sense.'

He suggests that I walk down to the post office, which also

serves as a newsagent, bookshop and stationers, to see if they have anything suitable. I'm told to get anything I want and put it on his account. 'Oh,' he adds, 'and put any books for Olivia on there, too. And if you can't get what you need, the office supplier in Cork can get it.'

I go to my room to fetch my coat, and glance out of the window. I can't see my cottage from here. It's obscured by a rugged raft of countryside dotted with pines, and beyond that, the skyline is dominated by the curve of the grey Atlantic meeting the sullen grey sky – not an auspicious start to the school holidays.

I'm keen to get my head around the project and advise Noel how best we should handle it. I've never been much into reading biographies but find myself itching to begin, because this isn't just a stranger's life. It's surprisingly intertwined with my own grandparents' lives, and that personal connection provides a drive, a spark; I feel I'm about to engage with their past, too, as Noel brings his early years to life.

15

GRACE

The next day, while I'm out and about without Olivia, I first walk to Grandpa's cottage, to see what kind of progress Sean has made on it. The weather hasn't been kind, so I'm expecting to see little change. But as I round the last corner, I stop and gasp. It had seemed like a wreck before, but now it truly is one.

The roof is entirely gone.

Well, not gone, I think as I get closer. It's on the ground, a huge pile of rotting slates and beams scattered with rusting nails. The building is now like the other wrecks I passed as I travelled south: an empty shell constructed of field stones. Its windows are blind eyes, its gaping doorway a cry for help, its gables exposed bones pointing sadly at the grey clouds. But the cottage is surrounded by a complex nest of scaffolding, suggesting that this state won't exist for long.

I walk in and look up at the sky through the exposed floor joists. I'm filled with sadness for this place that had once been a home, now unravelled and exposed to the elements, its history wafting away on the Atlantic breeze.

As I wander, my gloom is offset by the pile of new wood at

the side of the house: big timbers, surely for the roof beams, and a couple of pallets of new slates.

I hear the rumble of an engine and spy Sean's truck negotiating the twisting road towards me. The fast-scudding clouds have turned a sickly yellow – a warning that a deluge is imminent. Sure enough, just as he pulls up, the first spats of heavy rain plop onto the windscreen.

He leans over and pushes the passenger door open, and I run to get in. He's thoughtful and caring, and I've deduced that he's not married but wonder why. I feel that he's good 'father' material. Then I catch myself. I'm the one who's still married, and I don't know if any divorce I manage to obtain in England will be recognised in a country where divorce is simply not an option.

I shake droplets of water from my hair, smiling and breathless. 'Thank you. It seems you arrived in the nick of time, once again.'

'It's what I do best,' he says, adding, 'I was just checking the site. I'll have a couple of lads up tomorrow morning to help get the roof on. What do you think?'

'I think it's too wet to be building roofs. I'd hate for you to have an accident in this weather.'

'Thanks for your concern, but, sure, this is Ireland.' He flashes a smile. 'If I waited for a dry day, my work would never be finished. I need to get the roof on, and the windows in, or the rest of those floor joists will need replacing, too.'

'The rain won't harm them?'

'They'll dry out, as long as they don't stay wet. We'll have the roof timbers on in a day, and once the felt is laid and battened down, she'll be sound. Then we can wait for a dry day to slate the roof. You're right, that can be a bit hairy in the wet. I'll line the chimneys, too, while it's in this state. Then, when we have the windows in, we can warm a fire in the grate. A few days, and the old place won't know herself. Shall I give you a spin back to Noel's?'

I can't imagine anything as homely as a fire in that bare shell of a building. 'That would be good, Sean.' His name feels warm in my mouth, and I have to clear my throat. 'Thank you.'

He reverses with careless ease and heads off back down the road. 'So, what are you up to with Noel? Are you family?'

'No. He wants to write a memoir. I'm just to type it up. Noel said I wasn't to tell anyone, though.'

'Best if everyone knows that, really. It'll stop all the other rumours.'

I glance at him with amusement. 'What rumours?'

'That your mother was his love child, for one. That he's going to leave his fortune to you.'

He grins at me, and I choke on a laugh. 'I hope you can let people know that isn't true, at least!'

He drops me off by the garden path, gently caressing my cheek before I hop out. I stand in the rain and watch his truck head away down the slope; he waves out of the window as he disappears around the corner. I feel guilty, like someone caught out fantasising about having an affair. But I've left Graham and should feel comfortable with my thoughts, I reason with myself. I wonder if it's because Graham is unfinished business. Perhaps I should steel myself for the inevitable dialogue. It's got to happen, sooner or later. I wonder if I should go and confront him. The thought makes me shudder. I will, but not yet.

The pond is being churned into a frenzy by the wind-whipped rain. I realise I'm being soaked and run for the kitchen door. Olivia is playing snakes and ladders with Finola on a small table in front of the range in the kitchen. Their heads are close over the board, a statement of black and gold, and they're so engrossed I'm barely acknowledged.

'I got a bit wet,' I tell Jane, somewhat unnecessarily.

She takes my wet clothes. 'There's a line in the conservatory for the drying, but we'll put the coat by the range. You'll perhaps be wanting a stock coat, like Noel's?'

I assume she means the long, brown mac with an added cape over the shoulders for extra protection. It certainly seems like a good idea, for me and Olivia. 'Might I find one in Roone Bay?'

'The Co-op might have one. Noel would know.'

My coat is designed for city living, for running from the car to the house or the bus or the shops. It's most unsuitable for my present circumstances. In fact, seeing it hanging by the range, it's ludicrously out of place.

A bit like me.

I spend a couple more days working my way through the piles of papers but soon realise it's actually a waste of time without some method of cataloguing, as I can't recall from one day to the next what is where.

Noel comes in to find me standing in the middle of the room, frowning. He laughs. 'Now you know what I've been dealing with,' he says. 'But I came to tell you, help is on the way. The manager from the stationery wholesalers in Cork is going to visit. He's bringing some cards, and you can order anything else you need. Desk, chairs, filing cabinets, a new typewriter, a new-fangled coffee maker; anything.'

'A Dictaphone might be the answer,' I suggest, placing a hand on his pile of handwritten notes. 'Would you be up for reading these onto a tape? I can type more quickly from dictation.'

His brows rise. 'Are you suggesting that my writing isn't clear enough?'

I flush then realise he's joking.

'Well,' he says, 'I've never done that, but hopefully I'm not too old to learn. But there's no point starting until you have the right tools, so get away with you, now.'

'Jane mentioned a Co-op,' I say. 'Is it nearby? I got soaked today and could do with a waterproof. Olivia could do with one, too, and Finola suggested I get her some wellington boots, for when they go out with the dogs.'

'Ah, she means the milk co-operative at Drinagh. She's right – they have working clothes. We're largely a farming community, after all.'

I'm amused that Noel thinks of himself as part of the farming community still, but I suppose his connection is in his roots not his present circumstances.

'I should have thought of that. I'll drive you both over there tomorrow,' he says.

'I don't want to put you out.'

'No bother. I wanted to go anyway. I need a new wheel put on my wheelbarrow.'

I smile, thinking how grounded he is. For all his vast wealth, he's happy out in the rain, rescuing dogs and donkeys and parrots, while Graham's middle-class aspirations seem to weigh him down.

16

GRACE

We pile into Noel's Rover, which he drives with the careful concentration of someone who's not quite sure of the width. We pass two motor vehicles as we head back through Ballydehob, and, with a shudder, I recall the journey here. There were times I almost gave up. It's strange how utterly horrible a situation can be, but the moment stability returns, that trauma is relegated to the mental filing cabinet of past events. Back then, I never would have imagined myself seated in this solid tank of a car, with its walnut dashboard and upholstered leather bench seats, infused with a faint whiff of petrol and ancient cigars, being driven miles just to buy waterproofs.

Drinagh turns out to be a small town spread along half a mile of potholed road. As we approach, a strange horse-drawn vehicle passes us going the other way at a brisk trot. The driver is slumped down between two large wheels, and it seems as if he's asleep, but he raises a lazy salute with a crop as he passes by.

'What on earth is that?' I ask, astonished.

'A sulky, and a trotting pony.'

He sees my lack of comprehension and explains. 'They race, but only at a trot. I should bring you to Ballabuidhe Fair, in Dunmanway, in August. Travellers come for miles to sell horses and race. It's an experience, all right. Here we are now.'

Noel pulls into a layby in front of a spectacularly unimpressive block of a building, which incongruously overwhelms the neighbouring cottages. He leads us through a side door, straight into a large shop which no one would expect in a building that looks like, and probably is, a warehouse and a staging post for milk from small farms. A horse-drawn vehicle clops through an opening at the back and stops before a raised platform, where huge metal churns are noisily swivelled off the back. I'm enchanted. It's like stepping back in time. I suspect it was like this in England thirty years previously, and in a few years, I don't doubt this will all have vanished.

The shop seems to stock everything from huge farm machinery and gates to ham and eggs. Noel leads us to a small section with a couple of rails and shelves of practical garments. Jeans, shirts, pullovers, boots, outdoor clothing, and workwear such as milking gowns and overalls. Almost everything, even flat caps, come in children's sizes, too. Presumably children who grow up in farming communities are incorporated into working life as soon as they're big enough to carry a pail.

'You'll be wanting to cast your eye.'

Olivia glances at me, confused.

'We'll have a look around, while we're here,' I say in answer and explanation.

It's pretty much an obligation, though there's little to interest a city girl. We walk up and down aisles of gardening utensils, milking equipment, things for feeding calves and an amazing array of objects I can't even fathom a use for. The few toys have an agricultural theme – sit-on tractors and cast-iron miniature replicas of farming vehicles, threshers and hay wagons.

We gravitate back to the clothing area. Noel seems to enjoy shopping, and enthusiastically fits Olivia out with green wellies and waterproofs. She holds her arms away, looks down at herself and frowns.

'You look grand, girrul,' Noel states, which puts a slight smile on her face. 'Pretty as a picture!'

I love the way the Irish add an extra syllable into words: girrul, fillum, calluf. It's nice that his years in America, sometimes all too evident in his speech, haven't totally eradicated his Irish roots. But perhaps coming home has allowed him to sink back into the dialect, like shrugging into a coat left behind at his father's farm many years back.

I'm a bit worried about the cost and try to demur as he holds a coat up to me, but he insists. 'My treat,' he says, flapping his hands, almost embarrassed. 'Not a bother, not a bother.'

We carry our haul to a sales counter left over from the fifties; it's a huge slab of wood, marked and scuffed from years of iron accoutrements passing over its surface. Behind it, there are tall shelves stocking nuts and bolts and door handles and candles.

No money changes hands. Noel has the items added to his account, and we leave feeling as though we've added another layer to our immersion into the West Cork community.

In the car, Noel hands Olivia a small set of gardening tools and some packets of flower seeds. 'There's an old greenhouse out the back where you can grow some seeds on, when the weather's bad,' he says. 'Then when they're big enough, you can put them out in the garden.'

'What a fantastic idea,' I enthuse. 'I used to love growing things with my dad. Flowers for the butterflies, mostly.'

As we drive up to Noel's door, though, my new, safe world explodes into fragments, and my mind blankets with numb dismay. There's a car outside, with English number plates.

Noel stares at me then says quietly, 'You two slip on around the back; I'll check it out.'

'Thank you,' I say breathlessly, glad that Olivia is laboriously reading out loud the names on the seed packets and hasn't noticed.

As we take our purchases upstairs, resolve sets in my mind. It's over six weeks since I left home, so I shouldn't be surprised that he's here. In fact, it wouldn't have surprised me if he'd arrived a week after I did, so at least I've had some time to find my courage before facing him. But of one thing I'm sure: I'm not going to let him bully me. And I'm not going to let him take Olivia.

I bounce between the bed and the window, while Olivia, oblivious to my distress, reads *Danny, the Champion of the World* out loud, pleased to exercise her newly acquired skill of working out big words using syllables.

'*While I was still a baby, my father washed me and fed me and changed my di-a-pers...* What are *diapers?*'

'Diapers are nappies,' I explain shortly, still pacing.

'But daddies don't do that.'

'That's what makes this story different,' I explain, suddenly realising this wasn't the best book I could have bought. 'Danny's mummy died, so his daddy had to do everything.'

'Well, my daddy would have got a nanny,' Olivia states and carries on. '*He has to earn a living by repairing auto-mobile engines, and*— What's an auto mobile?'

I correct her pronunciation. 'Automo*bile* means a car.'

'Well, why don't they say that? ... *servicking customers with gas-o-line.* What's gas o-line?'

'Petrol, love.' I sigh. I hadn't realised it would be American English. The lady in the shop said it was a popular book, and Olivia's reading is fairly advanced for her age, but I suspect I'm going to have to do a lot of explaining.

I try to imagine Graham living in a caravan, changing

nappies, and I smile. Graham had liked Olivia presented fully clothed and smelling of talcum powder. Any hint of what went on down below, and he excused himself rapidly. I suppose I, too, thought it was women's work. I allowed myself to slip into the expected role of wife, and it's easier to slip into a pattern of behaviour than to climb back out of it.

There's a small knock at the door, and panic seeps into my throat. I go out into the corridor at Noel's beckoning, closing the door behind me.

'It's not your husband,' he explains in a low voice. 'It's a boy, a youth, called Arthur. Says he's your stepson?'

'Oh,' I breathe, my panic abating slightly. 'How on earth did he find us?'

'It seems your mother told him.'

'But why would she... she wouldn't...'

'Apparently, Arthur has fallen out with his father, something about his future. He seems to think you'll be pleased to see him?'

That makes sense.

I'd wondered when that particular dash of cold water was going to hit the frying pan. Arthur had tried to tell Graham in the past that he wasn't interested in working in an office, but Graham had insisted upon him majoring in business studies. I recall him saying: *After all, I'm paying for his education, and Arthur's going to inherit a dynamic and growing business. He needs to come into it fully equipped to run it.* It's strange how he assumed his son would be a clone of himself. It hasn't occurred to Graham that Arthur is his own man, with his own interests, and maybe some of his mother's bohemian disposition.

I don't voice my real fear: that Arthur has laid a breadcrumb trail to my door, whether he knows it or not, and one of these days, without a doubt, Graham will follow it. I know he'll find us, of course. I just didn't want it to be this soon. I wanted to weave a cocoon of independence around myself first, get Olivia settled into her new life, which would act as a buffer to the inevitable confrontation.

'So, shall I send him away?' Noel asks.

I shake my head. 'It wouldn't be fair, would it? After he's come all this way to find us.'

The bedroom door is flung open. 'Arty's here!' Olivia yells gleefully, and she's off, skipping down two stairs at a time. I don't even have time to admonish her for listening at keyholes.

We follow more sedately, and there, in the living room, Arthur gently puts his little sister aside and rises apprehensively from an ornate high-backed chair.

Olivia's face is shining with delight.

I smile a welcome and hug him, feeling his tension dissolve as he hugs me back. 'You found us then,' I say.

He gives a wry smile. 'I told your mother I'd walked out on Dad, too. She didn't want to tell me where you were. But I wanted to see you and Ollie, so I slept in my car outside her house for three days until she told me.'

'Oh,' I say. 'That would have done it, I guess. Thank goodness it's not winter. I'm so sorry, Arthur. I wanted to tell you, but I didn't dare tell anyone. He... he took it hard then?'

'He alternated between red-hot rages and the chill of an iceberg. I don't blame you for leaving. I don't know how you put up with him as long as you did,' he says. 'He phoned me up, asked if I knew where you were, which I didn't, of course. That's how I knew you'd done a bunk. Then, when I got home for the break, he was unbearable. I had to agree with everything he said, or he exploded! And he expected me to go into work with him, to earn some holiday money. You should have seen him when I said no! I don't know how many times I've told him I'm not interested in electronics, but he just doesn't listen.'

I give him another hug. Arthur might be in his early twenties, but to me he's a motherless child. It's kind of nice that he's run to me and his little sister. All those years when I was trying to be his stepmother, trying to provide him with the love that had been ripped away when his mother first absconded then died, thinking I'd failed. But here he is. Tears rise to my eyes. 'Oh, Arthur. I didn't mean to leave you, too, I hope you know that. It was just that I couldn't be with him any longer. He wouldn't let me be me.'

'I know all about that,' he agrees with a wry smile. 'He thought I had "carbon copy" painted on my forehead.' He grins. 'Anyway, I wasn't going to lose another mum, or my little sister.'

Noel slips out, leaving us to catch up.

Arthur looks around slowly and says, with a tinge of jealousy, 'It looks like you've done all right for yourself.'

When did he attain that strangled upper-crust articulation? I wonder if it's more noticeable because I'm now used to the softer Irish vowels, but I find myself cringing inside. Graham didn't do him any favours, sending him to a posh school. He'd adjusted to fit in, but here it makes him not just English but a descendent of one of the English overlords who'd let the Irish starve.

'Not really,' I correct, shaking my head. 'Noel has employed me to do some typing. It's temporary, while the cottage is being renovated, then we'll move in there. I expect Mum told you about the cottage? Well, it was in a worse state than we thought. Come on – we'll walk over and I'll show you. I can't offer you a room here, I'm afraid.'

'Oh, I have money. Dad was fairly generous while I was at uni, but I wasn't interested in drinking and daft pranks.'

Of course. Graham would have wanted his son to be seen to belong to the moneyed classes and probably provided him with a substantial allowance. No waiting on tables to make ends meet for *his* son. And if Arthur hasn't wasted his allowance, he could have accumulated a reasonable nest egg by now.

How strange that Arthur and I both did the same thing.

'Of course, it won't last forever, but it'll give me some

breathing space,' Arthur adds, confirming what I thought. 'I've applied to take a PhD next semester.'

'Does Graham know?'

'I told him. He wasn't happy. He thought I was going to leave and go to work for him this year, but I think he likes the idea of his son having a doctorate. I didn't tell him a doctorate in what, though!'

I'm guiltily aware that Arthur must have been the whipping post for Graham's ire after I absconded. In hindsight, there are many things about leaving that I could have organised better, but I truly wasn't thinking straight, and I'm pleased he seems to bear me no ill will.

Arthur and I had had an understandably rocky start. His childhood years had been divided between an austere home and a tough boarding school, and his mother was often away, from what I can gather. I didn't even meet him until after I'd been installed as the new mistress of his home.

That wasn't just unfair; it was brutal.

I tried to be a mother to Arthur, but it was strange, trying to make him feel welcome in his own home, where I was, in fact, the interloper, and my age being nearer that of older sister than mother didn't help. Arthur decided I was a gold digger and was utterly horrible to me, until the arrival of Olivia. His big-brother adoration of his baby sister came as a welcome relief after his initial, grating antagonism, and we gradually found common ground. During breaks from school and university, he became Olivia's champion, her unstinting protector and companion. I really hope Olivia and Arthur can retain their closeness.

He's almost a head taller than me now. I wonder when that happened. We sent him off to university as a teenager, arrogance and anger wrapped around his thin frame like a shield, and he's returned a man, fleshed out with muscle and height. His self-confidence, though, is that of a child pretending to be grown up. It doesn't yet sit well on his broad shoulders.

I turn to Olivia. 'Go and get your new raincoat, darling, and get mine, too. We're taking Arthur to Grandpa's cottage.'

'I'll drive us,' Arthur comments. 'It looks as if it's going to rain.'

He's right – the sky is definitely grey.

'This is Ireland. It'll rain the moment we step outside.'

'Why didn't you go somewhere warm? Majorca. Spain,' Arthur asks. 'Why here?'

'Because I have a house here. Besides, I don't speak much Spanish, and I need a job.'

'So this is permanent then? Dad was hoping you'd come around.'

'I know. That's why I couldn't tell him where I was going. He would have followed and made me return.'

Olivia runs back in with our waterproofs, which are still crackling with newness, and says gleefully to Arthur, 'Uncle Noel says to come for dinner tonight when you've got yourself sorted.'

'Uncle?' Arthur asks, raising one eyebrow.

'For politeness,' I explain.

He should know that. Graham, with his exacting standards, always required his children to call his friends 'auntie' or 'uncle' instead of just their first names. Perhaps he sees the intimacy as something more than it is, though; me worming my way into Noel's life for what he owns, for security and comfort. I smile to myself. Does he really think I would marry a man old enough to be my grandfather, for material benefits? But then, he thought I'd married his father for those. I think I disabused him of that notion, though, and I hope he thinks better of me than that now.

When we arrive at the cottage, Arthur grabs his greatcoat out of the car. It's a statement, very much something an Oxford graduate would be wearing. He frowns at the empty shell of the house I own. 'That's your grandfather's house? You're going to *live* here?'

I laugh at the arrant snobbery of this youth who, unlike me, grew up in a somewhat upmarket environment. 'It'll be fine – you'll see.'

I show him where our bathroom will be, and he shakes his head. 'And the job with Noel; how did that come about?'

I explain, and he nods. 'So, it's all worked out very nicely for you, hasn't it?'

There's a slightly sour note in his voice.

After I've shown him around, he drives us back through the town, past the post office, past the bank, to a small hotel at the top of the hill. Arthur books himself in for a week in the first instance, adding arrogantly to the receptionist, 'I don't know how long I'll be staying.'

'What will you do now?' I ask as he drives us back to Roone House.

'I've got a job for the summer, in Southampton. I like the sea. I'm going to work at the marina and take a sailing-instructor course part-time.'

I didn't expect him to stay in Cheltenham, under his father's eye, but this astonishes me. I thought he'd head for the metropolis.

Over dinner, Noel gently quizzes Arthur about his life at university, about his ambitions and his present situation. 'Grace tells me you got an honours degree in business studies? Well done. But have you any idea what you're going to do now?'

Arthur looks down at his plate, his hands frozen on the cutlery for a moment, before raising his eyes and staring at me, not Noel, as he answers. 'Actually, I got a degree in biology.'

I'm stunned into silence by that bombshell, the words *What? You're joking?* hovering on the tip of my tongue, but even as they're forming, I know he's not. I realise now why he never wanted us to visit him at university, or meet any of his friends or lecturers. He even elected not to receive his degree certificate in person, opting Graham and myself out of the ceremony at the same time.

'Oh dear!' I exclaim faintly. Then I burst out laughing. 'Graham is going to be *livid*.'

Arthur grins sheepishly. 'I know. I kind of don't know how to tell him. I've taken a master's in marine biology, and the PhD will be in either marine biology or oceanography, depending on which university will take me.'

'I had no idea,' I comment, astounded.

'That was the whole point,' he says. 'I've always loved the sea. Like Mum did. My biology degree included a module on sea life, and it fascinated me.' He shrugs as if to say *And that was that*.

And well it might have been. Small things tend to trigger big changes in our lives. I'd never found anything that I particularly wanted to do, so I'm pleased for him to have discovered that focus. But Graham is going to be furious. He has a business exploding into the new era of technology, and his son doesn't want to take it on.

'Anyway,' Arthur says, stabbing at his meat with the point of a knife, 'I'm not going to let Dad, or anyone, tell me what to do with my life.'

Noel is staring at him with a strange expression, and I get a chill of unease. Is it just because my previous life has come knocking at my door? Or does Noel see beyond the obvious? I suspect he's a good judge of character. He made most of his money working with horses, and I understand that the first tranche came from a skill in backing the right ones.

The dinner passes amicably enough, though, and we see Arthur off at the door, later, to drive back up to the hotel on his own. I don't sleep, though, churning over my marriage, and where it all went wrong.

It was partly my fault, of course. I was young, naïve, blindsided by his charm and, I admit it, his wealth. But I'm not so young now. And not so naïve. I don't feel as terrified as I did before about Graham finding us. I will make sure Finola knows my fears regarding Graham's arrival, though I suspect Noel has told her, and I'm determined to shed the weight of Graham's dominance. Noel and Sean have my back, so I just need to tell him, straight out, that I'm not going back. I want a divorce.

17

GRACE

Sean turns up the next morning while Noel and I are still chattering at the breakfast table, and asks if I'd like to go up to the cottage and discuss the renovations with him. Noel is paying Finola to look after Olivia, so that I can work, so I ask if it's all right.

'Sure, it's grand. Take your time,' he agrees. 'We can't really get going until Dickie's visited. He owns the stationery wholesalers in Cork. He grew up here and was at school with me, so he's taking the opportunity to catch up. And apparently he's bringing some kind of new typewriter to show us.'

'I'll be out in the truck,' Sean says and shuts the door behind him.

Noel glances at me. 'Sean's a good man; get to know him a little.'

I hope he doesn't notice the flush I feel creeping into my cheeks.

I briefly wonder whether Arthur will be expecting me to call at his hotel, but he was never an early riser. I'll catch up with him later.

Sean helps me climb into the truck, a big infectious smile on his face, and asks, 'Where's Olivia today?'

'Doing Very Important dog training with Noel's dogs.'

'Poor dogs!'

'Oh, they won't mind. It's all play to them, but listen, I have to tell you...' As we drive past the mill to Goosheen in bright sunshine, enjoying the overhanging abundance of fuchsia and the riot of orange montbretia that line the banks, I explain about Arthur's unexpected arrival.

He frowns. 'Are you worried?'

'Arthur's okay, but I'm worried that Graham will now know where I am.'

'I'll put the word out for everyone to look out for an English car. Will he drive the silver Rolls-Royce over? That will be a sight to see!'

'I don't know. He might use my blue Volkswagen.'

'Look, cheer up. There's no use working yourself into a fret over what hasn't happened. If he turns up, someone will get me, all right?'

I nod, the tightness in my chest easing at his reassurance. 'So, what is it you want to discuss?'

'Nothing, really. I just wanted to see you again.' His grin is mischievous as he reaches for my hand.

I wish I could control my tendency to blush. We stroll hand in hand, and I'm glad there are no other workmen around. Last time I walked up here, the cottage was a sad derelict, roofless, its windows staring towards the sea like sightless eyes. Now, the skeletal outline of a roof has been created with beams of wood, dragging the cottage from uncaring decay back to the promise of life.

Sean is standing by the gaping doorway, beaming at my amazed expression. 'I said the roof wouldn't take long,' he says with satisfaction. 'We'll get the roofing felt on later, then the building can start to dry out.'

His solid presence makes my heart beat a little faster. It's strange how attractive I find him. He doesn't have Graham's classic, stern good looks but rather a tendency towards those creases that come from a natural inclination to smile. His is a very calming presence, a rock of reliability in my turbulent mental state.

'You did promise,' I agree with a smile, 'but I didn't expect to see it done so soon.'

'You should listen to me, girrul!'

I laugh. 'I will, indeed.' But it's a shame the felt isn't on, as it's started to rain.

He guides me back to the truck, opens a catalogue and points to some windows. 'I've ordered those for the whole house.'

'Has it got to be plastic?' I ask dubiously.

'UPVC,' he corrects. 'It survives much better than wood in this climate. And double glazing will help keep in the warmth.'

'It doesn't look very traditional.'

'It's practical. And it's not going to look very traditional, anyway, once you get the conservatory on the front.'

'That's what you'd do if it were yours?'

'Absolutely. I'm all for tradition, but not when it comes to being warm and comfortable, which you could never accuse these old houses of being. Three-feet-thick walls might mean the wind doesn't get through, but neither does any warmth. They hold a constant temperature, like a cave.'

That sounds gloomy, I think.

'So, tell me about Graham. That is his name?'

I nod and tell him how naïve I was, and how he became unbearably domineering, but so subtly I didn't really notice it happening until it was just overwhelmingly part of my life.

'Hmm,' Sean grunts. 'So, you ran because you're afraid of him?'

'I'm afraid of his overbearing authority, more than anything.

I've never seen him violent, though I think he could be. But if he knew I was leaving, he'd certainly try to take Olivia away from me.'

'Can he, by law?'

'I don't know. I don't even know if I had the right to take her myself. I just didn't want to get into a fight about it. But if he finds us, how can I stop him?' Tears sting my eyes again.

He puts his arm around my shoulders and gives me a comforting hug. 'Sure, now, that won't happen. A girleen needs her mother most.'

Graham's biggest assets are his confidence and his money. What if he has a court order or something? It's comforting to have moral support, though. I draw away, slightly embarrassed, and wipe my eyes. 'So, how long will it take you to get the windows?'

'Don't be changing the subject. You know I like you, don't you?'

'I, ah...'

'Well, I'd like to kiss you, if that's all right.'

I gasp, not knowing how to answer. He leans in close, his breath tickling my face. I tilt my head just slightly in acceptance, and he pecks a kiss right on my lips. His grey eyes crinkle with amusement; he knows I'd half expected a little more. Maybe next time I'll be able to prove that his interest is reciprocated.

Meanwhile, the black cloud overhead has drifted on, and the day is looking a little brighter. I feel a bit more positive about the future, even though it's hard to believe that this empty shell, this building site, is going to end up as a family home. From what Sean tells me, he has other projects on the go, and blockwork can only go up a few courses at a time, as the mortar needs time to set, so it seems we'll be living with Noel for a while yet. Noel must have known that when he offered.

Sean glances at his watch. 'Can I tempt you to have lunch with me?'

'It's early, surely?'

'Ah, well. I wasn't doing so much today. Just say yes, and save me the bother of arguing.'

I laugh. 'Okay then, yes.'

He starts the truck, drives down to the main road and turns right. I glance at him, startled. 'Where are we going?'

'You'll see.'

After a few miles, he turns inland, up a tiny boreen, then onto a dirt track which has deep runnels either side gouged out by the rain. He drives through a pair of stone-built gateposts, bounces along a rutted track and pulls in by the side of an old farmhouse. He jumps out with the flash of a grin. 'Come on then!'

'Whose house is this?'

'My family's. It's where I grew up. My brother runs the farm, mostly, but Mam will have hot bread in the oven.'

I baulk. 'She doesn't know I'm coming?'

'It's fine.'

I slip down and follow, somewhat reluctantly. He opens a door made of nailed planks, and we enter a long, low room with exposed rafters and the wafting scent of baking bread. In my opinion, no scent is comparable. My mouth waters, despite myself.

There's a woman by a large wooden table, setting out a pile of plates and knives. She's neatly dressed in a tweed skirt and a hand-knitted cardigan. Her iron-grey hair is pulled back into clips, and she wears no make-up or jewellery.

Sean walks over and kisses her on the cheek. 'Mam, this is Grace; I told you about her,' he says.

I wonder quite what he told her.

She glances at me and smiles, as if it's the most normal thing in the world for her son to bring a stranger in for lunch. A streak of colour in her grey hair betrays the merest hint that she was once a vibrant redhead, and age has added depth to features that betray an inner calm. She must have been quite lovely once.

'Ah, you're the English one who blew in with the wind. Come in, come in, make yourself at home, girrul. The boys will be in from the fields soon, like a horde of locusts, God help us! So, you two get on, and help yourselves while there's still something on the table! The kettle's on the boil, so.'

She dumps a huge square of butter onto a plate, and proceeds to slice thick chunks of ham and cheese, while asking, 'Sean tells me you're staying at the Big House, doing some work for Noel? I wonder what that might be? And he tells me you have a wean? She'll be going to the school below? So, you're intending to stay then?'

Sean winks at me. 'Mam will be after knowing your life history if you're not careful.'

'Now, Sean!' she says in mock severity, hands briefly on her hips. 'Don't you be telling the girrul your tales now! So, eat up. And where is it you're coming from? And how is it you have the house given?'

She places a huge metal teapot on the bare table, which is weathered from years of scouring, and I find myself saying, 'I'm from Birmingham. The house belonged to my grandparents, Connor and Caitlin McCarthy. I thought I could just come and stay in it. I didn't realise it would be in such a state.'

'You have the papers for the house then?'

'Sure I do.'

She nods. 'That's good, but even so, you're lucky no one moved into it.'

'Lucky?'

'Land that had no known ownership was sold. And there's squatters' rights,' Sean says. 'What with the famine, and the Depression, and thousands of people emigrating, and land lying bare, the government had to do something. Of course, some politicians did rather well out of it,' he adds cynically.

'But isn't that always the way?' I murmur.

'Lord preserve us! I remember Caitlin – sure I do! And she's your grandmother? Well now! Wasn't she ever the wild one?' I'm sure I hear admiration in her voice. 'Her father never forgave her for running off with Connor, you know, but there's not a body blames her. Well, the place will be grand, as soon as it has a roof over. And how is it you know Noel O'Donovan?'

I find myself telling her how I need to earn a living so placed an advertisement in the post office.

'Ah, so he's no relation?'

'No,' I say. 'But it seems he was once a friend of my grandfather.'

'He was that. My mother was after telling me that the two boys were ever running wild together.'

I've eaten a single piece of warm soda bread smothered in butter, and a piece of mild cheese, but I don't much care for the ham, which is dark brown and overly salty. Sean whips it from my plate when his mother isn't looking. 'Home cured,' he whispers. 'An acquired taste.'

The door opens and three young farmhands crowd in, bringing a distinct farmyard aroma. They cast curious glances at me but dive into the fresh soda bread and cheese as if they haven't eaten in a month, cheerfully elbowing each other in the bustle for the best slices of ham. They talk of silage and milk quotas, and a young cow who's gone lame.

Sean looks over as he sighs and puts his knife down. 'Are you finished? We should head away, if so. I should be getting back to work.'

I rise and turn to Sean's mother. 'That was wonderful, thank you. I don't think I've ever eaten bread like it.'

She beams, kisses me on the cheek and says, 'You come again now. Don't be a stranger.'

But I am a stranger, I think, though everyone treats me as if they've known me all my life.

As Sean drops me back at the foot of Noel's drive, he asks, 'Will you be up later?'

Twice in one day? People will talk. But I want to see him, so I nod. 'But I'd have to get back to Noel's for dinner at six.'

'Okay.'

I walk up the drive, feeling strangely confused. Why did Sean take me to his mother's house? And I forgot to ask him which of those lads was his brother. Did they wonder why I was there? I imagine the banter that will have broken out after we left but somehow know it would have been good-natured.

I've just started to work on my afternoon editing when Jane calls up to say that Arthur is at the door. Olivia, who's working on spelling with Finola, is there before me. She screams, 'Arty!' and throws herself at Arthur.

He swings her around in a full circle. 'Shall we go and get cake? I saw a neat place in the main street.'

'Cake, cake!' Olivia sings out, jumping on the spot.

'You just had your lunch,' I protest, but cake wins the argument. I say to Jane, 'Do you mind telling Noel I'm out? I'll make up the time later.'

'Should I come, or should I wait here?' Finola asks.

'Come on down,' I suggest. 'Then I can leave you all to your own devices while I come back and get on with my work.'

As we walk down the slope towards the road, I glance over at the spit of rock that conceals my house and tell Arthur, 'I'm looking forward to moving into my own place. You should walk up and see the progress. It's amazing. They're building a whole new bit on the back so we can have a brand-new bathroom and kitchen.'

He's holding Olivia's hand. She skips along beside him and declares, 'Sean's making a bedroom for you, too,' as though there's no question that the third room is for her brother.

'Of course, you can come and stay any time. You know you'll be welcome,' I concur.

'Great,' he says, smiling down at Olivia. 'I'll be coming here a lot – you'll see. This place is just amazing.'

We walk down to the main road and stop on the bridge to look out across the bay. The sun is shining. There's a flash of paddles in the distance: a couple of canoes, so low in the water they're almost invisible. Not even the hint of a breeze ripples the surface, which moves placidly, reflecting the sky above.

'Not good sailing weather,' Arthur murmurs.

'No,' I agree. 'Good paddling weather, though. Maybe we should buy a couple of canoes when Olivia gets a bit bigger.'

'Maybe I could take you both out sailing, if the wind rises?' Arthur suggests. 'I talked to a guy at the hotel. I can get the loan of his Wayfarer 34.'

'Maybe,' I say, though I'm dubious. My experience of boating is limited to the ferry, and I don't like the way sailing boats tip over as the wind rips into the sails.

As we seat ourselves noisily by the window in the little café, which is almost empty, I wonder how it survives. We wouldn't find seats in Cheltenham, midday, without queueing.

Despite all my efforts, I'm unable to fully engage with Arthur. I'm too young to be his mother, too old to be his friend, so being married to his father adds a weird slant to my role in his life; besides which, he was away at school or university for extended periods.

It's useful to have Finola with us, bridging the gaps in our dysfunctional family, but I see her casting interested glances his way, which bothers me. To a teenager, he must appear handsome and worldly and rich. But she's too young to be getting involved, and it would be a disaster, besides, like my own marriage. His world and hers are like hot and cold streams of weather, never mingling but gliding endlessly over and around each other. I can't imagine her in an English city. She's too innocent to be dragged into the segregation of an English class system, which, though it's become less distinct over the generations, has never truly disappeared.

I'm jolted back out of my daydreaming as a girl brings over a tray of tea and mugs and hot scones and butter. 'Thank you,' I say, smiling at her.

'It's no bother, so.' She smiles back. 'Are you enjoying your holiday?'

Olivia states, 'We're staying at the Big House with Uncle Noel.'

The girl tilts her head in surprise. I quickly interject, 'Just until our house is ready. It's being renovated.'

'So, you'll be staying then?'

I nod, hoping Olivia doesn't see.

'Enjoy, so!'

Arthur chatters on and I realise, once again, how similar he is to Graham. He doesn't ask how we're doing. He grins artlessly at me and witters on about what he's going to achieve once he has his doctorate, and how he's going to sail his yacht across the Atlantic. I wonder how he'll afford this dream yacht. Does he think Graham will buy it for him? I doubt it, especially in light of his deceit regarding his education and future.

For a moment I feel sorry for Graham, then I harden myself. He is, after all, the instigator of his own loneliness.

After a while, I leave the three of them talking. There's little enough for youngsters to do in this tiny town, but hopefully they'll find pleasure in just being by the sea, if only for a short while. Despite the weeks sliding by, I still feel buoyed by this change from my urban background. I feel a shift happening inside myself. Like a neglected plant that's moved into the sun, I feel myself becoming sturdier, healthier.

I walk straight up the hill, having lost most of the day

already. Sean must have seen me coming. He's waiting, perched against the front wall, by the gate, which is hanging sadly by one hinge, the other long dissolved by salt-encrusted spray.

We share a smile, and I perch next to him. Together, we watch the water loop into the bay, glittering with flashes of reflected sunlight, with the colourful houses strung along its border like a necklace.

'It's a grand day, to be sure,' Sean says, reaching for my hand.

'It is,' I agree. 'It's beautiful today.'

'And every other day. You can watch the storms from here. That's why we need the conservatory on the front. This cottage always had potential,' he muses. 'It was sad to see it so neglected. It was strange the way Connor and Caitlin ran off, Ma said. Her father would have come around in the end.'

I notice that he's been stripping the old render from the walls.

'Will you leave it as stone?' I ask. 'It looks nice, exposed like that.'

He shakes his head. 'In the valley I might, but without the render, the building would be eaten alive by the salt scour. And the stones have gaps between. The wind would find its way in, with nothing but the inside plaster to stop it. The aim is to make the place cosy, not pretty.'

'Cosy I like,' I agree.

He pulls me by the hand. 'Come through to the back.'

Inside, the house is slightly gloomy. Grey render on the walls, grey concrete on the floors. The ceiling joists have been covered with a layer of plasterboard. He explains about the insulation that now fills the spaces between the joists and points to the underfelt that will seal the roof space from the clawing fingers of wind.

I shiver. 'This place must have been cold, when my grandpa was growing up here.'

'Sure; they all were. It was a hard life, but maybe not the worst. For those who survived the famine, you know. People are soft today. They don't know the half of it.'

'But you do?'

Did I sound slightly sceptical? Sean is, after all, much of an age with me. The skin around his eyes creases with amusement. 'Are you learning nothing from Noel?'

I feel chastened and also slightly irritated. 'He told me about his early childhood then skipped straight to when he was in America.'

'Ah. Strange. You'd think he'd tell the story in the order it happened, but no doubt he has his reasons. As for me, well, I like to hear tales from the old ones,' he says. 'They know to stop and count their blessings.'

As I've stopped to count mine, I realise – mainly, my freedom and Olivia's happiness. I just had to find a space to do it in.

He shows me around the new building, which will be a kitchen, a bathroom and a utility area, and I start to believe I might one day live here. My imagination is now slotting me into this place.

'So,' he says with an air of finality. 'The plastering will soon be done, the wood burner in. Then we'll leave it to settle before you decide about colour and carpets and the like.'

'So soon?'

'Are we good, or what?'

I laugh. 'You're a real find!'

'And so are you,' he says, colouring slightly. 'Might I walk you back up to the Big House?'

'I'd like that,' I say, warmth creeping up my neck, 'but perhaps you should stay here and get on?'

He laughs. 'Slave driver.'

I try to pull my hand free, but Sean tightens his grip fractionally before letting go. There's unspoken dialogue between us. I realise he likes me as much as I like him, but he knows I've been hurt and is too sensible to rush things. I feel as if we're consolidating some kind of unvoiced covenant for the future, and I'm filled with a sense of illicit excitement – I've never been interested in a man before, the way I'm interested in Sean, even though the last thing I should be doing is starting a new relationship, when I'm still trying to move on from the last, disastrous one.

I'm amused by my own capacity for feeling guilty, as though my interest in Sean is making me an unfaithful wife. It's been nearly two months now, but in my mind, I left Graham years ago. He was always married more to his firm and his own status than to me. At what point will my conscience allow me to move on and stop making me feel responsible for breaking up a marriage that was rooted in misunderstanding?

'Well, I'd best let you go and get on then,' he says.

'Thank you. For everything,' I say. What I mean is, *Thank you for understanding that I'm not quite ready*.

'No bother,' he murmurs, a shy smile on his lips. 'No bother at all.'

I feel his eyes follow me as I leave.

I walk up past the new hotel, which is near completion. It will be taking a few guests this summer, Noel told me. People he knows. But he isn't intending to push it through any agencies. He'll let it gather its own momentum; find a clientele who already want to come to West Cork. He's talking about the Irish diaspora, other immigrants he'd known in America during his entrepreneur years who want to come back and revisit the place they still think of as home, or their offspring, who are keen to discover their roots.

Almost as though Noel had heard my thoughts, the strains of Josef Locke singing 'I'll Take You Home Again, Kathleen' hit me as I enter the house. I slip into the main room and stand at the door to listen. Noel lifts the needle on the record player and starts the song again. There's a spit and crackle at the opening, as though he's done this many times before. I lean against the door frame, and Noel swivels, startled. I'm almost sure there are tears in his eyes.

'Oh,' he says. 'You're back. I'll just...'

He reaches for the needle, and I hold my hand out to stop him. 'Don't. I love that song. No one sings it the same as Josef Locke, do they? As if he really knew a Kathleen, who always pined for her Irish home.'

He nods then admits, 'I loved a girl called Kathleen, once.'

I recall his wife was called Sinéad and fumble with confusion before saying, 'I'm sorry. I didn't mean to intrude.'

'No,' he says softly. 'It's fine. You're writing my memoir. By the time we're finished, there will be no secrets left. I'll tell you about Kathleen, when the time comes.'

I leave quietly, but Noel doesn't put the song on again. He leaves the record to play out. Grandma is called Kathleen, too, though she spells it the Irish way, Caitlin. I think about Grandma as I've never thought about her before. She came from here, but I'd been so wrapped up in myself, my own growing up, coming of age, that it didn't occur to me that maybe, in some hidden corner of her heart, she might wish to come back. How she loves the pure sound of Josef's voice, too. She said it was like a spoonful of the sweet black treacle she'd been given as a child, when her throat was sore. Her eyes would twinkle as she admitted that, sure, didn't she complain of a sore throat a little more often than was true?

I smile at the memory, then another thought jolts me. Is my grandmother the recipient of Noel's unrequited love? Did he know her that well? The letters I'm sending to Mum mention Noel; how could they not, as we're living in his house. I suspect she lets Grandma read them. I wonder if she recalls him? I wonder if she would be brave enough to come back for a visit with Mum, or whether it would be too painful, in her twilight years, to see where she might still be living if Grandpa Connor hadn't had to travel to England for work. It must have been hard. Traumatic, even.

18

NOEL, 1932

When Noel O'Donovan finally reached Boston, the first thing he did was change his money at a reputable bank and get himself tailored up. His functional, mended farming clothes, fine at home, labelled him an Irish immigrant, and that was no good. In a new tweed suit, with a smart cap and brogues, he toured the city, discovering the best places for work – and the places best avoided. He knocked on doors, made it known he was literate and keen to work. And when he was rejected, he went back again and yet again. Despite what he'd put on his immigration documents, and despite his farming back-ground, he wasn't going to be a farm labourer, not if he could help it.

He was long-legged and slim, which made him look younger than he was, and eventually he was curtly asked, by a bank manager, could he run? Like a racing dog's dinner, he replied with a quick grin, and was given a message to run. The manager set his stopwatch going as he ran off, and when Noel got back, he was hired with a curt nod. His first job, as a runner for the bank, lasted six months, and he was happy enough being the errand boy, while awaiting the opportunity to get a job behind the counter. But he discovered a reward for his enthusiasm in quite a different way.

The bank manager was the proud owner of a solitary race-horse, and all the staff were taken on an outing to the races, ostensibly as a reward but mostly because the manager liked to parade his prize-winning mare, Scarlett River, in front of his staff. Noel suspected that he also enjoyed receiving praise for being clever enough to see her potential.

When they got to the stables, though, there was a bother going on. The mare was skittish, fighting the bit, not wanting to be mounted. The stable hands were milling about outside, afraid to go in. The races were already underway, and she hadn't even been warmed to the turf. Noel could see she was unaccountably distressed, rearing back from contact, the white of her eyes visible.

'What's with her?' the manager snapped, glaring at the horse.

Everyone shrugged helplessly. She'd never behaved like that before.

'Well, get in and sort it!' he said. 'That's what I pay you for!'

No one moved. Noel watched for a moment then grabbed the leading rein from the stable lad who was hanging onto it from a distance. He held out one of the sugar lumps he'd brought along and whispered the soft, sibilant Irish words he'd learned from Jed the blacksmith to shush the horses as they were shod, and gradually reeled her in towards him. When she was calm, he stroked her head and eventually cradled it on his shoulder, smoothing her neck until her great shudders eased. Then he climbed over the half-gate into the stall.

He learned, later, that the trainer had rushed forward to stop him, foreseeing a tragedy in the making, but the owner held him back. They'd all watched with bated breath, expecting the mare to rear and trample him. He was just another Irish immigrant, after all – it wouldn't have been a great loss.

He gentled her all over, stroking, feeling down each leg in turn, wondering why she was acting up. He found nothing, but by now the horse was calm, nuzzling him for more sugar, but when he put minimal weight on the stirrup, she played up again, so he unbuckled the saddle and ran his hand over the inside. Something pricked his finger. Further investigation revealed a sliver of metal embedded into a seam. Scarlett River must have been scratched as they tried to put the saddle on her. Nothing serious, but with the added pressure of a rider, it would have cut into her back.

'Sabotage,' he said, showing them.

The owner turned red with fury. 'Get her ready, and I want to know who did that – and how they got in here. You, boy, what's your name?'

'Noel, sir.'

'You're in charge of her until after the race.'

'Yes, sir.' Noel checked the saddle over then placed it carefully on her back.

'What a stunner she is, sir,' he added. 'Sure, I know it in my bones, the darlin' will win this race. I'm thinking I might put a dollar on her.'

She didn't win but came in second, and during the next week, Noel's manager asked if he really wanted to work at the bank, or would he rather work with horses?

For Noel, it was no contest.

He began as a stable hand and learned everything he could from watching the trainers, the jockeys, the vet and the bookies. Within five years, he was running the stables and had bought his own racehorse. Within ten, he was running his own stables, money piling into the bank faster than he could spend it.

19

GRACE

We make a little progress in organising Noel's piles of papers while we wait for the new typewriter to turn up, but my presence seems to have opened a floodgate of reminiscing. Over a glass of wine one evening, he tells me about his journey to Boston and explains how he became the manager of a racehorse stables, and how he laid his bet on his manager's horse.

'Now that was a lot of money in the day,' he says. 'She didn't come in first, but didn't I make enough to buy a new suit? Wasn't I the man? *Heh*. And that was when my career changed from errand boy to stable hand, then to stable manager. And from that, and a little luck with a mare I bought for breeding, I went from poor Irish labourer to the owner of a large stable of my own very successful horses. But I'm getting ahead of my own story.'

By his early twenties, I now know, Noel had already lived through poverty, marriage and the death of his wife. Then he emigrated, leaving behind everything he knew. It was a tale the Irish had become familiar with over a couple of centuries. These days, in England, with education being free, most chil-

dren have scarcely let go of their mother's apron strings by their
early twenties.

I'd supposed it was grief that had sent Noel running from
his home, as much as the hard life and lack of prospects, but
now Noel has hinted of an unrequited love for a woman called
Kathleen. What had stopped him from declaring himself? I'm
curious to discover the truth behind that titbit of information,
but before I can worm my way around to sly investigation, Noel
quizzes me about Graham. About how we fell in love and
married.

'It's boring,' I warn him.

'Tell me anyway.'

'It wasn't love,' I admit dryly. 'And everything was my own
fault, in the end.'

Noel smiles gently. 'People like to cast blame, but sometimes the things we do are simply a part of life, right at the time.
It's what brought you to this place at this time. Had it not, you'd
be somewhere else. So I'm curious how someone like you could
end up with someone I'm beginning to detest, though I've never
met him. In all my years, one of the most profound lessons I've
learned is that those who inherit expectations often have a
different set of values from the rest of the population. It doesn't
always make them bad, but it does make them different.'

He's right; I've thought that myself. I wonder what Arthur
would have turned out like, had he been the son of a metal-
worker, like my dad. I pause, thinking, then find a place to start.

'That first day at work, as his secretary, I knew I couldn't do
it. I was going to fail. I was going to be kicked out and sent igno-
miniously home by the end of the week. But Graham realised I
was nervous and did everything he could to make me feel at
ease, and it worked. A few weeks later, I was able to walk in
through that front door without wanting to be sick. And soon
after that, I wasn't only doing the job but doing it well.

'My office was adjacent to Graham's, though he tended to

call me on the phone if he needed me to go in. The office suites on the top floor were known as "up in the gods" by the workers on the other two floors. I felt special up there. I thought Graham was kind, but later I realised he was just ruthlessly practical. Helping me to settle in was in his own interest.'

Noel waits quietly. He seems engrossed in something happening beyond the window, but I know he's listening, taking it all in.

I carry on, reliving my mistakes. 'Graham inherited a small business that made electrical goods. It was failing dramatically when he took it over, and he immediately shifted into electronic components, seeing the way technology was going. From there, he shunted into handheld gadgets and the computerised games that were just coming onto the market. He got in at the right time, I guess.'

'Like me with the horses,' Noel states.

'Luck plus business acumen,' I respond. 'Some people have one or the other – or neither. Well, it didn't take me long to realise that he was attracted to me. Of course, I was flattered and began to imagine what it would be like to be married to this powerful man, to live in a big house, to be able to afford things without having to struggle. I mean, that's every girl's dream, isn't it? The fairy tale. To find not just the love of your life but one who can dump you into a universe made of ball gowns and chandeliers, like some Regency romance.' I give him a lopsided grimace. 'I'd challenge any woman who said their dream was to marry an ironworker and live in a damp two-bedroomed house, counting pennies to buy their children shoes.'

Noel smiles but nods for me to go on.

'Soon, he started to walk me to the door in the evening. That was unusual, in itself, but nothing spectacular. Then one day, when we reached the door, it was chucking it down, so he offered me a lift home. I'd never been in a car so plush, so quiet, with a polished mahogany dashboard and leather seats. I must have been grinning or something as he turned briefly from the road, and his features softened into the nearest thing I've ever seen to a smile. He asked if I liked his car, and I told him it was beautiful. *So are you,* he said. *May I take you out to dinner?* And that was that.'

I glance at Noel. 'You see, no one had ever told me I was beautiful before. He made me feel special. I recall all these details, because my first real romance was written in those few words. As is my greatest regret. I wish I hadn't applied for the job. I wish I'd never met him. I wish he hadn't chosen me. But I was young and impressionable. He wanted someone he could mould, but I didn't know that then. In hindsight, I guess I was pretty much a blank slate, but I would have discovered myself, eventually, had I been given the chance.'

'But it wasn't all bad? He didn't, ah, hurt you or anything?'

'Not like that. It sounds small, but he controlled everything. Of course, even at that early stage in our relationship, he betrayed himself many times, only I was too naïve to see it.'

'Betrayed himself how?'

I take a breath. Is it this hard for Noel, telling me about his past? 'Okay. For instance, he said he wanted *me* to get to know *him*, not the other way around. It's strange how, once I realised who he was, all the little things I'd missed when he was courting me rose up and explained themselves, afterwards.'

I curl my lip at my own stupidity. 'There were lots of similar indicators but, of course, I wasn't looking for them. And by the time I truly realised what Graham was, I was a young mother with a daughter, trapped in my gilded cage. I kept hoping things would get better, if I only worked at it and pleased Graham a little more. I decided, you see, that if I was unhappy with my situation, it was my fault. There were many girls who would have jumped at the chance. In fact,' I add with a wry grin, 'I'm sure there were many who tried. But Graham was, as far as I know, faithful.'

I pause for a moment, and another incident comes to mind. 'He proposed in the Savoy, on his knee, where we could be seen. He handed me a diamond ring he said had been his mother's, though I never quite believed that. He liked having money – and spending it. Can you imagine it? The low murmur of chatter from a *select* clientele, a deathly hushed moment, then the hullabaloo as everyone clapped and whistled like public schoolboys. I was embarrassed. Then there was the flash of a camera, and the next day our engagement was in print all over the country. He boasted, later, that it had all gone according to plan. I hadn't even said yes, but no one noticed.'

'You carried on and married him.'

'I felt obliged to go ahead with it, because everyone was congratulating us. I knew I didn't love him, even then, but I thought it would be all right. I mean, for centuries women have had arranged marriages and managed to respect their husbands; even love them.'

'Have they really?' His answer was slightly cynical.

'I guess they couldn't say otherwise,' I sigh. 'Anyway, Graham organised the wedding, even down to choosing my dress. I was just too awed by his status, his money, his personality, to do more than hint about things I minded, and he was always able to talk me out of whatever silly thing had upset me. Because didn't he love me? Didn't he want the best for me? That's how he gets on – by manipulating people.

'As I walked down the aisle, I saw tears in Mum's eyes. I thought it was pride, but later she told me it was because she was envisaging the heartache. But this was the first day of the magical rest of my life, so I was floating in my own fairy tale.'

'You were young, and what girl doesn't want to be the princess in the story?'

'My grandmother warned me not to marry him. It turns out she was right. I suppose she thought I had to make my own mistakes. But on my wedding day, she gave me a present, a large, old iron key. She'd tied a big blue bow on it and said, *Something old, something new, something borrowed and something blue.* I asked her what it was for, and she went all weird. She said one day it would unlock my future.'

'The key to the cottage?'

'I didn't know about it back then. I just thought she was being a little romantic. Graham, of course, told me to throw the filthy thing away, but I didn't. I brought it with me, hoping it would open the door to Grandpa's house, but when I got here' – I laugh – 'I discovered the house didn't even have a door any longer!'

Noel grins. 'One day the young might listen to the old ones, but I doubt it. So, you were saying...'

'Our wedding photographs adorn the grand piano in our best lounge – did I say I play a bit? No? Anyway, later, I would stare at them, wondering who that idiot bride was. How could she have been so naïve? How could she have not taken an interest in organising her own wedding, made a few decisions, instead of being a puppet?' I pause then grimace. 'The rest you can guess. The downslide from happiness to the realisation that this had been a disastrous mistake wasn't long in coming, and after that, it was a question of hiding my unhappiness, and coping, especially after...'

He waits, and my eyes meet his as I admit, 'I was told that he was questioned over the death of his first wife but wasn't convicted because there wasn't enough evidence. I was petrified.'

'Was that true?'

'I really don't know. But it changed everything.'

'Sometimes, we're told things we'd be better off not knowing.'

'I don't know,' I say doubtfully. 'Surely it's best to know things, even if it's something we don't want to hear?'

But Noel has drifted off, somewhere into the past.

20

NOEL, 1931

'Mother told me the news is all over that Caitlin ran away with Connor last night,' Sinéad told Noel over their evening meal.

He stilled at her words and hoped that the bitterness he experienced could be taken for surprise. He'd been forewarned, but now it had happened, it felt as if a piece of his soul had fled the room. Caitlin was gone. With Connor.

From the curl of her lip and the pleased tone in her voice, he wondered if Sinéad disliked the dark-haired girl who was her polar opposite. Maybe Sinéad, who was as pale-skinned and golden-haired as the angel she'd been likened to, and who never did a thing to upset the nuns, was quietly jealous of Caitlin's exuberance and zest for life. But it was also likely that she knew Noel carried a torch for her. Her expression was bland as she ladled broth from the cast-iron bastible into the wooden bowls and placed them on the table.

Noel's father cast him a sidelong glance. 'I heard that her father is ranting and raging to Connor's father, asking who'll care for him in his old age.'

'Well, we all know she was promised to Ben,' Sinéad said primly.

'Against her own inclination,' Noel reminded her.

'She should have done what her father asked. It was her duty.'

As it was your duty to marry me? he thought. But that wasn't really fair.

Until his final tryst with Caitlin, and the news that had knocked him sideways, he'd supposed, for some reason, that despite his marriage to Sinéad, she would always be there, in his peripheral vision, the shining light of her love there to keep him strong. It was strange that it felt like a betrayal, when it was he, in fact, who'd betrayed Caitlin.

Several months passed before he received a letter from Connor, telling him about their dreadful journey and recently improved circumstances. Connor evinced joy that Caitlin was with child, which made Noel jealous. Caitlin should be married to him, having his child! Sinéad was pregnant too, but with that jackeen Jacob's child, not his. It took great willpower not to blame her or the child – it wasn't their fault. Maybe, one day, Sinéad would bear his children, too.

But though Sinéad swelled gently under the weight of the child, she didn't so much blossom as grow ever more ethereal, as though the child was sucking the life from her. The women of the town whispered that she wasn't long for this world, that she was one of God's chosen. And then Sinéad's time did come, and far too soon, with a bright rush of blood. A nun was called to tend her, but what good that was, Noel thought, only Himself would know, as the panicked young woman spent most of her time on her knees, praying, while Sinéad silently issued forth a tiny, perfectly still baby boy then took herself off to Heaven.

Noel felt truly sad for Sinéad, because she'd been like a sister to him during their childhood. He hadn't been able to love her as a wife, though, and maybe the lost child was his fault, as if God knew that the few times he'd made love to her, he'd imagined it was Caitlin lying beneath him. Poor Sinéad. She hadn't always been sad. Jacob had stolen her innocence and joy in life, along with her secret dreams, and Noel realised that, in the end, his own actions hadn't saved her at all.

Noel wrote to Connor, telling him the sad news, adding that he was now a free man. He knew it was too late, though. Caitlin was Connor's wife, in truth, and having Connor's child, so Noel's regrets couldn't have been more poignant. Sinéad's mother had died not long after their marriage, and her father had followed soon after. Noel's father was unable to do much heavy work, and Noel found himself the lonely owner of a farm twice its previous size, with no family to grace it.

Then the bottom really dropped out of his world.

He received a letter from Connor to tell him of his own tragedy: that Caitlin had sadly died in childbirth too. Connor was also bereft, with no wife and no child. He hadn't been able to pen the words until his grief had dulled a little. Noel cynically thought that Connor would soon enough find another girl to marry; he wasn't one to live alone all his life. He grieved in secret, and though he tried to hide his sadness, there was one time, out in the fields on his own, when he howled his grief to the uncaring sky, for Caitlin had been the light of his life, and the light that had grown distant was now gone forever.

A short while later, his mother dropped dead, suddenly and unexpectedly as she was cooking the men's supper. Her heart had simply failed. This had been catastrophic for Paddy, a true believer, as the priest hadn't been able to administer the Last Rites, but Roisin was finally laid to rest, leaving Noel and his father without a woman of the house. Noel continued to work the farm with his father, but he'd lost heart.

All his youthful dreams had evaporated, and no matter how

many nice girls made it clear they would be pleased to marry him, he simply wasn't interested. He was bad news; everything he touched went sour. The girls were better off without him. He finally realised there was nothing for him in Ireland any longer. He was tired of the day-to-day grind; the milking, the loneliness, the deaths that surrounded him. He was working every hour God sent, just to keep the small farm going, and for what? Generations of Irish had worked their acres of land to pass them down to their children, and Noel was the end of his line.

He thought about his brother, Jacob, for the first time in ages. Jacob had been expected to take on the family farm before he ran away, and somehow Noel had believed he'd breeze back in one day, demanding his inheritance. But as time went by, it became more likely that he wouldn't -- or couldn't – return. They didn't know if he was alive or dead, in truth, but he was dead to Roone Bay and the little farm he'd left behind.

When Noel eventually admitted to his father that he wasn't happy, and that he wanted to go off to America, as he'd originally intended, Paddy simply nodded, as if he'd expected it. Neither man had learned to cook, and they missed Roisin's boundless energy, which had probably worn her out in the end.

'You go, son. Make a good life for yourself. This stony biteen of land has kept many generations of O'Donovans at starvation's door, and it's seen too much tragedy of late. Sure, it's time to let it go. The selling of it will provide for my old age and give you a good start in America.'

Noel had dipped his bread in the thin gruel he'd cobbled together, and it was hanging from his fingers, dripping back into the bowl as he asked, 'Are you sure?'

'You have the right of it, son. Make yourself a life away from this godforsaken country of ours. Sure, and haven't we been slave to this biteen of land far too long? Sell it, and take half with you to America. If you start with nothing, you'll always have nothing. Go and buy yourself that horse you've always wanted.'

Noel smiled softly. 'You knew I wanted a horse?'

'I've always known, son.'

And so the farm had been sold to an ambitious farmer who was buying up land around Roone Bay. 'Times are changing,' he explained, rather pompously, to the father and son. 'I've bought one of those new mechanical tractors, and it's going to take the place of a dozen men. I need bigger fields to make it economical.'

'These are small fields,' Noel said, frowning, indicating their land with a turn of his head.

'Not a bother,' the complacent farmer replied. 'I'll take out a few ditches is all.'

Paddy put his hand on Noel's arm, sensing that he was about to argue, and whispered, 'Make your choice, lad! Either stay and work the land, or sell it and don't look back. The land has been like this since my grandfather's day, and his before him, and never a fortune came of it.'

Things had gone too far for him to change his mind now.

His father had already made arrangements to marry a widow in Bantry who would cook for him and keep him, as Noel's mother had done for so many years in return for him providing for her. Perhaps he'd chosen to remove himself from Roone Bay, so that he wouldn't see the changes that were going to rip out the old ways.

Noel nodded once, to himself. His father was right. He should move on not look back. He turned and walked away, through the fields he'd known since childhood, leaving his father to complete the deal with a spit and a handshake. He stared around, committing this life to memory, as he would never see it again. There was the boreen he'd travelled with the donkey cart, on his way to the dairy. There was the little stone shed where his mother had kept the chickens from the foxes. He looked over at the roof of their house, where his childhood had known nothing but happiness, despite the hardship; the house that would be allowed to fall to ruin or be used for sheltering animals.

And there beside him was the field where he'd courted Caitlin, in those long summer days before he'd married Sinéad, to his everlasting sorrow. How easily everything he'd taken for granted had fallen apart, like winter swooping down ahead of its time. Yes, it was good that he was leaving. The memories here would surely kill him in the end.

So the land was sold. Noel had seen his father married, and his portion of the sale had been sewn into his pocket by the widow, who seemed kindly enough. Noel had tears in his eyes when he waved his father goodbye, but he turned away resolutely and didn't look back, because father and son both knew it would be forever. He wasn't the first, and wouldn't be the last, to disappear over the water to America to seek, if not a fortune, a different kind of life.

Gone were the days of mass emigration; the US authorities limited immigration these days, but he'd been lucky enough to get a visa, though he thought it had a lot to do with the money he was taking with him, which seemed like riches to a lad who'd never had a farthing to call his own. It took him a long day to get to Dublin by public transport, where he had to wait another few days before sailing across to England and travelling south to Southampton. There he boarded the steamship RMS *Queen Mary*, which would pass by the Bishop Rock and take maybe five days to get to Ambrose Light in Canada. From there he would travel to Boston, where a distant relative would give him board until he could support himself.

As he boarded the ship and took his place in a cramped cabin shared with three other men, he'd never felt so alone. He'd never, in fact, been further from his home than Cork city, and that only once in his life.

For two days, he fought light-headed nausea whenever he tried to stand, then on the third day, the sickness passed, and he was able to rise from his bunk and walk the deck. Leaning on the rail on that third evening, crossing a serenely benevolent Atlantic, the sky was so hypnotically filled with stars, it seemed he might drown in them. He watched the ship's wash churning below, and the thought of throwing himself in briefly crossed his mind. He wouldn't last long in those chill waters. The mammoth disaster of the *Titanic*, gone these twenty or so years, still haunted Atlantic crossings. It was a sobering thought. He'd never much liked swimming anyway.

He shook his head, smiling at his own dark humour. He wasn't really suicidal; he was simply leaving behind everything he knew, and giving up was a weakness he wouldn't allow himself. He wasn't afraid to die, but, equally, he wasn't afraid to live. Though the latter might be harder in some ways, now he'd been boosted into this different life, he was going to make the most of it.

21

GRACE

The weather has taken a turn for the worse, and for several days Olivia and Finola have warmed themselves by the range. Arthur is still up at the hotel, writing letters, he says, but he's intending to move on soon. After three days, the downpour slows and grinds to a fitful halt. The low cloud base that drifted in and settled over Roone Bay has lifted slightly, and small patches of blue have broken through. It's atmospheric enough, lending the sea a steel-grey coat and partially exposing Mount Gabriel, which reaches into the clouds behind us.

Finola decides to take Olivia out on the soggy hillside to dispel the frustration of having been trapped indoors by the weather. The exuberant dogs weave a pattern of excitement around their ankles as they get ready. They, too, have been avoiding their usual haunts, deterred by the torrential downpour. I marvel at the weight of all that water hanging over our heads, and wonder why it doesn't just fall out of the sky at once, flattening us and obliterating everything.

'Be good,' I say, kissing Olivia lightly before shooing her out of the door. 'Have fun. Do as Finola tells you.'

I can't help worrying. But she's livelier than she'd been in

Cheltenham; happy to go out and get dirty and wet, and her quick wit is more evident, away from the dampening effect of Graham's displeasure. She'd been anxious in his presence, trying to please him, be the daughter he wanted her to be, grateful for the odd word of praise. Of course, he wanted her to be a little lady, perhaps marry into the higher echelons of society that he could never penetrate.

I go on up to the office and find Noel standing at the window. 'Dickie will be here soon,' he says, glancing at his watch. 'Did you phone him with a list of what you needed?'

'I did. He's bringing it with him. A few reams of paper, a typist's chair, but most importantly, a decent typewriter.'

He glances at the old, black monster and says, 'I'm rather fond of that, actually.'

I flush faintly, 'I'm sorry, I just can't—'

He grins like a child. *Gotcha!*

I crack a smile, and shake my head.

His next question, I sense, is more serious. 'What do you think about your stepson, Arthur? I mean, arriving here, like this.'

'I honestly don't know,' I admit. 'There's no harm in Arthur, but his finding us might lead Graham here.'

'Would he harm you, this husband of yours?'

'He's a bully, and controlling, but he's never laid a hand on me in anger, though I think he has the capacity. He doesn't like his will being crossed. I've never challenged his authority, so he never had cause to get cross with me until now. I don't know what he'll do, really. I'm more afraid that he'll take Olivia.'

'Could he do that?'

'Legally? I don't know. Physically, probably, but I don't want to put it to the test. He's arrogant enough to take what he wants.'

'As is his son.'

I smile. 'True. Poor Arthur is a product of his upbringing.

Spoiled rotten with money and expectations but given little love or attention. He was hurt badly when his mother ran off and left him behind. I understand he visited her a few times in America when he became a teenager, but she never wanted him to live with her. I think she was as self-interested as Graham, in her own way. He was on holiday with her in Spain when she died in a boating accident – that was before my time. I couldn't be a mother to him, though I did try. I wasn't old enough. He was horrible to me, actually. Then Olivia came along.'

'Put his nose out of joint, did it?'

'Quite the opposite. I think she helped bring us to an understanding. He's quite protective of her, in his own way.'

'But for Arthur to not have told his father what he was studying is a bit, ah, strange?'

'Not really; that's why I didn't try to explain why I needed to leave.' I flush slightly. 'Once Graham has made up his mind about something, you can't change it. He would have refused Arthur's funding if he didn't approve. Educational grants are all based on the parents' income, so Arthur would have got no financial assistance if Graham had pulled the plug.'

'He'd have had to get a weekend job, like the other students,' Noel remarks.

'Maybe, but why make life harder for yourself when your father has so much?'

'Pride, perhaps? Deception has a way of turning on a person. And he's involved you, now, in this deception.'

I grimace agreement. 'Graham will be angry enough that I've left him, but what Arthur's done, and then him coming here, makes it seem as though I've been complicit.'

'I'd say Arthur is quite capable of looking after his own interests,' Noel says.

'I guess there must be some of his father in him. He certainly fooled me about his studies.'

'Well, it will unfold as it must. But if you need help, don't hesitate to ask. I don't accept bullying.'

'I don't want my personal situation to impact on your life.'

He waves a hand dismissively. 'If it does, it'll stop me from getting bored.' He looks out of the window and changes the subject. 'The sun's making a valiant effort, and the forecast is good. Sean will be able to make good headway on your house.'

'That will be a relief. The sooner we can move in, the better.'

'Don't you like living here?'

'Of course we do!' I stop and smile. There it is again, that underlying dry humour. 'It's just that I fear I'm taking advantage. And it's going to be difficult to prise Olivia out of this house!'

'Children are resilient. She'll recover. It's a novelty to have a child around the place, actually. Though I have plenty of distant relatives, of course. Finola is one of the best of them. A few generations in a backwater like this, and we're all related somewhere along the line.' He grins. 'And they're all itching to know who I'm going to leave everything to. Oh, look. There's Dickie now. He must have gotten an early start from Cork.'

A car crunches up the gravel driveway, and within minutes, a man erupts into the office, his whirlwind presence much larger than his diminutive, wiry frame. He's followed in by a young man puffing beneath the weight of a huge cardboard box.

'In here,' Noel directs, steering him into what will be my workspace. The box, which seems far too big to be a typewriter, is lowered carefully onto the desk. The young man scurries out, presumably to bring in more equipment.

Noel is amused, obviously echoing my confusion. 'What, in the name of all the saints, have you brought me?' he asks.

'A computer!' Dickie says with pride. 'All the top companies are investing in them, and in a few years every company will have one, sure, and aren't I always right?'

I must have looked terrified, because Dickie pats me on the arm. 'It's easy. I'll show you.'

'But I just need a typewriter!' I exclaim.

'It is a typewriter. You write into it, and when you're happy with your work, you can print it off. No correcting ribbons. No wasted paper and ink. It's pure gas, you'll see.'

As he's talking, he scores the tape on the box and lifts out what looks like a small, bulky television. His lad scurries back in with another box, and within moments they're plugging in a tangle of cables that link the screen, the box, a separate board with keys on and a little box on a wire on the right-hand side. They plug it in, switch it on, and there are a series of internal scratching sounds before the screen attains a ghostly green hue.

'Voila!' Dickie says, like a magician. 'The electric pencil!'

Noel and I glance at each other and share a conspiratorial grin. We haven't a clue what's going on.

'Sit, sit,' I'm instructed. 'Now, type something.'

'What?'

'Anything.'

I type, *Hello. My name is Grace.*

A little flashing square on the screen precedes every letter, and there's what I typed, sitting boldly on the screen! Fascinated, I type some more. *I'm here to assist Noel in writing his memoir.*

'Oh,' I say faintly. 'But won't it disappear when we switch it off?'

'No, you save it. Move the cursor with the bug – that's the thing on the wire, there – click that button. That's right. Now, give it a name, something meaningful, like Test Number One.'

I follow his instructions.

'Now,' Dickie says, 'I'm going to turn it all off. See, it's off. Now I'm going to turn it back on again. Wait a minute... and here's the menu, and here's Test Number One, that you wrote. See? It's still there. Click on it, using the button on the bug.'

And there are the words, exactly as I typed them.

'Like magic,' he says, no doubt pleased by my dumbfounded expression. 'So, type in something new, with a mistake in it. Okay, so. Now press that button, and it will go backwards and delete it all, one letter at a time. Now type it in correctly. Or you can just click on the error, like so, and change that one letter. Then, to be safe, before you shut it down, create a copy on a floppy disk. This,' he says, waving a little square folder in front of me, 'just in case the computer goes wrong, or you have a power cut or something. Then you haven't lost everything.'

There's a silence as we digest everything. 'Shall I get Jane to wet a pot of tea?' Noel asks, sensing a lull in the sales spiel.

'Sure, that would be grand.'

'Grace, would you mind asking her to bring it to my study?'

'Of course.'

I'm overwhelmed by my elevation from typist to user of space-age technology, and hope I don't let Noel down by finding it beyond my capabilities.

I'm invited to join the men for tea and biscuits but take my leave, saying I need to check on Olivia. I slip out, sensing a connection between the two men. I suspect they have a history, and that Dickie was happy to drive all the way down from Cork not just to make a sale but also to catch up with an old friend.

I go back down to the kitchen, to make good my excuse. Olivia and Finola are still out with the dogs, I'm told. Jane adds, darkly, that my stepson came calling while we were busy with the computer. Jane keeps her gaze on the pastry she's rolling as she says, 'I told him you were busy with Noel. I think you should explain things to him.'

I sense an undercurrent to her words. 'What do you mean, explain things?'

She stops, wipes her hands on a towel and reaches for a baking tray. 'Explain how it is. He walked around the back and into the kitchen. You and Olivia are Noel's guests, but that doesn't mean he should presume...' She tails off, her cheeks reddening.

I can see that Arthur, used to his father's position in society, would have made certain assumptions. Despite my distant family connection to this town, this community's past, I'm definitely a blow-in, a stranger. I've chosen to live here, and hope the community will one day absorb me. But Arthur has no connection at all. He certainly hasn't got the right to walk into Noel's home without being invited. But how can I say these things without upsetting him? I always thought Arthur must be more like his mother but more and more I'm seeing his similarity to Graham: his expectations, his arrogance, his sense of superiority. I'm left with an uneasy feeling that this isn't going to go well. I always felt sorry for Arthur, the unloved son from Graham's first marriage. But I've recently learned that Arthur doesn't need my pity. He's very capable of choosing his own future.

22

GRACE

It's been just over a week since Dickie's visit, and as Noel's busy this morning and our work won't begin until the afternoon, I wander up with Olivia to see how the building work has progressed.

'Oh my goodness!' I exclaim. There's now a door on the front, and the gaping holes have been filled with modern, double-glazed windows. 'We'll be moving in in no time.'

Olivia's lip trembles. 'I like the Big House,' she says. 'I'd like to stay there, with Uncle Noel, and Auntie Jane, and the dogs.'

I swallow a sigh, foreseeing the problems moving might bring, but I'll take each day as it comes.

Sean walks to the gate to greet us, wiping his hands on his jeans. He holds his hands out and gently squeezes one of mine then releases me, before Olivia sees. Unlike Graham's hands, which have never known a day's hard labour, Sean's are rough and briefly reassuring; everything is all right between us.

'What do you think?' he asks with a smile, indicating the roof. 'I put pigeon roofs on the front.'

'Pigeon roofs?'

'Aye, those little pointy bits above the windows. Like wee gables, only they don't change the room inside.'

'Do pigeons sit on them?' Olivia asks, staring at them.

'Seagulls, maybe. Or jackdaws. You have to watch those jackeens – they can be determined, and if they can't find a hole, they'll make one.'

'Why did you do that?' I ask.

'It makes the house pretty as well as functional. It wasn't so much bother, and appearances matter if you ever want to sell.'

'You think I'll sell?'

'I think it's best to keep your options open. It's a big move, from city life to as rural as it gets. Living in the Big House, with Jane and Finola to help, isn't the same as being on your own, with Olivia at school for most of the day.'

'Am I going to school here?' Olivia asks, turning to me in surprise.

Oops. 'Maybe; if we're still here when the school term starts.' I change the subject quickly. 'I owe you for the windows, don't I? And for your labour. Give me an invoice, and I'll get the bank to do a transfer.'

'Thank you. That would be grand. Now, let me show you where we're at.'

He explains that the chimneys at either end have been lined with ceramic pipes, as the jackdaws have chipped away at the inside, building nests and creating large holes in the stonework. It's all been back-filled with lime plaster that will suck in the damp atmosphere and set hard once the fires are lit. Now the windows and doors have been fitted, and the roof is sound, he can get on with the inside.

But it's the back of the house that makes me stop and gasp. It looks like a war zone, with a large trench heading away from the house. He waves a hand. 'Rory brought up his digger and dug the trenches, because I helped him out with his fencing last winter. When money changes hands, the taxman wants a cut, so we do it the old ways, on charity and luck. Every farmer's son is a builder when he's not a farmer. The septic tank will go down there, away from the house and well. Once we've laid the pipes, the grass will grow over, and you won't even know it's there.'

He turns to where the extension has been started, almost up to windowsill level.

'Goodness, I didn't realise it would be done so quickly.'

'You'll want this extra space, trust me. It was all very well, back in the day, to live in a house with no facilities, but not now. If you didn't have the washing machine and the shower, you'd hurry yourself back to England in no time.'

I shake my head, faintly echoing his broad smile. He's right, of course – I would find this simplistic life overwhelmingly difficult without some modern accoutrements. I'd told myself I'd just get on with it, get used to it, and I would have, too; but the idea of lowering a bucket down the well for water on cold and windy days isn't attractive.

'But you grew up in a house like this,' I say.

'I did. And as soon as I was old enough, I built a lean-to on the back for Mum. It had a corrugated iron roof, like the cattle shed. She cried when she had a scullery and running water in the house. Dad scoffed while I was doing it, saying it had been good enough for his parents, and why did we need a toilet indoors, for the love of God? But he's not above taking a shower now, after the milking.'

'But you must have built a house for yourself by now?'

'I did, but then one of my sisters got married and needed a home, so I started another one...'

The look on his face speaks volumes.

'And how many sisters have you got?' I ask, laughing.

'Five. All younger. And they're all eyeing my new building with a gleam in the eye. There's going to be a catfight, I tell you! And me after being too old to build one for myself to keep by the time I have them all sorted!'

I wander back to the big house with a secure sense of reassurance.

I seek out Arthur at his hotel the next day, to try to explain things to him, as Jane put it. But Arthur has his own plans, and none of them include returning to Graham. 'Father wanted me to work in the business for the summer. He said it was time I got involved, but I couldn't bear that. To work in an office, with him breathing down my neck? It would be a nightmare, so I told him my professor had found me a work placement at a bank in London. He wasn't pleased.'

'I can imagine,' I say dryly. 'But I thought you said you were going to Southampton?'

'And so I am – but I don't want him finding me.'

'Wouldn't it be better to tell him the truth?'

His glare snags me. 'Do you realise how daft that is?'

I grimace. I do, but stringing things out isn't going to make it any easier. The truth will land in Graham's lap one day, like a brick through a window – suddenly, without warning. And again it occurs to me that Arthur is a chip off the old block, after all – he'll make his own decisions regardless of what Graham wants or expects. And I get that Arthur doesn't want to cut himself off from his rather generous allowance, and will string it out as long as he can, salting the money away, as I did. I want to tell him that he can't have both worlds, the freedom and the money, but maybe now isn't the right time for home truths.

I'm thankful I decided not to bring Olivia.

We're in the main bar of the hotel, the remains of a light lunch strewn over the table. An impeccably dressed young man comes over and asks if we've finished. Arthur waves a dismissive hand at the debris, giving him unspoken permission to clear up. I feel embarrassed at his attitude and bite down on the urge to apologise on his behalf. Instead, I ask, 'So, when do you leave for Southampton?'

'Soon enough. I got my Yachtmaster certificate last year, and the instructor training I've booked in for means that when I start the PhD, I can teach sailing to earn a bit of income if Dad gets mad and stops my allowance, which he will, sooner or later. I thought maybe I'd volunteer for lifeboat crew, too, for the experience. That would be cool, but I don't think they get paid.'

'Good Lord!' I'm stunned for a moment then beam, lean over and give him a hug. 'Wow! Arthur! You've been hiding yourself from all of us! Saving lives! Where did your love of the water come from?'

'It was when I went to America and stayed with Mum.' He was silent for a moment, contemplative. 'Before you came along.'

I put my hand over his. 'I'm sorry about what happened.'

'Yeah, well. I guess I didn't get to know her too well, at that. But anyway, she took me waterskiing and diving. She paid for me to do the PADI diving course, probably to keep me out of her hair for a few days, and that was the start of it. I just love the sea. In it, on it, under it. Must have got that from her.'

'I wish I'd known that earlier.' Arthur had been with her when she died, apparently. It must have been awful. I don't know the details, and I don't like to ask.

He shrugs. 'We didn't exactly speak much when I was home, did we? I guess I resented you a bit to start with. It wasn't your fault, though.'

But maybe now I've left Graham, he can relate to me as a friend, the mother of his new sister, rather than an interloper into a home life he'd never had. I glance at my watch. 'I need to move. Noel and I are working on his memoir this afternoon.'

'Can I come and collect Olivia? I can look after her for a few hours and drop her back up at the house later.'

For some reason that makes me nervous, but I don't have the

heart to refuse. 'Okay. Drop her off by five, then she can be cleaned up ready for dinner. Noel likes to eat early.' This is my chance to tell him what Jane said, but I find myself reluctant. Arthur has been hurt too many times for me to add to his burden. 'Just drop her off at the drive – she knows her way up to the house.'

Noel is waiting for me when I get back. He has a pile of papers in his hands and is lost in contemplation. I bustle in and press the button that turns on the computer. He glances up, startled. 'Oh, you're here. I thought I was early. I must have been reminiscing. Sometimes I find an hour has gone by, and I have no idea where I went.'

'I've been like that all my life,' I say. 'Especially after I'd been reading. Mum used to say I was off with the fairies.'

He smiles. 'I recall Caitlin saying that. She was younger than me, but I was at school with her brother, Rory, before he took off, as so many did, if they didn't have land to inherit.'

I was about to ask him if he could tell me something about her early life, but he cuts me off before I've done more than take a breath. 'So, shall we make a start?'

I nod. We've now decided that he'll read from his notes, and maybe mention things he forgot to write as they come to him. I'm to type it out, interrupt if I don't understand something, but leave editing. I'll shape his words into good English in my own time, and then we'll both work on the document to bring it up to standard once I've done that.

I was born on a small farm in Roone Bay, on the south shores of the Mizen peninsula, in West Cork. My mother had me at home, in their own bed, as she bore my brother, Jacob, before me. It was always her regret that God didn't see fit to send her any more children, and she saw that as a failing on her part, seeing the other families with countless children running bare-foot about the place.

We were poor, but not the poorest, because my father had ten acres and five milking cows, and grew rows of cabbages to keep us fed. We had one apple tree that he called his orchard, and he minded it like a special child. Indeed, it was a good source of bartering, for the scraps of fabric that Mother used to make our clothes from, or for bits of farm equipment, or the like. One of my earliest recollections is sitting with Dad on the donkey cart, taking the milk to the creamery. I must only have been around three, because I was wearing a dress, as boys did back then, before starting school...

I find myself engrossed in the romance of a childhood brought up on the land. Bartering was conducted on a daily basis between families, and what couldn't be bartered for was bought at the one local shop, which stocked everything a small community needed. Noel's parents were industrious from morning until night, and the kitchen – the main room in the house – was filled daily with the warm scent of fresh soda bread, which was served with great chunks of salted ham. City folk would think it a hard life, I suppose, but the way Noel tells his story makes me think the children were happy and healthy, despite the deprivations.

Noel stops, and I wait, hands hovering over the keyboard. It's surprisingly easy to use this keyboard as the buttons don't have to be pressed so much as touched. I glance at the wall of writing, which scrolls away above as I write. It's strange not having to worry about carriage returns, although I'm startled when the word I'm typing suddenly disappears and puts itself on a new line, below. It's not magic, as Dickie said, so much as disconcerting. But I'm sure I'll get used to it. I don't like not being able to print it out, though – at least not right now. What if it does all disappear? That reminds me, I'm supposed to save it!

It's a couple of hours later when Noel says, 'I think that's enough for today. I'm fair exhausted. Do you have it saved?'

'I have,' I assure him, slightly guilty that I almost forgot. It would have been ghastly, seeing these ethereal words blip out of existence.

'Okay, so,' Noel says, rising and stretching. 'How did that go for you?'

'It went well, I think. But it's a strange way to work, and I didn't stop to correct anything, as we agreed, so don't look – I don't want you to judge my typing on it!'

'Sure, I won't. Tomorrow, if it suits you, we'll start our new schedule. After breakfast we'll work, then after lunch you can go through what we've done in the morning, make sure you have it all. It'll be a pattern, yes? We can work for four days, and have Friday and the weekends clear. When we have the first week done, we'll get a better idea of how long it's going to take.'

I let the computer whirr its way to sleep. What a useful typewriter this will be in offices!

Noel accompanies me downstairs, and I check my watch. 'Olivia should be back soon,' I say.

'She's out?'

'Arthur's taken her out.'

My feelings must be written plainly on my face. Would Arthur run off with Olivia, take her home to her father? He has little love for his father, but a little demon of doubt tells me he might do something like that for money. I see it clearly now, for the first time.

We walk on down the wide staircase in silence, each immersed in our own thoughts. I'm infinitely relieved when I find Olivia in the kitchen. She's sitting by the range, with Goldie's head in her lap. The collie is staring up at her with something akin to adoration. They seem to have bonded, which is nice, but also another worry. When we leave here, she can't take Noel's dog with her. Perhaps I'll find a puppy for her, when we move in. We have the space and the land, after all.

'Did you walk up the drive on your own?' I ask.

'Arthur drove me up to the pond. He said it wasn't safe for me to walk up on my own. There are builder men working on the hotel.'

'The men aren't a bother,' Noel says mildly. 'I know them all – and their parents. I'll take a cup of tea, Jane, if I could, please? I have a thirst on me after all the talking.'

'And just who are you writing about,' she snips, crashing the kettle onto the range. 'I'll not be ending up in your book now, you mind!' She glares at him, but I sense it's in exasperation rather than anything more lasting. Maybe Jane, too, has secrets she doesn't want the world to hear.

Noel chuckles. 'Everyone's going to end up in my book, Jane, *a chara*, but you'll have your words spoken before it ever sees the light of day.'

Arthur calls around for Olivia just as we're having lunch the next day. He's been here a while now, and I try not to let my hint of unease spill out. 'Have you any plans for today?'

'Not really,' Arthur says. 'Just get to know the place a bit better.'

'Then take Finola with you,' Noel suggests. 'She's being paid already to look after Olivia, so she might as well earn it.' This was accompanied by a smile, taking the sting from the words. 'She can be showing you the way. She has my telephone number remembered, too, so if you're going to be late, or get into any difficulties, she can call.'

Finola smiles and nods. It'll make a change from traipsing around wet fields with the dogs, but as they leave, my smile fades. 'Thank you,' I say.

'Not a bother,' Noel replies. 'She's too precious to leave to chance.'

We both understand the subtext: Arthur can't run off with Olivia if Finola is with him. But as I slip back to the office to begin work, I realise his kindness echoes my concern, which is deeper than a simple matter of trust. Why is Arthur really here?

A day later, thankfully, Arthur takes himself off on a visit to some marine centre in Galway. I'm amazed by his interest in this stuff, but I'm equally as disturbed to realise how little I know of my own stepson. I feel I've failed him by my ignorance. And as I type up another section of Noel's past, he mentions some friends, people he grew up with. Connor, for instance, my own grandfather, who ran to England with my grandmother to save her from a marriage her father had arranged.

23

CAITLIN, 1931

'Are you sure about this?' Connor asked.

Caitlin nodded firmly. 'It's best for us all.'

'I know you love Noel.'

'He married Sinéad for the farm,' she said bitterly. 'That was his choice. Knowing that, I must be away from here. I promise I'll be as loyal to you as a wife could be, and Noel's name will never cross my lips. You're a good man, Connor. I'll bear your children and be a good wife. Is that enough?'

He grimaced. 'It's enough for now. You know I've always loved you. Perhaps you'll grow to love me.'

He kissed her inexpertly, and because the promise had been made, she allowed him to make love to her. Her breasts were sore, and she winced as he explored them with a kind of wonder. She closed her eyes and tried not to mind his inexpert fumbling. She couldn't love Connor back, but she had to think of herself now. And she would be faithful, try to make him happy. She guessed he'd never been with a woman, as he showed no surprise when she didn't cry out or bleed. But men were young, somehow, and a bit daft when it came to relationships. She felt like a mature woman, with all her experience, though she was still but sixteen.

Connor made his plans secretly and secured passage to England. When it was time to leave, Caitlin packed her belongings in her shawl and walked through the moonlight to Connor's house. It wouldn't be a problem, Connor said wryly – his father would be dead from the drink.

As she slipped through the back door, she suddenly recalled Noel's ring and pulled it quickly from her finger, pushing it deep between two of the crumbling stones that surrounded the fireplace. Tears welled unbidden as she left the token behind her and looked determinedly towards a future. Let it stay in the house where she'd cried her farewell to Ireland and all that she loved.

Connor crept silently down the stairs and hugged her, probably having a very good idea of why she was crying. They slipped out, his father's drunken snores echoing behind them. He would have no one now. His wife dead these seven years, one son gone to America and now Connor slipping out in the night like a thief. She felt a brief moment of sadness for him, but he'd never been a kind or loving father to Connor, and they had a life to lead.

Caitlin was sick all the way to England, hanging over the rail. She was light-headed and faint, in a way she'd never experienced before. She hated herself for that weakness. She'd never fainted or been sick in her life before this.

Connor stood behind her, rubbing her back during bouts of sickness. It was a rough crossing, and she wasn't the only one suffering. It was lucky that he wasn't affected; she was retching so hard he had to physically stop her from tipping over into the unpredictable troughs and whitecaps.

Between waves of sickness, he held her hand, patted it comfortingly and said, 'It'll be over when we land. You'll see. It's just the sea sickness.'

But she knew it wasn't. She'd known pregnant women be sick like that, and had wondered if they were taking folk medicine to make the baby go away, but now wondered if it meant she was going to lose the child, anyway. She didn't think she'd ever feel well again, but after a few moments on shore, she did feel marginally better. Aside from feeling weak from the continual dry retching, and the hunger in her belly, her head cleared. 'So, where do we go now?' she asked.

'We find the train station,' Connor said, pointing at a sign.

His friend in Birmingham had obtained him an unskilled job in the steelworks. They had just enough money to get there.

Connor carefully counted out the fare, and with what remained he bought bread and a flagon of small beer. It took five tedious hours, the heavy steam locomotive chugging through countryside and towns that were subtly different from home. Caitlin had never been on a train before, and she was enchanted by the noise and the smoke and the speed. But she was also so tired she could barely keep her eyes open.

When they arrived, with no money left for buses, Connor led her through dreary streets for too many miles, after being misdirected several times, and was as kind a companion as she'd believed he would be. Some people were helpful, but others spat and jeered at them. There were advertisements for lodgers in some windows, some with the rider: *No Blacks, No Dogs, No Irish*. It didn't take Caitlin long to realise they looked exactly what they were – Irish immigrants – with their rough, home-made clothes and a single cardboard suitcase between them: yet more immigrants from Ireland, there to steal jobs from decent working Englishmen. She bore it stoically. She would show them. She would learn how to make nice clothes, and do her hair, and change her speech until she no longer looked or sounded like a stranger in that strangely grey and dirty city.

When night was falling, they eventually found Connor's friend's house, and were shown into a tiny room with a single,

narrow bed and a chair. 'It's only temporary,' Connor said, a
trifle hopefully, as Caitlin sank onto the bed with a sigh. Her
feet hurt, and she was fighting back tears of exhaustion.

The next day, Connor was made to stand, cap in hand, until
the fireman came to get him, and instruct him on the most
menial and gruelling job there was: a stoker for the big foundry
furnaces.

It took Caitlin a while to get used to being called Mrs
McCarthy, but they told people right from the start that they'd
been married in Ireland, and either people believed them or
didn't care. Eventually, they were able to make good that claim
and signed the church register as man and wife. True to her
word, Caitlin locked Noel away in a corner of her mind and
made her life with Connor. For a while they barely had a living
wage. She hated living on charity and got work as a cleaner in a
shop, but she knew that the moment it became obvious she was
pregnant, she would have to leave. It was a relief when Connor
came back one day having acquired a job as a trainee riveter in
the foundry. He would work for two weeks before he got his
first pay. Gradually, their lifestyle improved, as they saved
enough for a deposit on a better room.

'See, I said it would work out,' Connor said, with satisfaction, after they'd moved.

'I don't know if I've ever told you how grateful I am,' Caitlin
said.

'I know you wanted Noel, but I make you happy, don't I?'
he asked anxiously.

'You do,' she said – and meant it.

Her child, a healthy girl, was born a few weeks later and
was the most beautiful thing she'd ever seen. She felt a flood of
love reach out over the water. *Oh, Noel! What we could have
shared.* But life could be worse. Noel was lost to her, and

Connor was a thoughtful and considerate husband and father. She would be content with her lot. She knew Connor wanted her to say she loved him, but she couldn't lie. She would never love him the way she'd once loved Noel, before he betrayed her, so Connor would have to be content with that.

It was a couple of years later, when the child was no longer a babe in arms, that Connor came and kneeled beside her, where she was sitting, mending his trousers yet again. His eyes were shining with unshed tears. He handed her an envelope, and she took out what seemed to be a bank draft for a large sum of money.

'Where on earth did you get this?' she asked, worried. 'Connor, what have you done?'

'Nothing, sweetheart,' he said. 'I promise.' His tears fell, unashamedly, as he said, 'It's from Noel, but sweetheart, he's gone. He died in an accident with a horse, and he'd told the man he was working for in America that we were to have it if anything happened to him. It's enough to buy a house, Caitlin. We don't have to live like this any longer.'

Caitlin gasped. *Noel's dead?*

Connor's dark eyes assessed her strangely. 'I love you, Caitlin. I've always loved you. I'd do anything for you. You know that, don't you?'

Consumed by the unexpected weight of overwhelming grief, it didn't occur to her to question Connor's words.

24

GRACE

Another month has drifted by, and September is fast approaching. Sean and I aren't making any secret, now, of our budding relationship, aside from being circumspect in Olivia's presence. She knows I like him but probably has no idea of the possible outcome. She asks less, now, about when we're going home and when we'll see Daddy. I have the feeling she's quietly relieved he's not here. She's certainly changed from the unhappy child I thought was being bullied at school, to an outgoing child who loves a rough and tumble in the wet grass with Goldie.

We go down to the school on enrolment day, and Olivia plays happily with two or three girls while I speak to Angela Daly, the headmistress. I discover that Olivia's teacher will be Finola's mother, and I'll meet her in due course. As Noel said, there's a web of connection between the people whose kith and kin are rooted in the wider Roone Bay community.

I'm open with Angela about my situation, and she smiles, assuring me that Olivia will have no problems with bullying in her school. Next week I'm to take Olivia to meet some of the other children, for a play day before school starts. Mothers are advised to stay until the children are involved in play then discretely leave for an hour or so.

Arthur left for England this morning, which is a relief. His being here has made me think a lot about his relationship with Graham. I'd chosen to walk away and take nothing but my daughter, but Arthur has too much to lose. I don't doubt he'll want to preserve his inheritance; in fact, he said as much. I hover between pity for his loneliness and annoyance that he found me, because I'm trying to fit in, to belong, and he was like a crusty barnacle on the side of my ship, tearing wounds into any craft that drifted too close. Now he's gone, tension I wasn't aware of slides from my mind. With his absence, I can breathe again. And that, too, makes me feel guilty. I didn't choose to be his mother or his confidante, but he has no one else. He was a disruptive influence, though, with his air of misplaced superiority. He wasn't just a summer visitor but a threatening storm cloud that passed over without dropping its load.

He didn't fit in and didn't want to.

I kept my distance from Sean in Arthur's presence; after all, I was – am – married to his father, so it seemed crass for him to see me staring with adoration at another man.

With a lighter heart, I walk up to the cottage, where Sean is working. I knock on the front door, amused that I even feel the need to; it is my house, after all. He thunders down the stairs, opens the door and envelops me in a massive hug, before kissing me hungrily on the lips. 'I can do that, now he's gone,' he says then steps back and tips his head in quizzical enquiry. 'Do you mind?'

I smile. 'No. I've been itching to do that for a long time.'

'You have?'

'You know I have.'

He smiles back. 'Ah, you English don't give much away, you know.'

'I'm trying to change.'

'Actually,' he says, tipping his head down to kiss me again, longer and more intimately than before, 'I like you just the way you are.'

This pleases me enormously. Over the months I've been here, I have changed; I've become me, the person I should have been before. I look back and wonder at myself. Why did I stay with Graham so long? Why did I fear him? Yet there's a niggle in the back of my mind suggesting I wouldn't have feared him without cause.

The internal plaster is drying, and Sean quizzes me about colour as we walk through the finished rooms. 'I think blue would be nice in the bedroom,' he says with a faint grin.

'You do, do you?'

'Well, you know, if I'm going to live here, I should have a say in the decor.'

I turn to face him, a query on my lips regarding the church and marriage, but he stops the words with his finger then kisses me. All my nonsense about waiting flies out of the window.

'I'm still married, you know,' I say eventually.

'I know. But you've left him.'

'What will the people here think?'

'There'll be a few grumblings, but they'll get used to it.'

'Noel said that I could do worse.'

He looks pleased. 'He did, did he?'

'So, why aren't you married?' I ask lightly.

'I never found the right woman.'

'I'm a blow-in, a stranger, English in every way that matters.'

'You're a woman in every way that matters,' he corrects. 'I knew I was going to marry you when I picked you up from Skibbereen, that first day.'

'Good Lord,' I say faintly.

'You looked so tired and sad and lonely. I wanted to give you a big hug. Then, once I knew you owned the McCarthy place, it was signed and sealed. I've had my eye on that for a while. Sure, it's the only way I'll get it now.'

I give a responding smile then become serious, and hold him a little away, to see his deep eyes properly. 'Sean, I... I want this. I want all of it, all of you. But I have unfinished business with Graham to get through first.'

'I know. And there's little Olivia to consider. She's found a way into my heart, for sure, but I don't particularly want to be stepdad to Arthur.'

I grimace. He's right – Arthur is my problem, too. Mine and Graham's. I instinctively knew it was wrong with Graham but didn't listen to my own misgivings, and I instinctively know it's right with Sean. Something deeper than mere thought is at work here. I don't have a shadow of a doubt. And when my divorce comes through, we'll marry and have children. I don't need to ask if that's what he'd like. I just know.

He leads me through the rest of the rooms and we discuss plans, imagining colour and warmth, and companionship. The house has been transformed from the sad shell I'd discovered into the place I'd imagined it to be before arriving here.

Later in the year, when the external rendering has settled, it will be sealed with hardwearing paint, and that will brighten the house. I'm pleased that Sean built the little pigeon roofs on the front, adding a tweak of artistry to what might have been an oblong, grey block. But even if he hadn't, it's my oblong, grey block. My future. And when we're inside, warm and dry, warming our toes before a fire, what it looks like from the outside will be immaterial.

25

GRACE

The next morning, Noel seems flustered by the whole memoir issue, so I try to jog him into just chatting, in case I can pick up on anything to get him motivated again. 'You said maybe start from the present and work back, but I'm curious about why you came back to Ireland,' I say. 'I mean, you've told me why you left, and it sounds to me like you simply wanted to leave everything behind and start over. So something must have brought you back.'

He mulls that over.

'My decision to return to Ireland had mixed roots,' he says finally. 'I never stopped missing my homeland, but it was also about coming to terms with myself, making peace with the past. If I'd married in America, it would have been a different story. If I'd had children and grandchildren, I might have had reason to stay in Boston, but in the end, I thought I'd come home to die.'

He sighed. 'It so nearly backfired. When I got here, I found that the house I'd grown up in was gone, totally, not a stone left behind. That upset me more than I can say. The man who bought the land from me and my father had taken out the boundaries, made bigger fields and had the boreen widened into a real road. He built a big ugly house with false pillars, up the hill; you must have seen it! It must have a good view of the bay, but when I saw that, I nearly got straight back on the plane to America. Then I noticed Roone Manor. It had always been there, of course, but like part of the scenery. Only now I saw it as a romantic wreck, and I had so much money I didn't know what to spend it on, so it seemed like a good project. I had dreams of creating a racecourse in Roone Bay, too, of bringing money into the town, but I decided it would change the town too much.'

'But do you feel that this is your home now?'

'After nearly fifty years in America, I never quite felt as though I belonged there, but returning to Roone Bay didn't feel like coming home, either. I felt like an alien, displaced in either location. Maybe it was because I had no family to call my own.'

'What about your brother – Jacob, wasn't it? Did you ever look for him?'

He nods. 'I found the ship he'd sailed on, and where he'd disembarked, and that was the last trace I ever found. I got a detective onto it, but he found nothing, except a brief stay in a guest house. When he left there, it was as if he vanished into thin air. When I got rich and famous, and my name was in the newspapers, I thought he might come and find me. When he didn't, I knew he was dead.'

We get down to another tranche of childhood recollections from Noel, who somehow makes the hardship of those days sound like the start of a fairy tale. Maybe it was. He doesn't dwell on the hunger, the cold, the hand-me-downs, the mattresses of straw and the sheets made of flour sacks. He dwells on the community spirit, the love and kindness he recalls, which carried him through those early years. And after being helped on my way through Ireland by complete strangers, that resonates.

I was a little afraid that my English accent would set people against me; atrocities committed by the ruling classes have ever been the bane of the poor. But, on the whole, I find the Irish a kind people; inclusive and tolerant. Noel's extended family, I learn, worked hard, and shared everything, despite struggling on the edge of poverty. And one by one, many left: brothers, sisters, cousins, friends. They went to England, America and Australia, seeking work, seeking a living, seeking a life. Noel lists them, name by name, then is silent.

I glance up from the keyboard. 'Did you find out how they got on? Did you hear from them again?'

He startles out of reverie, lifts his eyes from his notes and glances at his watch. 'Is that really the time? I have a hunger on me now. Let's go and see what Jane has prepared for us.'

I thought he hadn't heard my question, but he adds softly, 'When I could, I traced my family. Some I'm still seeking. But we'll come to that in due course.'

I save the work and follow him down the wide staircase. Finola and Olivia walk up from the kitchen stairs to join us, and we find the table in the dining room laden with far more than the four of us could eat. I wonder how Noel reconciles this abundance with the frugality of his childhood?

Olivia prattles; it's the only way I can describe it. I've never heard her so verbal, so easy with her words. And here, there's no one to tell her to think before she speaks, to just get to the point! Until now, I hadn't recalled just how often Graham had taken her to task for 'rabbiting on'. She tells us about the ruined cottage in the woods, with no roof, covered so much in ivy that the house is indistinguishable from the surrounding woods unless you know what to look for. She tells us about the red squirrels with huger tails than the grey ones in Cheltenham, about the fox with two cubs, playing, just over the ditch. 'They saw us but didn't run away,' she adds, 'because we stood very still and quiet, oh, for ages.'

'You did that?' I say, impressed.

Noel hides his smile. How far we've come, Olivia and I, not in miles, but in our relationship with this gaunt stranger. He's not only invited us into his home but has enveloped us under his protective wing. I was afraid, when we first came here, that Olivia would disrupt his quiet, somewhat introspective lifestyle, and he would be irritated by our presence, but it seems the opposite has happened. He's enjoying his interaction with us. Perhaps living the dream might have turned just a little sour with no family of his own to share it.

Perhaps he regrets having spent his life in the acquisition of wealth, instead of rearing children and grandchildren. I don't know the full story – yet. But perhaps he never married again because he could never replace Sinéad. Yet I wonder how to reconcile this with the knowledge that he was once in love with a woman called Kathleen, which is slightly at odds with him carrying a torch for his dead wife.

As if reading my thoughts, Noel, reaching for a slice of fresh soda bread, says contemplatively, 'I did think, when I was young, that I would be a father. It would have made all this a little more meaningful.' He waves a hand, encompassing more than the room we're in, then adds, 'But I do have an extended wealth of distant and very interested relatives wondering who's going to inherit everything when I die.'

I smile with him and ask, 'And have you made that decision?'

'Most assuredly. My solicitor has the details, and a copy is also lodged with the bank. It would be a shame if this turned out to be another Bleak House, don't you think?'

'Oh, yes, indeed! I read that a long time ago. The solicitors used up everything, didn't they, and then the will was discovered when it was too late.'

Noel casts a glance that suggests he's surprised I've read the classics. Perhaps he thinks women these days are more attracted to romances. Noel's books take up a whole wall in the lounge. Has he read them all? Many have wonderful bindings, and might well be first editions. I'd been summoning up the courage to ask, but it seemed an impertinence; after all, we're temporary guests in his home.

'We're finished, so,' Finola says. 'Shall we go on? I thought I might take Olivia up to meet my aunt Mary. She's an artist. If you don't mind, of course?'

'Of course – that would be lovely,' I say.

After they're gone, Noel grins at me and says confidentially, 'Well, it's not what I'd call art, but she's happy out, so. And a child won't know the difference.'

I laugh at his irreverence.

'So, what is it you haven't told me about your Graham that explains why you're quite so scared of him, and what Arthur has to do with it?'

He throws this remark in so quickly, I'm left with my mouth hanging open for a moment then tell him quietly about Margery's revelation at the art exhibition, adding, 'I'd taken her sly implications regarding Graham's involvement in his wife's death as malicious gossip, but a few months ago, I was tidying out Arthur's room and discovered a folder containing newspaper cuttings and police reports on his mother's death, as if he, too, had been wondering... I don't have much Spanish but enough to confirm that Graham had been brought in for questioning. I knew he was a control freak, but then I wondered whether Margery was right, if he was a sociopath – or worse. After all, just because he wasn't convicted of a crime didn't mean he didn't do it. There was no proof, of course, but the worst thing was, I thought him capable.'

'Ah,' Noel says pensively. 'But you couldn't read the cuttings, so?'

'No, but I recognised the odd word.'

I thought for a moment and elaborated. 'I'd seen the ruthless way he dealt with people who crossed him in business, and our marriage was, as it transpired, a business transaction. If he'd had any inkling that I was thinking of leaving him, I was afraid he'd stop me. At the least, he might have stopped me from going, or stopped me from taking Olivia with me. But voicing this fear to anyone would have made me sound paranoid. Even my mother, who was pleased I'd left him, didn't know what I'd discovered about the man I'd married.

'And the worst thing is, I should have known it before Olivia was even created. There was a moment on our honeymoon, when we were lying in bed. He was leaning on one elbow, looking down at me with a self-satisfied expression. He stroked my hair and murmured, *I'm infatuated with you. So fresh and young and beautiful. And you're all mine. If I can't have you, no one will.*' I grimaced at Noel. 'I thought that was so romantic. I recall laughing at the time. I don't know how long it was before the thought trickled into my mind that it wasn't funny. It's actually frightening, being the object of possessiveness; it's dehumanising, turning a person into an object.'

'You were young. He was rich and manipulative.'

'I know, but I'm ashamed of myself – for marrying him, and then not having the strength to leave sooner. Then I thought leaving him would harm Olivia. Also, I thought of marriage as a lifetime commitment, for better or worse, like the vows I made.'

'It certainly is here, in Ireland,' Noel comments. 'What God hath joined together, let not man put asunder...'

'Quite,' I agree.

I recall my grandmother quoting that phrase. But those archaic, lofty words blanket countless lives filled with unhappiness. Marriage 'endured' by women is wrong, plain and simple. No individual should belong to another. Companionship, loyalty and fidelity should be born of choice not compulsion. But it's all right for Grandma and her platitudes, I find myself thinking. She married her childhood sweetheart and loved him to the end of his life, which must have compensated in some ways for the years of hardship she struggled through when they first moved to England.

'Life takes us down some strange roads,' Noel says somewhat pensively, making me wonder what past event has slipped into his mind.

26

NOEL, 1931

Noel was at market when Caitlin appeared before him. Both stood stock-still for a moment, then Noel recovered his manners. 'Caitlin,' he said, nodding a greeting.

'Noel O'Donovan, how are you?' she said primly.

'Are you on your way home? Here, let me carry your basket. It's heavy enough.'

'I'm well, thank you,' she said, surrendering the basket. Then her face fell, and she almost cried as she whispered, 'Noel, how could you marry Sinéad?'

They walked side by side for a moment on the long road to her house, he with the basket crooked in one elbow, his heart full of grief, for it was Caitlin he loved.

There had been murmurs about the strange, sudden disappearance of Noel's brother, Jacob, who'd absconded overnight, everyone knowing Jacob and Sinéad were promised. The two families had been pleased at the proposed union, as it would join the two farms. And with Jacob gone, and Noel set to inherit, it was widely believed that Noel had married her for the same reason.

Their silence was filled with her unanswered question, because he couldn't tell her the truth.

'I will regret marrying Sinéad for the rest of my life,' he said honestly, but the look she cast him was one of cynical sadness: he wouldn't be the first man to abandon his true love to marry for gain.

Finally, she said, 'My father is set on me marrying Ben Dowd and has instructed the priest to say the banns, even though I've said I won't.'

'What will you do?'

She shrugs. 'Run away. Connor's going to England and has asked me to go with him.'

Connor, Noel's best friend, who'd long coveted his Caitlin! 'Does anyone else know?'

'No. And you mustn't say it, either! My father would have me married to that dirty old man, and I won't. I wanted you to hear it from me.' She stopped abruptly and faced him. 'I thought we were going to be married, Noel? I thought you loved me?'

'I did. I do,' he said hoarsely.

'But you betrayed me,' she wailed and fell into his arms as though propelled.

He held her close, tears filling his eyes. 'I'm sorry.' What else could he say? 'I wish...'

'If wishes were horses, beggars would ride,' Caitlin said snippily, pushing away.

He smiled. That was the Caitlin he knew and loved; the one who wouldn't be pressured into a marriage she didn't want, as he had. 'Do you love Connor?'

'He's a good man, and he knows I burn the candle for you. But he's loved me all his life and knows I'll be a faithful wife.'

Noel nodded, but deep inside, grief weighed down his heart. Not only would Caitlin be married to another, but he would never see her again. 'Where will you go? America?'

She shook her head. 'I can't go so far from my home. Connor has a job waiting in Birmingham, in the steelworks.'

'Then maybe we could meet...'

'No. We mustn't. You know that. Look, we can cut across the boreen here.'

There had been a soft rain, and the fields they skirted were green, edged with buttercups and fading bluebells, but his mind was consumed by the girl walking beside him, who should have been his. She led him to a tiny grove speckled with wild flowers. She took the basket from him and reached up to kiss him. 'Lie with me, Noel.'

'You don't know what you're asking!'

'I do. Before he ran off to America, my cousin told me what happens between a man and a woman. It's not as if the nuns ever told a girl the truth, and what do they know of such things?' she said dismissively. 'I'm going to be married, but I'd like my first time to be with the man I love. Will you do that for me? It will be our final farewell.'

She'd flushed scarlet, but Noel reached for her face with both hands and kissed her. He might be married to Sinéad, but more than anything, he wanted to possess this woman – and have that memory to carry him through the years.

She tried to stifle her little cry of pain as he entered her body, but it was too late to change his mind. When it was over, he said, 'I'm sorry. I wouldn't have hurt you for the world.'

'I love you,' she said. 'And I'm not sorry!'

He stood to tidy his clothes as she pulled her skirts down and made herself decent.

'Connor is a good man,' Noel said. 'He's a good choice.'

She nodded and turned away. 'Go home, Noel. I think we shall never meet again in this life.'

'Caitlin?'

She stopped and turned back. He pulled a ring from his finger and held it out. She took it and grimaced at the initials he'd scratched inside. Her eyes glistened as she turned and walked away fast.

'Oh, Caitlin,' he whispered, but she was gone.

He turned and stumbled away, grief-stricken.

27

GRACE

Olivia and I have been here, in Roone Bay, for three months now, and the old life is receding, along with my fear of an unknown future: whatever happens, I'll deal with it. Noel's memoir is well underway, and I have a handle on the piles of notes and documents. We're in the office, and Olivia is out somewhere with Finola, when Jane knocks and puts her head around the door. 'There's an Englishman here to see Grace,' she says.

I hadn't heard a car pull up outside, but I know who it is by the look on her face. I thought I was ready for this, and I'm surprised it's taken this long, but I begin to shake. Noel and I move silently to the window and peer out. Parked on the drive is a silver Rolls-Royce.

'Show him into the lounge, Jane, if you'd be so kind,' Noel says, 'and wet a pot of tea?' His gaze levels at me. 'Do you want me to deal with this?'

I take a deep breath, try to control my erratic heartbeat and pull my shoulders back determinedly. 'No. This is something I must do for myself.' Then I add, 'But I'd appreciate you being in the room.'

I take a step towards the door. His hand falls gently on my shoulder. 'Give Jane time to bring the tea in. It'll break the ice.'

'Thank you.'

We wait a few moments while I gather my courage. I've known this moment would come, but I'm still finding it daunting. 'Ready?' Noel asks, and I nod.

I follow him downstairs and into the lounge.

He stretches his hand out. 'Mr Adams, I presume? I'm Noel O'Donovan.'

Graham, immaculate in a severe, dark suit, takes his hand and nods curtly, but his eyes are on me. I try to avoid meeting his gaze but catch an expression I've never seen before. He's feeling uncomfortable, which wasn't at all what I expected. His discomfort floods me with confidence.

'Take a seat,' Noel suggests, indicating the easy chairs and a sofa which surround a small coffee table by the unlit fire.

Jane places a large tray on the table, and lays out cups and saucers.

'That's grand, thank you, Jane,' he says, dismissing her. Then to Graham: 'Will you take tea? And a biscuit, maybe?'

We all sit stiffly, nursing our saucers and munching self-consciously on our biscuits. Finally, Noel asks, 'How did you find the drive down?'

'Tedious,' Graham says, with a curl of his lip. 'The roads are awful.'

'And that's the new ones,' Noel says with a faint smile.

There's another awkward pause, then Graham looks at me. 'You're looking well, Grace.'

'People have been kind. How did you find me?'

I meant, how did he know where to find me at all, but he says, 'There was a girl down by the bridge; she said I'd find you here.' His glance takes in the impressive room in a sweep. 'You've fallen on your feet.' The snippy comment smacks of displeasure. If he thought to find me destitute, grateful to be rescued, he's learned otherwise.

'I'm only here temporarily,' I say, noting the apology in my tone and hating myself for it. 'While my house is being renovated. I'm working here. A kind of PA job.'

'I know.'

I look at him blankly. 'You know?'

'Of course I know. This isn't the dark ages. I had a private detective find out where you were. I thought I'd give you time.'

Time to what, reconsider? 'That was thoughtful.'

He nods, as if it's his due. 'You chose a most inconvenient time, when we're so busy. Why did you do it? Run away like that, I mean. If you were unhappy, why didn't you just tell me, and we could have talked it through?'

I shake my head. 'You've never discussed anything with me. You don't listen. You never have. You simply expect me to agree with everything you say.'

'I've always—' He bites off the words. 'So, I'm here now. I've given you plenty of time to think about what you've done. You've had a holiday. You've made your point. Now it's time for you to come home. You need to think of Olivia. The school term is about to start.'

I stare at him in astonishment and say, slowly, 'Graham, Grandpa's cottage is being done up for us to live in. It's not a whim. It's not a holiday.'

There's a silence while he digests this, then he gives an exasperated sigh. 'You don't know what you're saying.'

'I do.'

I find the words a little amusing, given that the last time I said them I'd been in church, marrying him, but he just gives a little moue of irritation, not catching the humour. 'I thought you loved me.'

And there it is. He doesn't say he loves me or has missed me. I lie, feeling a little sorry for him, because he has no idea what he is. 'Maybe I did, once. But I've been lonely and frustrated for quite a while. I tried to tell you that, to discuss it,' I said, throwing his words back at him, 'but you said, *Nonsense, of course you're not!*'

From his look of confusion, I gather he doesn't recall that dialogue at all. 'And where is Olivia?' he asks finally. 'I'd like to see my daughter.'

'She's out with a girl who's caring for her while I work. If you wait a while, they'll be back. But, Graham, she's not going back with you, either.'

'She's my daughter. I have every right...'

I give him a hard stare. 'You said she's to start school. What school, Graham?'

He has the grace to look slightly embarrassed. 'You know what school. We discussed it. She needs to have a good start in life, get to know the right people.'

'And get the right accent?' I suggest gently. 'I told you I wasn't going to send her to any boarding school. She's little more than a baby. But you went ahead and registered her, didn't you?'

'I know what's best for my daughter. You haven't the least idea. I knew you'd come around after you had a chance to think about it. It didn't do Arthur any harm, did it? It put him in line for a good career.'

'I know what it did for Arthur,' I snap. 'More than you do, I expect!'

'He loved the school, when he got used to it. He said he was happier there than at home.'

Which says more about his home life than the school.

I try to make him understand. 'Arthur was unhappy. He was lonely. He felt unloved, and at least at school he knew exactly what the score was. He just learned to hide his unhappiness. I'm not putting my sweet daughter through that.'

'You're mollycoddling her! You don't understand how the

world works, Grace. If she's to get on, get anywhere, she has to meet people in her own social bracket. You have to let her go, so that she can learn to stand on her own two feet.'

'She's a baby!' I snap, then take a breath and lower my voice. 'She can find her feet when she's grown up. And what if I don't want her to "get on" in your world? What if I just want her to grow up happy, as I did?'

He glares and leans forward aggressively, hands on his thighs. 'Happy? Your father died because he was a manual labourer in a filthy job! Your mother worked in a shop! Do you think I want that for my child?'

'Olivia is my child, too. I want her to be happy.'

'Were you happy when I met you, scratching a living, sharing a dirty home with that other girl? Do you think I didn't check up on your background? I rescued you! I gave you the opportunity to rise above the hoi polloi, and you jumped at it. You knew exactly what you were doing!'

'You think I married you for your money? And your status?' I ask, stunned. 'You think our marriage was a contract for the future?'

'Well, what else is marriage?'

'Good Lord!' I mutter and shake my head. 'I think this discussion is over!'

He stands up. 'Right. That's the first sensible thing you've said. Go and pack your bags, and we can finish it at home.'

I stand in amazement. 'Graham, do you ever listen to anyone except yourself? Did you hear a word I said? Listen carefully. I've left you. I'm not coming back. Olivia and I are going to live here. She's going to school here. That's final.' My hands are clenched at my sides. 'Do you hear me now?'

We stand facing each other, and for the first time I wonder why I was so afraid of him. His face is set in the petulant expression of a child who hasn't got his own way. I'm no longer the silly, impressionable girl he married, or the wife who agreed with everything to keep the peace. He sees that I've changed but is totally baffled by it.

'Legally, you can't stop me from—'

'Don't you *dare* threaten me with court action! I'm her mother. I can support her. I have a house. I've cared for her since she was born! If you push that, I'll go for full custody, and you will never see her!'

He says, with slightly less confidence, 'I was going to say, I have the right to see her.'

I take a deep breath. 'You can see her, of course, before you leave. She's really looking forward to seeing you. You're her father. I don't want to take that away from you. When she's old enough, she can choose whether she wants to come and stay with you, for holidays, or to live, and if she wants to work for you in the end, I certainly won't try to stop her. But right now, you can speak to her in my presence. Then I'd like you to leave Roone Bay, leave Ireland.'

Noel, who had also risen when we did, quietly interjects. 'There's a hotel up the road, Mr Adams. Why don't you book in for tonight? It's too late to face that long drive.'

Graham nods curtly, white with anger, so I add, 'I'll bring Olivia up tomorrow; we can have lunch together. Olivia will be delighted that you're here.'

'It would be nice if someone was,' he says nastily, turning abruptly and striding to the front door. He pauses to ask, a little glumly, 'You haven't seen Arthur, have you?'

I don't know why I'm compelled to lie. 'Why on earth would you think that?'

'I don't know. But if he does turn up, will you let me know? He was supposed to be working at a bank in London, but he's not there. I haven't a clue where he is. I just wish he'd be honest with me.'

I wish he would too, but I'm a fine one to think that. I feel slightly sorry for Graham, in all honesty. His first wife left him, his second wife ran off with his daughter, and his son has gone AWOL.

He strides to his car without looking back.

'That wasn't so bad, was it?' Noel comments, his supporting hand on my elbow.

'It was bad enough. Can't you feel me shaking?'

'Well, it wasn't obvious while you were having at him.' He grins fleetingly. 'I was expecting more of a roola-boola, to be honest.'

I smile at his words, which would more usually describe children having an argument, but I tremble as the adrenaline leaves my body weak with shock. 'Thank you for your support, anyway.'

'Not a bother, girrul, but you were doing all right on your own, never you mind.'

From the window, I watch the silver car glide quietly down the drive, and a moment later, Sean is knocking on the door. He gives me a kiss and a hug, before asking, 'That was him? The husband? Good-looking fellow, altogether. Are you going back to him?'

'Don't be daft! What are you doing here?'

'Someone told me about the flash car, so I parked across the road down below, in case he was trying to abduct Olivia. But she wasn't in the car, so I let him pass. Unless she was in the boot?' he adds with a fake gasp of horror.

I laugh. 'Well, he might have tried, if she'd been here, but she's out with Finola. He's gone to book into the hotel.'

'He didn't get violent or anything?'

'Noel was with me, so he behaved himself. But I'm walking up to the hotel with Olivia, tomorrow, to have lunch with him. I don't suppose you're free? I mean, just to be there, discreetly?'

'Of course,' he agrees. 'And I'll follow you home.'

I breathe out a shaky smile. 'You have no idea what a relief that is.'

'I think I do. It'll be best for all when he drives north again.'

I nod. 'I'll certainly feel safer.'

When Olivia comes in, and I give her the news, she dances around the room ecstatically, chanting, 'Daddy's here, Daddy's here! We're all going home!'

Oh dear. She thinks we're all going to climb into the Rolls-Royce and sing happy songs all the way back to Cheltenham. I could have handled that better.

The weather has descended the next day, and just before lunch, Sean pops in to drive us up the road. Save us getting drowned, he says. I'm grateful, because his windscreen wipers can scarcely keep up with the sudden torrential downpour. I laugh as we run to the hotel door, squealing at the chill splatters that drench us, leaving Sean to park up.

'We should have brought raincoats,' I say.

'A little wet never did a body any harm!' Olivia quotes grandiosely. Will we ever lose Grandma's sayings?

Graham is waiting in the hotel restaurant, dressed impeccably in a suit, with a white shirt and a tie shot with silver. He stands to greet us, as out of place here as a prince in a cowshed. Olivia rushes over, and he picks her up in a brief hug, before depositing her and smoothing his jacket. 'How's Daddy's princess?' he asks, pulling out a chair for her.

Olivia begins to tell him, and I wait for the usual demand for her to slow down, think before she speaks, but he manages to contain himself. Maybe he's missed her, in his own way. Or perhaps he's realised that he doesn't want to lose his daughter, as he's lost everyone else in his life.

During the lunch he tells me he's booked in for a couple of days, but he has a meeting to go to in Belfast on his way home. I warn him quietly that he can meet with us here, or at Noel's, but only with me present, and Olivia is going nowhere near his car. He looks miffed, but I add, 'If that happens, I promise, I'll call the police and say she's been kidnapped.'

Graham's brows rise nearly to his receding hairline when I state my terms, but he doesn't quibble. Maybe he thinks two days should see us back on track. Or maybe he's realised this is one battle he's not going to win.

He pays Olivia more attention than he ever did at home and subtly reminds her about the big house, her lovely bedroom and the expensive clothes hanging in the cupboard, waiting for her. I glare at him, but he's playing his own hand, so much so that she begs me, her eyes big with unshed tears, 'Can we go home with Daddy, Mummy?'

Graham casts me a look of vindication. 'It seems Olivia would like to come home with me,' he says. 'Wouldn't you, princess?'

'Yes, please!' She bounces in eagerness.

'Would you want to go home with Daddy if I didn't come?' I ask gently.

Her lip trembles. 'I want you to come home, too.'

'No, darling,' I soothe. 'School is starting soon, remember? We went and visited, and you played with some of the other girls, who were nice.'

'But I had a school to go to at home. I don't need to go to school here.'

'Do you remember that Arthur used to go away to school?' I ask. 'And he was unhappy there. Do you remember what he said about it?'

'How he didn't like it, that he was unhappy and everyone was horrid, and he wished he could come home?'

Graham starts, leans forward and hisses at me, 'Grace, don't!'

I glare back at him. I'm done with being nice when he's being manipulative. 'Well, if you go home, Daddy wants to send you away to boarding school, the same as Arthur. You wouldn't be in your nice bedroom. You'd be in a bedroom in the school, and you'd only come home on holidays. That's why I brought you here, love. I want you to live with me, not go to some horrid school all on your own.'

Her lip trembles, and she looks up at Graham, hoping he's going to deny everything I just said.

'Not all boarding schools are nasty, Olivia,' Graham explains. 'I went to one, too. Arthur was just being silly. You'd be fine, really.'

'I don't want to go to Arthur's horrid school.'

'It would be a different one, for girls,' Graham continues, not realising he's shooting himself in the foot.

Olivia stares at him for a moment, and the hovering tears erupt. 'I don't want to go to board school!' she cries. 'I want Uncle Noel!'

Before I can stop her, she's scraped her chair back, shot to the door and is out into the street. I leap up. Graham leaps up. Sean, who'd been sitting behind us, leaps up, and we all scramble for the exit, chairs flying behind us.

By the time we get out, there's no sign of Olivia.

'Where did she go?' I ask frantically, struggling to be heard above the noise of the torrential rain. 'Oh Lord, she'll get soaked!'

Graham is hesitating, just inside the porch, reluctant to run out into the downpour.

Sean takes charge. 'She'll have gone to the Big House. You go on that way, down the main street; I'll take the lane behind the bank in case she went that way. Don't worry. She can't have gone far.'

I run down the street, past a few surprised shoppers hurrying through the rain, and up to the Big House. I run to her room then downstairs, but there's no sign of her. Sean, who's come in through the kitchen door and up the internal stairs, shakes his head. Finola and Jane exclaim in distress as we quickly explain what happened.

Noel joins us, brought by the commotion, and quickly gathers what's happened.

'I think I know where she'll be, though,' Finola says. She's pulling on her wellingtons as she speaks. 'There's a wreck of an old house up in the forestry, where we made a kind of den. She called it her secret hiding place. If she's not there, I don't know...'

I grab my waterproof from the mudroom and thrust my feet into my wellingtons. I snatch Olivia's waterproof from the hook so quickly the hood rips.

'Follow me,' Finola says.

Noel calls, 'Sean, take my coat. Take the dogs. I'll go and get help from down on the building site. Jane, can you stay here in case she comes back?'

Lanky and Jack look askance at us and back away from the door as we try to usher them out into the angry Atlantic squall, but Goldie follows us out, if a little dubiously. 'Good dog,' I say. 'Find Olivia!'

The rising wind is howling beyond the door, causing the trees on the hill to ripple like a fitful ocean. I'm hit by a biting slash of rain and shield my eyes. I scan the overgrown shrubs, screaming, 'Olivia! Where are you?' but the wind steals the sound as it leaves my lips.

Finola is younger than me – and fit. She turns back, fleetingly, to where I'm struggling against the bullying wind, then turns and heads up the slope. I slip, stopping myself with a cry, my hand hitting the rutted path, which has turned instantly into a stream.

Sean pulls me upright without pausing. 'We'll find her,' he yells.

We push past the wrought-iron fence, into the wild landscape beyond. There's a path of sorts. I've been up it a little way with Olivia, but I'm soon at the remnants of a stone wall and into unknown territory. Why had I no idea of where Finola took Olivia on these rambles? And why would Olivia want to go up here when the weather is so bad? Are we wrong? Is she running the other way, towards Colla Quay? I imagine her on the shore, the waves crashing in, pulling her... *Stop it*, I tell myself. Noel will have sent someone that way to look, and I'm trusting Finola's instinct.

The wind drives the rain onto my skin like knives. My feet slide as I clamber over an exposed raft of bedrock, and I fall heavily, banging my knee. I curse and push myself to my feet.

'Are you all right?' Sean yells over a crash of thunder. His bare head is slick with rain.

'Yes. Go on. Where's Finola?'

He shields his eyes from the onslaught and says, 'She went that way, into the trees.'

There's a shrill whistle behind us, and I glance back to see three young men tumbling over the stone wall. Presumably builders. They wave, and Sean indicates up the hill. They separate, two going on up to the ridge and another traversing the hill in the opposite direction to us.

'Should we split up, too?' I shout.

'Hell, no. I don't want to be out here searching for you, too. We'll find her. She'll be wet and cold, but it's not Antarctica.'

'It feels like it,' I say, shivering.

He grins. 'Good that you can still joke. Come on.'

'How on earth will we know if someone finds them?'

'Whoever finds them will get someone to ring the lifeboat station. They'll send up a white flare, which is a signal but not a distress call.'

'Will we see it in this weather?'

His teeth glint in the half-light. 'You'd see it from space.'

We hit the edge of the forestry, and the full onslaught of the driving rain is diminished. Heavy drops of rain gather and fall from the branches.

Sean stops short, holding up his hand. 'Did you hear something?'

'No.'

'It was Goldie's bark, I'm sure. This way.'

We're sloshing through puddles of bog, and Sean stops abruptly, listening again. He starts to run, and I run after him, not knowing what he's heard. Then I hear a faint cry. We come to a wall of green, and I realise it's the wreck of a house, a gable end covered in ivy so thick it's just the shape that gives it away.

I shove my hood back to see better. Under the forest canopy, we're out of the worst of the wind, but the trees are shedding water like taps. I swipe at my eyes to clear them. We scramble across a pile of stones, where the wall has fallen, but I can't see anyone. We both scream at the same time.

'Finola?'

'Olivia?'

Goldie barks somewhere nearby.

'Over that way,' Sean yells, pointing.

All I can see is forestry, ranks of dark pine marching away in uniform lines. 'Over here...' Finola's voice is weirdly muffled.

'Where?'

Goldie is barking frantically at the forest floor.

'Holy Mary, Mother of God,' Sean mutters, yanking on my arm to hold me back. 'It's a well.' He kneels and peers down. 'Finola? Are you down there?'

Her voice comes echoing back. 'Olivia's here. She's cold. She was barely holding on, so I climbed down, but I can't get her out. The stones are too slippery. The water's about four feet deep, so I'm not about to drown, but it's fierce cold.'

The breath I didn't realise I was holding falls out of me like a train whistle. *She's alive. Oh my God, she's alive.*

'Finola, can you lift her onto your shoulders?'

I hear the sound of sploshing, then a stone rattles down into the water. There's a long pause, then Sean leans right down and is hauling Oliva out by one arm. She rises like a fish, dripping with water, covered in algae and slime. She's gasping, shivering, and her teeth are chattering.

I run over, sink to my knees and hug her, tears mingling with the rain dripping down on us. In that instant of relief, my mind manages to fill with a whole alternative scenario: of us not finding the girls in time, of them drowning, of Olivia being brought home still and white. I would regret selfishly stealing her from her home, regret coming to Ireland. I would blame myself for everything, and nothing would ever be the same again...

'Grace, wise up! Get that coat on her. I'll carry her down to the Big House,' Sean commands as I struggle to get her warm. 'You get her into a hot bath, and I'll get word to the lifeboat station, so those boys on the hill can come in and get dry. Fino-la,' he yells down, 'can you climb a little higher? I might be able to pull you up.'

'No,' she calls back. 'There's nothing to grip.'

'I'm going to send a couple of the lads up with a ladder. Hang on in there, girrul.'

Olivia clings to me like a leech, so cold she's gasping for breath. I unpick her fingers from my clothes and stand, forcing her arms into the coat. 'Olivia, stop!' I snap. 'Sean has to carry you. I'm not strong enough! I'll be right behind you.'

Sean picks her up and runs. I follow on, scrambling down the pitted slope, more often on my backside than my feet.

As we break out of the forestry, a youth comes bounding down the hill. Sean points behind us, directing him to the well.

By the time I get to the house, I hear footsteps pounding upstairs and follow Jane to a bathroom I've never seen before, where the hot water is already running.

Sean comes out, swiping his wet hair back from his brow.

'Darn, girrul, I'm fair drowned,' he says with a grin. 'She'll be fine. Don't you mind now.'

Jane has stripped Olivia's waterproof coat off and dumped her in the rapidly filling bath, clothes and all. *Thank God for Noel's big boiler*, I think. 'I'll stay with Olivia,' I tell Jane. 'The lads have gone to rescue Finola. She'll need hot water, too. I hope there's enough.'

Jane pounds away downstairs.

Olivia's gasps gradually slow, and pink trickles into her cheeks. I run more hot water. As she gazes up at me, wide-eyed in the aftermath of her adventure, the panic I'd been holding back erupts in a choked cry. What if we hadn't found them in time? What if Finola hadn't climbed down to hold her up?

'Are you all right, Mummy?'

Olivia hesitantly puts her hand on mine where it clutches the side of the bath. I wipe my eyes with the back of my other hand; I'm so used to hiding my feelings, I doubt she's ever seen me cry.

'I'm just so glad we found you, that's all.' I take a deep breath to calm my shaky voice. 'Why did you do that, darling? I wasn't going to let Daddy send you to boarding school. That's why I brought you here, to Ireland, you know.'

She thinks about that for a bit. 'I like the school we went to see. Do you think we can stay here instead of going home with Daddy?'

'I think that's a very good idea,' I say. 'But we still have to go and live in Grandpa's house when it's finished. Is that all right?'

'I'll have my own bedroom?'

'You will. It won't be big and posh, like Noel's house, or like Daddy's, but it's ours, yours and mine. Will you be all right if I go and find you some clean clothes?'

She nods and grins. 'I'm wearing my clothes in the bath!'

'Yes.' I laugh. 'You are, aren't you?'

There's a knock on the door. 'May I come in?' It's Noel.

'Sure, we're all decent in here.'

He says to Olivia in mock annoyance, as if he really is her kindly grandpa, 'You know you're supposed to get water from the well for the dish of tea, not dive in it for a swim?'

She laughs. 'I didn't dive in! I was standing on the floor, and all of a sudden it was gone.'

'That must have been a shock.' He turns to me. 'The boys have brought Finola out. She's fine. She's a real trouper, isn't she? Climbing down there like that. Apparently, it was Goldie who heard her yelling, and then Sean heard Goldie barking. What an amazing dog. Oh, and your husband was here. I sent him back to the hotel. Seems he didn't want to go rushing around the countryside to rescue his own daughter.'

His tone of deep dislike is one I'd like to cultivate.

Later, when Finola had been collected by her mother, and the young men who'd run over to help had all gone to get dry, Sean and I are toasting ourselves in front of the living-room fire, sitting close together on the sofa. Noel is quietly watching Olivia, who's wrapped in a blanket, cuddling Goldie on the carpet in front of us.

'I feel chastened,' Noel says finally. 'I knew the wreck was there, and just about every house had its own well. It must have been capped, years back, with wood, but over time it got covered with leaves and forgotten about. I'm going to get the well filled with stones and capped with concrete.'

'But, look, all's well that ends well,' Sean says with a smirk.

We all burst out laughing. I think mine was slightly hysterical. He puts his arm around me and pulls me close.

Olivia shoots us a look of disgust. 'You're not going to kiss, are you?' she asks. 'Yuk!'

After I've put Olivia to bed and read her one of her comfort bedtime stories, I spend the evening with Noel and Sean, just quietly discussing the future, and I try not to dwell on what might have happened. Human lives are so fragile, I think drowsily, as their murmurs rise and fall in quiet companionship. So many pitfalls to negotiate, so many dangers lurking beneath the still waters of our fairly suburban lives. I don't doubt that Olivia will cause me a few more panics in the course of our lives, but, sure, isn't that the way it is?

I smile inwardly. Sure, I'm getting very Irish!

The next day, Graham makes his farewells in a civilised, but slightly chill, voice. He won't be late for his meeting in Belfast. Even now, he's organised this visit to me around his business. He kisses Olivia perfunctorily on the cheeks and tells her, 'See? That's what happens when you don't do as your mother tells you. But I suppose you've learned your lesson.'

I am astounded that he can proselytise, even at the last hurdle, but Olivia just says, 'Yes, Daddy,' and I realise that was always her stock answer to anything he directed at her.

Sean is like the lighthouse rock, battered by the Atlantic: solid, immoveable and trustworthy. Graham has been sculpted from the sand that speckles the shores, its grains packed tight into a package that glitters and sparkles but would be whittled away in the face of a storm. I didn't come to Roone Bay to find love, but it has found me, and I'm glad.

Graham tells us stiffly that he'd love us both to come on a visit when we feel up to it. I like the way he says that, as if his home is the holiday destination. That suits me fine. After the last debacle, Olivia seems almost as relieved as I am to see her father off.

Finola helps by suggesting, 'Wave goodbye to your father, and will we go and get an ice cream?'

Olivia nods, her father forgotten in an instant. Graham's visit, which I'd been dreading, has cleared the air. I no longer have that black anvil cloud hanging over me. I'm not sorry to see the silver Rolls-Royce glide away. It caused some comments in the town, as did Graham's attitude, and I guess it's no secret that it was my husband who'd been visiting, and that I've left him.

I'm not looking forward to instigating divorce proceedings, even though Graham has grudgingly agreed to make it as hassle-free as he can. I guess it's in his interests to do so. It frees him up to find Mrs Adams number three. I hope he finds an older woman this time, one who enjoys being in his social circle, but it wouldn't surprise me if he goes for another younger model, one who'll produce him the son and heir he hasn't discovered in Arthur. Some people never do learn by their mistakes.

Divorce is still not legal here. Gran says *married is married for life*, in Ireland. Never mind that your old man beats you half to death and starves you, when you're joined by God, then nothing except death will free you from that pledge. That's got to be wrong, in just about every way.

Thankfully, I'm English and can get a divorce. If Graham's not going to contest it, maybe it won't be such a nightmare of legislation and blame. Do the Irish authorities recognise a divorce settled in England? And when I'm divorced, will I be able to marry Sean? I'm sure there's been no end of gossip about myself and Sean, but it doesn't seem to bother him. He has a philosophy that tides him over all of life's hiccups: Sure, it'll be grand!

I heard it whispered that Noel married Sinéad for the land and wonder if that's why he pined for his Kathleen. He married the wrong girl and simply couldn't get out of it. He wouldn't have been the first to make such a mistake. But I know now, from his quiet reminiscing, that his decision hadn't been about the avaricious acquisition of land.

28

NOEL, 1930

Noel knew Sinéad like a big sister and had assumed she would one day be his sister by marriage. His brother, Jacob, had been courting her relentlessly. Though he seemed to be hesitant to take the final plunge and ask for her hand, it was a deal in all but the wedding. Noel was aware that Jacob lusted after Sinéad, who was undoubtedly the most beautiful girl in Roone Bay. With her porcelain skin and yellow hair, people whispered that she was an angel, a changeling or a fairy child. They ribbed him about it, wondering what he was waiting for, because he was in his mid-twenties, and so was Sinéad – too old, surely, to still be unwed.

Then, out of the blue, Jacob walked out one day and didn't come home. No word to either his family or his fiancée. Noel's father was stunned, and his already greying hair grew white over the next month. Some supposed Jacob would send money, asking his love to follow, assuming he'd gone to America, but Noel knew Sinéad would never abandon her family. Her father was after saying that Jacob had gone wrong, and secretly, even though it was his own brother, Noel was inclined to agree. To abandon her, after she'd waited so long for him, and her now considered an old maid, was a dastardly deed.

But when her father, Tim Roycroft, called one morning to speak to his father, Noel had a premonition that things were about to change. The two men walked the fields together, the low murmur of their words hanging on the still air, not loud enough to be heard. It was no secret that Mary Roycroft was dying of the consumption, and that no amount of praying was going to save her, so he wondered if she was on her final call, and the priest had been called to give her absolution. Maybe Tim was asking for the loan of their donkey cart, to see the poor lady down to her final resting place.

No doubt he would learn in time.

He bent his back to his task of clearing the shed for the next milking while he was waiting for his father to help load the heavy churns of milk onto the cart. He never minded the earthy smell of cows, or the pervading scent of warm milk, but in the back of his mind he always believed he'd leave it all one day and go to seek his own place in the world, because the farm would be Jacob's. Now he didn't know what to think.

When the men came in, Noel's mother served a dish of tea, and the men passed the time talking of the harvest, the weather, the birds coming in from the south and the state of the world. They knew about things beyond their little corner of Ireland, because the priest would read the news every week, and the men would gather to listen and take the tales home to their wives. The Depression was real, but talk of fascism and war was too distant for poor farmers to comprehend, like a cloud that never spilled. How could life be any worse than when the great famine had swept through the land? But still, they liked to listen. And the priest never lost a moment to keep his avid flock in check with tales of everlasting fire and hell and damnation if they didn't listen hard enough, so there was plenty for the two men to discuss.

Then Tim Roycroft nodded at Paddy, and left, so lost in his thoughts he forgot to take his leave of Noel and his mother. Roisin glanced sharply at her husband, but he shook his head and went back out to complete his chores.

The turf was smouldering in the grate when Paddy came in for his supper, stamping the mud from his boots at the door frame as he always did. The old house, built of field stones, kept a constant temperature, cold in summer and winter alike, so there was no point in shutting the door, except when the bitter east wind flattened the grass. Noel's mother swung the skillet pot on its davit and ladled the food out, proportionate to their needs: the most for the man of the house, the next for Noel and the smallest for herself.

'That was Sinéad's father.' Patrick O'Donovan stated the obvious but didn't lift his eyes from the plate as he slurped the broth. 'He's finding the days difficult now and is after needing a favour.'

Roisin frowned. 'Not Mary, then?'

'Oh, aye, the good Lord will take her soon enough, but no. It's Sinéad.'

Noel was shocked. 'Is she ill? Has she the consumption, like her mother?'

Paddy briefly compressed his lips, as though not wanting the words to pass them, then looked directly at Noel. 'Sinéad will be needing to wed. With her mother ill, and Jacob gone, she'll have no man to look after her soon enough. As you're going to inherit the farm now, he was thinking you'd marry her and inherit his fields, also.'

Noel knew, instantly, what his father was talking of. After Jacob had run off, it occurred to him that the farm would one day be his, and that maybe Sinéad, who'd waited for Jacob longer than a maid might be expected to wait, might be hoping for his own hand, instead.

'No,' he said. 'I don't love her, and I won't marry for their biteen of land, never mind that Jacob would do so. I have a fancy to marry Caitlin. You know that.'

'You always were twice the man Jacob was, despite the good looks on him. I've never asked much of you, son. I'm asking this now.'

'I don't love her!'

'You don't know...' Paddy stopped and started again. 'Sinéad is a good girl. She wouldn't lie with him until they were married.'

'Yes, but...'

'Son, hear me out. Jacob made her a promise. He said if she lay with him, he'd call the banns and make it happen. He swore on God's love that he would do this, and if she didn't, he would go away.'

Noel's heart dropped; he knew what was coming.

'Your brother seduced the girl with his promises. Then, when she was with child, she asked him to make an honest woman of her, do right by her in the eyes of God. That's why he ran. Jacob is no son of mine,' he added bitterly.

Noel closed his eyes briefly, and when he opened them, his mother and father were staring at him hopefully.

'It's not for the farm,' his mother whispered. 'It's for her honour – and ours. If anyone knows she's with child, she'll be cast out of the community, and it was our son who did this to her. She's a good girl. She doesn't deserve this.'

'I'm asking you to be the son Jacob wasn't,' his father added, staring down at his dish. 'To right the wrong done by your brother.'

Noel thrust his chair back angrily as he stood, his supper cooling unheeded on the plate, all his own plans fled to the winds. 'No, she doesn't deserve that. I'll go down tomorrow and make my promise.'

His father nodded his approval. 'Tim can spread the word that the two of you had a long-standing arrangement, that it wasn't Jacob at all that she was to wed. You'll come to see the sense of it, in time,' Paddy said slowly. 'She's a good girl, so maybe it's not such a bad deal after all's said.'

Noel grimly completed his tasks, but the happiness was gone from him. The wedding was sorted in a hurry, by the priest, who, guessing the reason for the hurry, had read him quite a lecture on the evils of fornication outside marriage. No one even suspected that the apparent long-term romance was a lie, and his friends had butted him with their elbows, calling him a sly lad! Why would they doubt it? The Roycroft and O'Donovan farms met where the stream fell, and he could have seen her many times, with none the wiser. As had Jacob.

And him, Noel, never having lain with a woman in his life.

Sinéad, he had to admit, had looked utterly beautiful on her wedding day; like a wraith, tall and blonde and almost insubstantial somehow, but he didn't fancy her, not one bit. She spoke her vows clearly and calmly, with no hint that she was unhappy with the arrangement. And Caitlin had been in the church, her stunned gaze on him the whole time, as if she couldn't believe he would really go through with it. Tim paid for a good shindig, and Noel and Sinéad had gone home, amidst much ribaldry, as husband and wife.

And not long after that, his Caitlin fled to England with Connor. Even though the marriage had been forced on him, he'd decided to make the best of the situation, but their flight had quietly rocked his world. Despite everything, he thought she would always live close by, that he could love her from a distance. But now he was living a half-life, married to a woman who didn't want him, while the woman he wanted was so far away, she might as well be on the moon.

His new wife was spending most of her time nursing her dying mother, while looking increasingly fragile herself.

Rumours began to circulate that she was too good for this world, too religious, and God might call her to his side before she carried to term.

Noel tried not to mind that he was carrying the burden for his own brother's lack of honour, that no-good jackeen, but he was furious. His whole life had been irrevocably changed because of Jacob's actions.

29

GRACE

Olivia will start school in just over a week now. I'm impressed by the keen professionalism of the two teachers and the light, airy classrooms. Olivia seems happy enough and hasn't once talked about going back to live in Cheltenham.

Despite the fact that he's paying me to work for him, Noel has given me a week off to get settled into our house, before Olivia starts school. Finola soon won't be able to help out. She's mentally preparing herself for school, and her final exams, before, hopefully, going on to Galway University. She wants to be a teacher, and I have no doubt she'll be an excellent one; she has a real knack with Olivia.

We've been lucky with our first summer in Ireland. Sometimes there are soft days, filled with a drizzle so fine it's more like mist than rain. Often, the mornings feel damp to the skin, before the sun sucks the dew into the air and burns it off. Those atmospheric mornings, sometimes with the merest hint of a rainbow, reveal the magic of Ireland, the superstition, the legends, the fairy folk creeping out of the raths in the half-light. But often the day is bright, with an arc of sunlight traversing the glinting sea, the distant sky drifting with a light swish of mare's-tail clouds.

A veritable flood of tourists had invaded over the short summer season, while Olivia was running wild, Sean was building my extension and I was busy typing out Noel's memoir. The normally quiet town came alive and was bustling for a while, but the visitors are fast disappearing, along with the sailing craft that had moored in the bay, leaving the town to sink into its sleepy acceptance that another winter is fast approaching. Then we'll see the full might of the Atlantic from our bedroom windows, which are, thankfully, double-glazed.

Sean tells me I've changed since Graham's visit; found my confidence, become more assertive. I think he means that in a nice way! I do feel as though I've finally planted my feet in a place where I can grow roots. I certainly feel more at home in Roone Bay than I did in either industrial Birmingham or upmarket Cheltenham.

Noel's memoir is creeping on slowly, day by day, and I'm almost sure that the Kathleen he mentions in passing is my grandma, but I get the feeling his story is leading to some big exposé that will free him from a burden he's kept hidden from the world but now wishes to share; with whom, I'm not sure, because I'm just the conduit for this cathartic undertaking. I hope that its eventual exposure isn't something that will destroy him.

I felt compelled to leave, in some way, but conversely, I always longed to come home. America simply wasn't Ireland, though it was the place where I made my fortune. I didn't apologise for being poor Irish when I arrived in America, and I won't apologise for being wealthy now I'm back in Ireland.

I stop him with a gesture. 'Why would you apologise for being wealthy? Isn't that the dream come true?'

He lifts his eyebrows in a gesture that I now recognise conveys amusement. 'My dear girl, haven't you realised that we Irish wallow in tales of woe? Poverty isn't our enemy; without it we'd have nothing to gripe about! The poorer you are, the more Irish you are.' He laughs. 'I'm a cultural curiosity, don't you see? I left as a farm boy with one pair of shoes to my name, and I've come back wealthy. I'm no longer part of the community I grew up with, because they don't know how to deal with it.'

He echoes my own thoughts about how I fit – or don't fit – into this tight community. I was warned that hatred against the English lingers beneath the surface of this historically wronged people, but I've never experienced it. The fact that my grand-parents all came from here probably helps, but that I'm 'seeing' Sean has surely tipped the balance. I guess Noel and I both sit somewhere in the middle, neither blow-ins nor locals.

'Let's delete that last sentence,' he suggests, 'and write,

I am hefted to the land of my birth, to my kith, and also to my kin. In America I was always a stranger. I was born in Ireland, and that's where my heart has always been.

'Just like the Kathleen in Josef Locke's song,' I comment.

'Exactly. Kith, of course, means the place in which you were born, where your feet have roots clawed into the land, like those of a mature tree. You knew that, didn't you?'

I nod, but I didn't.

I wonder if there's something in us that roots us to a particular place on earth, more than just familiarity. Could that pass down through generations? Noel's roots are here, and he came back, but I have no compulsion to return to Birmingham, where my roots lie, according to his theory. I never felt any attachment to the place. Instead, I'm grasping for my grandparents' roots, wondering whether they'll be strong enough to nurture me. These thoughts are fleeting, and

Noel carries on, his words drifting between memoir and personal philosophy.

I find his comments relieve my own feeling of isolation a little. I might never quite fit in, but nor does Noel, who was born here. However, Olivia is young enough to meld into the community. Already, her precise English vowels are softening, and she asks less about going *home*.

'I think that's it for the day,' Noel says finally. 'It must be lunch time. It's surprising how exhausting it is, delving into the past. Is this vain of me? Am I doing this to attain some kind of immortality?'

I smile. 'You're doing it because you want to. You don't need to justify it. As social history, memoirs are important. History books tend to deal with important people, politics and larger issues. Memoirs provide a much deeper understanding of how the big things impact on the lives of ordinary people.'

'You are right, of course. But,' he adds pensively, 'autobiographies allow for distortion of the truth. There are things I won't write, because they're too personal or might be hurtful to others. Talking of which, soon it'll be time to talk about my marriage and what happened to make me leave.'

'The lost baby and your lost wife,' I comment.

'Ah,' he says. 'Sure, they were sad days. People died who would be saved today. Like your grandfather's first wife, Caitlin, who never lived to see her grandchildren, but such is life.'

I'm stumped for a moment then say, 'Grandma Caitlin isn't dead. Did I say something to make you think she was?'

He's so still, I think he's stopped breathing, and when he moves, he's sucking air, as though it can't reach his lungs. I jump to my feet. 'Noel? Are you all right? Noel?'

I run over, but he lowers himself into his executive office chair, and I hover uncertainly, wondering whether I should run for Jane. His head drops into his hands, and when he looks up, his face is wet with tears. 'Caitlin O'Driscoll? She's still alive?'

'Yes, I told you, that's who gave me the cottage. Grandpa Connor inherited it when his father died, and when Grandpa died, it became hers. My grandmother's.'

He sighs, long and low, before saying, 'Your grandfather, Connor... He told me she died in childbirth, along with the child. He sent me a letter... I thought he must have married again.' He takes a long, shuddering breath. 'Grace, could you fetch a couple of glasses? Will you have a whiskey with me? I need to tell you something.'

'Of course.'

I'm not a great one for the whiskey, but I think maybe I'll take one anyway. I collect the glasses and bottle from the cabinet, and set them down. He pours generous measures, and indicates for me to sit. 'This isn't going to be easy for me.'

I give a rueful smile. 'You don't have to tell me anything. I've guessed already. You were in love with my grandmother.'

'Indeed I was,' he says. There's a pause while he searches for the right words. The office window is wide, letting in the smell of the sea and the cry of the seagulls. I realise I'm about to learn the real reason he's writing his memoir, and a sense of expectation trickles through me.

'There were two farms, you see. My parents' and the one along the valley from us, Mary and Tim Roycroft's. They had one daughter, Sinéad, who was a few years older than me.' His accent thickens as he drifts back into the past. 'She was a nice girrul, hard-working and beautiful, but I didn't love her. Her father came to us one day and told us she was with child. They asked me to save her, from the shame and everything.'

'Poor girl, but it wasn't your fault if she got herself pregnant!'

'No, but there's more. Sinéad was like a sister to me. She was supposed to marry my brother, Jacob, but he disappeared one day. Ran off, over the water. We never heard from him again. I know he got to America, but I never found any trace of

him when I went searching. It would have been poetic justice in
a way, if he had died. You see, Sinéad was deeply religious and
wouldn't lie with him until they were married. Jacob said she
should have been a nun. It was all her fault, he said. If she'd
taken the veil, he wouldn't have seen her. But because she was
so close, so beautiful, he coveted her.'

I'm confused. 'But who made her pregnant then?'

'Jacob. I thought they'd just made love, which is what Dad
told me, but after she died, he told me the truth. Jacob raped her
as she went to the well for water. That's why he ran away after.'

I gasp. 'But why didn't he just marry her, make it right?'

Noel grimaces. 'That's the crux of the matter, isn't it? I don't
think he ever wanted to marry her. She was just so beautiful, he
wanted her. He lied about loving her and got engaged, just
hoping she would sleep with him.'

'And you married Sinéad because of your brother's actions?'

He nods. 'I was already in love with Caitlin – we'd been
seeing each other – but when they asked me to save Sinéad,
what could I say? You can't imagine what it was like, in those
days, for a girl to have a child out of wedlock. She would have
been ruined, sent to the nuns, and the Lord knows what would
have happened to the child. Father said it would be useful,
besides, to amalgamate our two smaller farms, but for me it
wasn't about the land. I married her to put right what Jacob did,
even though I didn't realise quite how bad it was at the time.'
He sighed. 'Caitlin thought I'd married Sinéad for the land, and
I couldn't tell her. The ironic thing is, Sinéad lost the child, so I
needn't have married her at all. Our parents were pleased, of
course. It was what they'd hoped for, for the two farms to be
brought together by marriage, and they didn't mind that it was
me, not Jacob. But me, I was heartbroken.'

'And you never saw my grandmother again?'

He pauses and holds the glass up, watching the amber

liquid sparkle behind cut glass in the stream of sunlight. 'Sure, Sinéad and I hadn't been married long when I met Caitlin again, at the market. Since I'd last seen her, she'd blossomed into a fine woman. It was then I realised what love was, what a fool I'd been, and it was too late. I couldn't divorce Sinéad, even if I'd wanted to. Caitlin told me her father had promised her to an older man; she was just sixteen then. So, she told me she wanted to have a life and was going to leave Roone Bay, maybe leave Ireland. She wasn't going to marry to please her father. I was angry, but she was right. She had to leave and have a life. Eventually, she left, with Connor, who I thought was my friend. I was devastated.'

He's lost in thought for a moment then adds, 'When Caitlin ran off with Connor, I thought maybe I'd get over it, eventually, that Sinéad and I would grow closer with time.' He sighs. 'We didn't, really. She hated being a wife. Jacob was right – she should have been a nun. She was ever married to the church. When she died, I wrote to Connor telling him I was now free, but Connor eventually wrote back and told me that Caitlin, too, had died in childbirth.' He pauses for a moment then adds, with a kind of angry acceptance, 'Now I find she's still alive, that she and Connor had a long, happy marriage, and their child, Anne, got married, and there's a grandchild, you, and even a great-grandchild, Olivia. How very, very strange that is. After all these years. How could he do that to me?'

'The song,' I say softly. 'I'll bring you home, Kathleen. It was for my grandmother. But for Grandpa to tell you she'd died... That was just downright cruel.'

He sighs again. 'I should have guessed. You see, Connor loved her, too. We grew up together, close, like brothers. We both fell for Caitlin at the same time, but it was me she fancied. Lovely, she was; dark-haired, blue-eyed and vivacious. She wasn't afraid of anything, not the priests or the nuns, or convention. It's no wonder we were smitten. She said she loved me, first, and Connor like a brother.'

'That's sad.'

'I said I'd marry her when she turned sixteen. She said she'd wait for me, but then this thing with Sinéad happened. It was tough on Sinéad, too, because she knew I loved Caitlin. I wasn't very good at hiding it, you see.' He sighs again. 'When Sinéad died, I decided to leave Roone Bay, because the memory of Caitlin was everywhere. On the boat, in the middle of the Atlantic, I thought of throwing myself overboard. I felt empty, used up. I wanted to join her in Heaven.' He gives a brief chuckle. 'It would have been a shock to find Sinéad there but not Caitlin!'

I laugh with him, but he becomes serious again.

'Life was too strong in me, anyway, so I got to America and made my fortune.'

'But you never fell in love again?'

'I met some nice women, but I couldn't love anyone else, no matter how much I tried.'

Noel's face goes blank as he drifts back into memory. 'When that letter came, telling me she was dead, I was past reasoning with for a while. Connor was my friend. It didn't occur to me to check to see if it was true. All these years, and she was still alive?' Disbelief and anger flitted across his face at the betrayal, at a lost lifetime.

I put my hand on his arm and smile softly. 'I'm glad you didn't throw yourself overboard!'

He says, with a faint grin, 'So am I, actually. The older I get, the less sure I am that Heaven exists. But it's a shock to find out Caitlin's still alive, so it is.'

'Is that why you employed me?' I take a gulp of whiskey, and my eyes are blinded by tears for a moment as it catches my throat. I cough until I've regained some kind of composure.

He shakes his head. 'I heard about Sean starting to renovate

Connor's house, and I was curious. When I saw your notice in the post office, looking for work, it was the excuse I needed to find out about Connor's life, of course. Strangely, when I met you, I felt we had a connection, and then you confirmed that you were Connor's granddaughter; I assumed from a second wife. Now I find you're Caitlin's true granddaughter, too. Oh my.'

It's obvious, now, why Noel had been drawing my story out of me when we should have been writing his. 'Well, Noel, I need to tell you something, too.'

He inclines his head enquiringly as I sit back down and lean my elbows on the desk.

'Mum and Grandma are coming over here. They thought they'd have a holiday, see what I've been doing. I think Grandma felt a bit nostalgic about Roone Bay, but the thing is, I've mentioned you in my letters to Mum. I don't doubt Grandma has read them. She must know who you are and that you're back in Ireland.'

'Good Lord,' he mutters. 'Saints preserve us. Oh Lord.'

'Well, it's in motion,' I say. 'And if Grandma has decided to come over, nothing will stop her. She's a force to be reckoned with.'

'Is she still?' He's joking but looks panicked. 'How can I ever see her again, now, after all these years? What will we say?'

My body flushes with a profound, unclassifiable emotion, something I'd experienced only once before in my life, when I first set eyes on my child: love and fear and a sense of being inadequate, all bundled up into one uneasy package. I was exhilarated by the thought of these one-time lovers meeting again. But time changes everything. What if the passion is long gone – if they're just strangers closing a door on the past?

Tears flood into my eyes and I smile shakily, saying, 'I think something will come to you.'

He's staring into space when I leave the office. At dinner,

later, I see Jane glare at me, as if wondering what I've done to upset him. But what I do know is that next week, things are going to get very interesting.

30

GRACE

I stand at the window of my cottage looking out over a calm, blue sea twinkling under a sky brushed with mare's-tail clouds. The storm has scrubbed the air clean, leaving the damp land bathed in a soft glow.

A weight has been lifted from my mind. The worst that could happen has already happened: Graham knows everything, has gone home and I didn't fall to pieces. I'm in love for the first time in my life. Olivia could have drowned in the well but didn't; she's happily rebuilding the front wall – to help, she said. Graham would have a fit if he saw her piling up the stones in a somewhat haphazard manner.

I turn to Sean, who's standing quietly behind me. He's a quiet presence in my life, wrapping me with a sense of completeness. 'I want to move in now. Is that all right?'

He seems concerned. 'Is everything all right between you and the man in the Big House?'

I nod. 'Of course. But I've accepted his charity long enough. It doesn't feel right to stay there, expecting Jane to cook and clean for us, not when my house is liveable. I want to have my

own space again. I want to move in before Olivia starts school,
so she can settle in.'

'I suppose you've noticed that there are no carpets or tiles
on the floor, nothing is painted, the kitchen isn't ready and you
have no furniture?'

'Well, the latter is easily solved, and the painting and
finishing can be done around us. As long as everything is working, and we have a cooker, I can cope!'

He scratches his head, thinking, then says, 'Okay, so.
There's a place in Bantry that has second-hand furniture. I'll
drive you over there so you can choose what you want.'

'That's really kind, thank you.'

The other reason for wanting to move in, of course, is that
Mum and Grandma will be arriving soon. I want to be able to
meet up with them on my own terms, in my own house. Noel,
also, has his own obstacles to overcome, and maybe he'll deal
with those better without our presence in his home. I don't want
to be a bystander if everything goes belly-up. I mean, it's all very
well for Noel and Grandma to have been madly in love in their
youth, but that was half a century ago, and people change. Noel
might be carrying a torch that burned out years ago. They'll
meet up after two vastly different lifetimes. Will they still love
each other? Will they even recognise each other?

In Sean's truck, later, we drive up winding, potholed lanes
towards the Bantry road, through acres of young forestry and
past several dilapidated farms. Here and there, new houses are
being built alongside old ones, and I imagine the families will
just shift themselves over, leaving the old home, perhaps
without even a hint of regret.

'Sad,' I comment as we pass another one, and it seems that
Sean doesn't need me to explain.

'Maybe,' he says. 'But people want to move into the modern

day. The old houses are small and damp, and never as warm as the new ones. People's expectations have changed. They want straight walls, central heating, and modern kitchens and bathrooms. The old ways are going, sure enough.'

'Why don't they pull the old houses down?'

'Sure, and why would they bother? What would they want with a huge pile of stones?'

He laughs, and I laugh with him. He'd mentioned that the houses were built from stones lifted from the fields. This part of Ireland seems to have stones growing up through the soil. If you lift one, another rises to take its place. No, better to leave the old house to slip naturally back into the landscape, a romantic ruin to remind people of the past that shaped them.

O'Malley's is a strange place, a mishmash of rooms that seem to have been built on to a central building in some ad hoc fashion. It's roofed with corrugated iron, which I think must be noisy when it rains. The main building used to be a creamery, Sean tells me, where small farmers used to bring their milk churns in donkey carts, to be then hauled by truck to the bigger depots. There are derelict creameries all over, since the milk cooperatives started. That's progress, I suppose, though it will eventually put all the small farmers out of work. It's what happened in England, thirty years back. I can see why Noel's family had the foresight to want the two smaller farms amalgamated.

Olivia had been strangely silent during the drive over, and I find out why when we're standing in a room with furniture packed in at all angles, new at the front, old at the back, some beds on top of each other, some on their end, propped against the wall.

'What about that one?' I suggest. It's the new style: pine, with a slatted base. There are some old ones with a metal mesh base, like the one I grew up with as a child, but I hated the way the mattress would slump into the middle of the bed. It must be worse in a double bed, the couple shunted together by gravity.

'It's okay,' she says, somewhat dismissively.

I know she'd like to stay in the Big House, so I take that as a yes. 'We can't stay with Uncle Noel forever. We're only there while I'm working for him, and it's nearly finished. I said it was like being in a hotel on holiday, didn't I?'

She sighs. 'Our house is grubby!'

I bite back a laugh. Where did she get that from? Arthur, maybe. He's hugely antagonistic towards his father, but they certainly came out of the same mould, with a weather-eye on size and status. 'Well,' I say firmly, giving her a one-armed hug. 'Once your room is done, and we've painted it and lit the fire, it'll be nice, you'll see. And I did think, once we're settled in, that you might like a dog.'

That perks her up enormously. 'Like Goldie?'

'It might not be exactly like Goldie. We'll have to find one that needs a nice home. We can be dog rescuers, like Noel.'

She nods seriously. 'That would make us good people, wouldn't it?'

'I like to think so!'

Eventually, Sean loads the truck: two new beds and mattresses; a small cottage sofa; a second-hand kitchen table with a Formica top and metal legs; an electric kettle, some pans and tableware; four metal chairs with plastic seats. I plan to buy new bedding in Roone Bay with the money Noel has paid me for the work to date; he absolutely refused to deduct a consideration towards board and lodging.

Olivia is sitting quietly in the centre of the seat, resigned, I suppose, to the move, when Sean claps his forehead and says, 'Hang on a moment. I forgot something.'

He lopes back into the building. A few minutes later, he climbs back in and hands a small, orange, furry bundle to Olivia. She takes it automatically. A small face peers up at her, with wide blue eyes. Then the mouth yawns widely to emit a plaintive yowl.

'Oh!' she exclaims in wonder.

'Tuck her inside your cardigan,' Sean advises. 'She'll be missing her mother for a few days and will need to be cuddled.'

Olivia unbuttons her cardigan halfway and slips the kitten inside. Almost immediately it begins to purr loudly, working away at the wool with its claws.

I glance at Sean in amused exasperation. 'What are we going to do with a cat! We aren't even living in the cottage yet. We can't take it to Noel's house – what about the dogs? They might kill it.'

'Sure, it'll be fine. The dogs won't hurt her, you'll see. So, girrul,' he continues to Olivia, 'will we stop and buy the cateen something to eat on the way home? And a box for her to do her business in? And sure, won't it be better for her in the little house, after all, because that big field at the back will be her own.'

He glances down at Olivia, and his wide smile makes my heart jolt. It's like we're a real family already. But a cat and a dog? Graham would have a heart attack. All that fur... and maybe we'll be allergic... I almost laugh out loud.

By the time we get back to the Big House, the kitten is fast asleep against Olivia, who's cradling her, a faint smile on her lips.

Sean lifts them down gently. 'I'll go on and get the place sorted,' he says. 'Two days.'

'Thank you,' I say, and as Olivia isn't watching, he smacks a quick kiss, right on my lips, before jumping in the truck and heading off down the drive. I put a finger to my mouth, touching the place where he kissed me, as excited as a teenager with a first crush.

· · ·

But the day before the planned move, dark clouds roll in from the Atlantic, and the temperature plummets once again. There's a brief, heavy squall that lashes the windows, and I'm sure I hear distant thunder. I shiver and wonder why it feels like the portent of doom. I must stop letting my imagination run away with me. Olivia's spending the morning in the kitchen with Jane and Finola, reading, playing games, or creating something with glue and paper. Hopefully by the time they don their waterproofs and take the dogs through the garden and up into the wild scrubby land beyond (but not as far as the forestry!), the storm will have blown itself out.

Mum and Grandma are due to travel soon, so I'm a bit worried about the weather and the state of the sea. I can't imagine that the ferry from Holyhead to Dublin will be a very nice experience if the Irish Sea is rough, and it might even be cancelled if the weather is truly bad. It's Murphy's Law, I guess, that the storm has come down days before they're due to travel. But they aren't coming to lie in the sun. They're coming to see me and Olivia – and Noel. They'll come south by train and bus, as I did, and Sean will pick them up from Skibbereen in Noel's car, so we're all playing a waiting game, while getting on with things, as if this visit isn't going to be out-of-the-ordinary weird.

Noel reads through another section from his notes, and I type without stopping for an hour or so. He's focusing on his story to avoid thinking too much about what might transpire, and I feel the same way. There's a sombre feeling in the air, as though we've all been affected by the adverse weather.

I pack our belongings in anticipation of the move, surprised at how much we've accumulated already. Noel is disconcerted that I feel the need to move out, despite my explanation that Olivia needs to set her roots before school starts. I'll miss the Big House, too, though. I've enjoyed being here – the sense of prestige, the decor, the high ceilings, and the big boiler downstairs that heats the whole place. As a child, in the winter I'd scraped ice off the inside of the window with my fingernails, but it's easier to get used to luxury than it is to have been used to it and then do without. I fear Olivia has accepted her place in this prestigious building as a right, and the sooner we relocate to our own house, the better.

On the day of the move, Sean turns up after we've had lunch, which Jane insisted we stay for. I give her a hug for looking after us so well, and she tears up, as if we're going the other side of the world. I guess she's enjoyed having extra company in that big house; Finola and Olivia have practically lived in the kitchen with her while Noel and I have been working in his study. She gives me a hearty hug in return, as does Noel. I've become extraordinarily fond of the old man and know that he'll find his solitary existence so much harder, having had us invading his space for nearly three months. But as he said to me yesterday, our relationship won't just peter out. It had become deeper than that of boss and employee. He thinks of me as the granddaughter he never had, and do I mind that he becomes Olivia's surrogate grandfather?

Do I mind? I asked in my best phoney Irish. Sure, wouldn't we both be thrilled!

As I walk into our cottage, I'm stunned at what Sean's achieved in just a couple of days. His face is the picture of delight as he sees my amazement. The ceiling lights are on, the bare bulbs hanging, waiting for shades. The sofa is sitting smack bang in front of a wood-burning stove, which is cheerfully alight. I wander to the kitchen, where the little table and chairs I bought have been placed beside fitted units, a small fridge and a gas cooker that works from a bottle on the outside wall.

'Why gas?' I ask. I've never liked gas – it scares me.

'It's just practical. Electricity here is temperamental. It can go off for a week at a time, especially after a storm when the trees bring the lines down. You can cook on gas, and have candles and lamps for light, and the wood burner for heat. The water is run from an electric pump, but if the electric goes, you can always draw a bucket from the well. I should have got you a torch. I didn't think of that. I'll pick one up, for next time I'm passing, which will be tomorrow morning.'

Upstairs, I find he's painted the bigger bedroom forget-me-not blue and laid a blue carpet with a tiny yellow fleur-de-lys pattern. He's put both beds in there. 'It's a bit of a squeeze,' he says, 'but I thought the girleen might be happier in the same room with you for a few nights. And it leaves the other two rooms clear for the decorating. We can make her room nice for her, let her help choose the colours.'

'God forbid!' She'd probably choose purple or orange, which are very fashionable at the moment. 'But where did you get the carpet?' I ask. 'I didn't order it!'

'Ah, it's just an old bit I had lying around.'

'Strange that it's absolutely perfect for the room.'

'Yes, isn't it?' he says innocently.

He's hung a print of Van Gogh's *Sunflowers* on the wall, to brighten the room up a little. Olivia is with us, assessing, listening, and I hug her to me with one arm. 'Isn't this lovely?' I say.

'Where's Sophie the kitten going to sleep?' she asks.

'Well, we can have her in with us to start with, but when she's bigger, she can live downstairs, on the sofa by the fire, I expect! It'll be too cold in our kitchen.'

As Sean had suspected, the dogs had taken a brief interest in the kitten then ignored her. I'd worried particularly that Lanky might take a snap, but she'd put her nose to the kitten's face, taken a deep sniff then stalked away. I wonder if she understood that the kitten was family, not to be eaten.

Later, after Sean's gone and we're getting ready for bed, I contemplate the view from the bedroom window. The storm has gone through, but the wind has yet to die. Dark clouds are scudding manically across the sky, now and then fleetingly exposing a full moon, which sprinkles the sea with moonbeams. It's hard to describe the sense of serenity that settles on me. I feel lighter than air – and in love. I know this without a doubt. I don't know whether Sean will be able to move in with me before my divorce is finalised – it's something we haven't fully discussed yet. The future is wide open and smiling. This is our home. We'll be happy here, even if we have to wait a bit. And though I can't see into the future, if everything works out the way I envisage it, this is surely my happily-ever-after, the one I dreamed of as a teenager.

I don't fall asleep easily, though. I've grown used to the lack of traffic, but it's almost too quiet, without even the eerie knocking and gurgling that Noel's central heating system emits. I lie awake for a while, my eyes adjusting to the darkness and gravitating towards the dark square of un-curtained window where stark moonlight intermittently flashes on the glass. Olivia sleeps deeply, enclosed in her insular, childish space, where every exhausting new experience is quietly processed and stored for future use.

We wake up in the morning to eat breakfast in our own kitchen, with its view out over our own field. It's kind of surreal, that this is really our home from now on. Olivia lets the kitten out of the back door and follows her protectively as she explores. The kitten is still slightly wobbly, and her little nose bumps into the things she's sniffing. It's amusing to watch, and hard to imagine that this wavering little creature will soon be a confident preda-tor, keeping the mice from the pantry, to echo Sean's words.

Two days, Sean says, and we can put carpets down in the other rooms and go shopping for more furniture. To my relief and surprise, Olivia chooses green for her bedroom. Later, I might hint that the lovely sunflowers would look nice on her wall. His decorators turn up and begin to paint the other two bedrooms. My next job, I think, will be to buy fabric to make curtains. No matter how lovely it is here, I like to be enclosed when the dark falls.

We leave the decorators getting on with things and walk around the perimeter of our field, which is full of dock and gorse. Whoever's been using the field hasn't approached me yet. Perhaps he's afraid I'm going to ask for thirty years' back rent! We snack at lunch time, and I cook a simple meal for the evening. I've yet to build up a good stock in the larder, and it seems the time has come for me to invest in transport. Not just for shopping but to see Olivia to school and back. It's a nice walk when the sun is shining but won't be so pleasant in winter, or when the storms break in from the Atlantic.

Later, Olivia and I snuggle companionably on the little sofa, Sophie between us. I always thought cats were independent, not caring who looked after them as long as they were warm and fed, but Sophie seems to have attached herself to Olivia; maybe because she's so young, Olivia has become her surrogate mother. I see a grown-up, maternal side to my daughter emerging with the arrival of the kitten, and she's enjoying the responsibility of taking care of something.

I remind myself that I'm still a young mother, learning as I go along. Perhaps with my next child I'll have a better idea of how to do it.

I'm glad Olivia doesn't see the flush that rises in my face at the thought I hadn't intended to think. Yes, Sean and I will make a go of it. And I have no doubt that he wants a family. I wonder at what stage Sean realised he was renovating this cottage for himself to move into, and how much of it he paid for himself.

I've been reading aloud to Olivia, but my eyes are tired. I stifle a yawn behind my hand. 'Bedtime,' I say, closing the book.

'When can I have a TV?'

'When we're settled.'

'You say that about everything. When can I move into my own bedroom?' she asks, adding cheekily, 'When we're settled.'

'Soon,' I say. 'We'll give it a few days for the paint fumes to go.'

'I like the smell of paint.'

'So do I, but it's not good to breathe in.' I shunt her from the sofa. 'Go on. Clean your teeth, get into bed and I'll follow you up.'

I bank up the fire, close the glass door and damp down the airflow. It will smoulder quietly, generating heat through the night. Although it's not quite autumn yet, the house doesn't feel warm. Sean mentioned putting a conservatory on the front again this morning. I'm beginning to see the attraction. I check the kitchen. I hate the empty windows at night. I keep catching movement and glance nervously at my own reflection. Although there's unlikely to be anyone out there, I imagine secret eyes peering in out of the darkness. I'll put curtains up as soon as possible. Or blinds, maybe.

I lock the front door and slowly ascend the bare wooden stairs. I'll be pleased when Olivia is in her own room, too. Then I can put in a wardrobe and maybe a dressing table. I'm sure the house will feel warmer, even if it's just an illusion, when I've cluttered it up a bit with fabrics and carpets, but I won't be in a hurry. I'll take my time to discover things I like. Mismatched treasures rather than the artistically arranged decor of Graham's showhouse that never felt like a home.

I lie awake for a while listening to the little snuffling noises Olivia makes, and the intermittent loud purring of the kitten, who's no doubt under the covers with her, despite my instructions to the contrary. I smile. It's a small concession in her world of confusing changes. How adaptable she is, I think proudly.

I finally drift, feeling peace in my soul, at last.

31

GRACE

Something clinks downstairs, and I'm jolted into a state where sleep and consciousness are confused. Had I really heard something? Maybe a log shifting in the wood burner. I'll check around in the morning. I'm comfortable, warm, dozing and think no more of it, not willing to risk the chill air, only to find nothing. I probably dreamed it, anyway. A car passes slowly outside the house, going down the hill towards Roone Bay, and I think kindly of the driver, who's obviously mindful not to rev the engine at this time of night in case people are sleeping.

I drift off again.

The muffled whoomph of an explosion pulls me into semi-wakefulness, the vibration tingling through my body. Why would I dream that? I don't know how long I lie there – seconds, minutes – before the realisation hammers into my mind that it wasn't a dream. I jump out of bed, barefoot on the carpet, in full-alert mode. I go to the bedroom door, a shadow in the strange red glow of moonlight, slip my feet into slippers and grab my dressing gown. I'm about to open the door and turn on the landing light so as not to wake Olivia, when I hear a distant roaring, like the sea when the storm is down.

I reach for the handle but halt as I see a flicker of light in the gap beneath the door. A blast of heat hits my ankles. 'Olivia,' I scream, pulling the covers back and heaving her out bodily. 'Wake up – now!'

It takes a moment for her eyes to focus. She comes to, slowly, groggily, safe because she's always been safe. I grab her dressing gown and carry her to the window. The garden is lit red by the flickering of a fire, and Olivia is fully awake, her eyes wide with fright.

'The house is on fire,' I say. 'Downstairs, and maybe underneath us. When I open the window, it might create a draft that sets this room alight.' While I'm warning, instructing, I'm ripping sheets from the bed. 'You need to hold on to this sheet, really tight, with both hands. When I open the window, I'm going to lift you out and lower you to the ground. Don't let go until your feet are on the ground. Do you understand?'

I speak in a strong, determined, no-nonsense voice that seems to come from someone else. She doesn't argue but clenches her fists firmly in the fabric. I wrench the window open, thrust her out and begin to lower her.

As I feared, the moment I open the window, a belch of flame rips under the door from the landing. The stairs, made of old wood, must be going up like kindling. I feel heat warming my slippers as I pass the sheet through my hands. Then the weight drops from the sheet. I lean out. Olivia is backing away from the house, safe, screaming, 'Mummy! Mummy!'

In the flickering light, her face is turned upwards, streaming with tears. I know a moment of relief, and throw out her slippers and dressing gown, and she runs forward and grabs them. 'Get right back to the road,' I yell.

There's nothing to tie the sheet to, so I heave the bed onto its side, and wrench it to the window. I don't waste time trying to rip the sheet. I tie the corner to one leg of the bed and pray it holds.

The bedroom door is ablaze.

The sheet isn't long enough, but it might lessen the height I have to drop. The terror of burning overrides any fear I might have of breaking bones. Then I remember Sophie. Oh God. Do I risk my life to save a kitten? But how can I not? I can't see her. There's only one place she can be.

I don't know where I find the strength. I leap across the room, flip Olivia's single bed on its side and grab the kitten, who's trying to claw her way into the carpet, terrified by the smoke and the smell. I throw my legs over the windowsill, fold over onto my stomach, the kitten in one hand, the sheet in the other. I slither over the edge, wrap my legs around the sheet and slide.

There's a blast below me as the living-room window explodes. Then flames are reaching up through the gaping hole. The sheet is on fire. There's a massive rushing and crashing inside as, presumably, the bed slips through the burning floor. I'm jerked upwards several feet, and the sheet is ripped from my grasp. I land heavily and hear something snap. I think it's my leg. My clothes are on fire. I use my hands to tamp out the flames and howl as the pain bites. Suddenly Olivia is beside me quenching the fire with her dressing gown. Her face is red in the firelight, blotched by tears and heat.

'Get away from the house,' I scream. 'Move! Move!'

She backs away, tears streaming down her face, her mouth open in a silent scream. Cinders fall and smoulder on my skin; the fire is too hot, I'm too close. I have to move. The pain is horrific as I roll over. I heave myself on my elbows towards the gap in the stone wall, grunting with the flashes of light that claw my skull every time my broken leg is dragged. When I'm through the gap, I flop, my cheek pressing against cool tarmac, fighting the blackout that's threatening to consume my consciousness.

My lungs hurt. Everywhere hurts. Olivia is almost hysterical, but she's in one piece. 'Come here,' I rasp and grab her hand as she crouches. 'It's okay, love. I'm alive. You're alive. It's going to be okay.'

'Oh, Mummy! Sophie,' she wails.

'I brought her out. I dropped her when I fell. We'll look for her in the morning. She'll be scared, hiding. We'll never find her in the dark.'

I hunch onto my elbows and turn my head in dazed fascination towards the raging fire. I shiver, recalling the boom of an explosion and the incredible speed with which the fire had taken hold. How I had known what to do is a miracle. I don't recall even thinking, just acting.

There's a car speeding up towards the house, its twin lights carving through a drifting cloud of black smoke. I don't know the elderly man who slides out and hobbles to us with a limping gait and worried expression. 'Are you all right? Is there anyone inside?'

'We're fine,' I say and give a hysterical laugh, because I'm not. 'I think I've broken my leg. There's no one inside.' If there had been, they'd be beyond help.

He bends to pat my shoulder. 'Good girrul, yerself. I heard an explosion, and I saw the flames from my bedroom. My wife has called the fire brigade – they'll be coming from Bantry – and an ambulance. Sure, you'll be grand, so you will.'

He stated that fact with righteous certainty, but actually, we're not going to be grand. We're alive, but I'm stunned. My dreams, my home. *My home*. Almost all of my money spent on the renovations, consumed. There's nothing left in me but fear for the future. The whole house is aflame, from the ground floor up through the roof. Even as we watch, part of the roof caves in, making the man beside me jump. 'Holy Mary,' he mutters and crosses himself.

Other cars arrive.

People jump out, and wrap me and Olivia in blankets. A

guard arrives and squats beside me to ask, 'Is there anyone inside?'

'No.' I shake my head.

'Okay, so. What happened?'

'I don't know. We were asleep. There was an explosion. But I don't see how. I damped the wood burner down. There's no way fire could have escaped from there. I thought I was dreaming then knew I wasn't. We got out of the window, and I fell.'

'Well, thank the Lord you got out,' he says.

But it wasn't the Lord; it was me. I did it. I got us out.

He's musing as he watches the fire. 'It must have been the gas. Seeping out, filling the room, then boom. You had no candles lit?'

'No, nothing.'

And it wasn't gas – I turned off the gas to the stove; I remember because I'm afraid of gas. With good reason, it seems.

Wailing sirens echo off the hills. I close my eyes. I'm almost incoherent with pain by the time I'm lifted onto a gurney and loaded into the ambulance. Someone asks, can I see two fingers or three, and did I bump my head at all? Then they're giving me something to deaden the pain. I hear them joke, wasn't I warm enough, and sure, did I have to light up the whole of Roone Bay?

'Olivia – my daughter?' I ask, light-headed as the drugs take hold.

'She's right here, don't panic. She has burns on her hands that need treating, but she'll be fine. She's here, with us.'

'She put out the fire on my clothes,' I murmur sleepily.

'Did she now? Well! What a brave one she is!'

Everything goes blurry. I'm vaguely aware of being driven somewhere, of being lifted from the vehicle and trolleyed through to an operating room. Kindly eyes peer down at me from behind a mask, and I'm told to count backwards from ten.

32

GRACE

I wake groggily to find myself in a recovery ward, being checked for vitals every few moments. Then I'm wheeled into a ward with several other beds, and eventually Sean is there, beside me, stroking the hair back from my face. 'Welcome back,' he says, smiling.

'Where am I?' My voice is croaky, my throat sore. I'm not sure whether that's from the operation or smoke from the fire.

'Bantry Hospital.'

'Olivia?'

'She's fine. They kept her overnight, then Jane came and brought her home. She's in good hands.'

Tears steam down my face at what might have been. I don't try to hide them. His rough hand rests on mine, strong and comforting, as he says, 'She was allowed to visit before they left. She knows you're all right. She saved you from some serious burns you know. What a great girleen she is! But, Jesus, woman!' he says as my eyes focus on his, and his hand tightens on mine. 'You just nearly gave me a heart attack. Don't you ever do that again!'

I try to smile. 'I'm sorry about the house. All that work you did.'

'No matter. It was fixed once; it can be again. And you got yourself and Olivia out, and yourself with just a broken leg. Holy Mary, you could both have died.'

'My leg – is it bad?'

'The doctor will tell you the details. They had to put pins in, or a plate, or something, so you won't be dancing in a hurry. But what in Heaven's name happened?'

I tell him what I'd told the guard then add, 'I remember, now, hearing a noise down in the house, before drifting back to sleep. I thought I'd imagined it, but maybe I didn't. And a car passed down the road. I don't know what time that was – after midnight, in the early hours. I could see the moon. And stars.'

He's silent for a moment, contemplative.

'The investigator from the insurance company is coming down to check the site. I'm wondering what he might find. And the guard will be in to take a statement from you soon. Be sure to tell him about the noise you heard, and the car.'

'I will, though I didn't see anything useful.' Then I latch on to the first part of his sentence. 'Insurance? My house wasn't insured. I hadn't got around to that yet.'

'I always insure the job I'm working on until it's signed off. It's a legal requirement, but this is the first time I'm grateful to have paid out that cursed premium. But what's bothering me is how darn close it was. It doesn't bear thinking about. The fire officer says the explosion was under Olivia's room, from what he can tell, so if she'd been sleeping in there... God almighty!'

I shudder, feeling sick. If she'd been in her own room... My imagination is too good at writing a whole scenario in an instant.

Sean says, 'It was lucky I'd put insulation between the floor joists, too, and under the stairs. The old houses never had that. It must have held the fire back from the bedroom just long enough...' He peters into silence then adds, 'So, who would want you dead?'

A noise starts to buzz inside my head. 'No one,' I say in bewilderment. 'Maybe it was some vandal who hadn't known I'd moved in. No one would set fire to a house with people in it, surely? And a child. Does Graham know what happened? Olivia's his daughter – he should be told.'

'The guards have sent word to England, to check out where he is.'

'*Graham?* He... he... No, he wouldn't...'

He shrugs. 'Who else?'

I think out loud. 'Perhaps he didn't know we'd moved in. Perhaps he thought if the house was gone, we'd go home. Olivia is his daughter; he wouldn't harm her.'

'I have to go now,' he says, looking beyond me. He pecks a light kiss on my cheek. 'I've outstayed my welcome, and the hospital cops are about to kick me out. I'll bring Olivia in tomorrow. Oh, and I went up to the house to have a look around. I just couldn't believe it was something I did wrong, with the gas bottle and the cooker, or the wood burner, I mean. No way; I've done loads. But while I was there, I found Sophie. Not a scratch on her. I took her back to Olivia. They both seemed pretty happy about that!'

'Thank you.' I tear up again.

I blink hard as the surgeon advances, a clutch of nurses in attendance. I'm kept in for two days, for observation, as I have a nasty gash on my head, which has been stitched up, and which I don't recall getting. Maybe when I dropped to the ground. I have a splatter of cuts from the exploding glass, but thankfully I wasn't in the direct line when the window blew. I have some second-degree burns they'll want to keep an eye on, and although the hospital staff don't seem too worried about them, they hurt more than my leg. Apparently, I was lucky with the broken leg. The jagged bone didn't snag any major vessels, which could have killed me before the ambulance got there. I'm lucky to be alive on many counts.

The guard, Sean's second cousin it turns out, comes and asks searching questions about Graham and Arthur, and about my reasons for running from my husband, and why I came to West Cork. I'm as honest as I can be but wonder whether Graham is really the kind of monster who would burn his wife and child to death. Surely not. But then, his first wife died under mysterious circumstances. I tell the guard about that, too.

I'm let out on the third day, and Sean comes in with some clothes that Jane bought, to take me home.

'Where's home?' I grumble.

'Noel's, of course. He won't hear of anything else.'

I have to accept a nurse's help to get dressed, and they had to cut the leg of the new tracksuit trousers to get it over the cast that immobilises me from ankle to thigh.

I should count my blessings, as Grandma would say, but what I am, truly, is shocked. I know how controlling Graham is, and I knew to be wary of him when I tried to leave; but to try to burn me and his own child to death rather than lose some of his wealth in a divorce? The more I think about it, even after Margery's horrible revelation, I don't want to believe Graham capable of such an act. He's a pretentious social climber with no natural empathy when dealing with people, but could I have lived with him for seven years and failed to see the monster beneath the single-minded workaholic?

Sean has borrowed Noel's car to take me back. He helps to heave me onto the back seat and settles my cast along its length. 'Comfortable?'

'Not really.'

'Hmm. Well, it's your own fault. If you will go jumping out of upstairs windows.'

He drives back to Roone Bay slowly, navigating around the potholes to avoid jolting me.

When we arrive at Noel's, he pulls the door open, and Olivia tries to throw herself on top of me. I wince as she bumps my burns and wraps her arms so tightly around my neck that I'm half strangled. Her hands are so thickly wrapped in bandages they look like white boxing gloves.

There are tears on both our faces as I untangle her. 'Your poor hands,' I say.

'It's not as bad as they thought,' Sean comments.

'Shall we go in first and cuddle after?' I ask.

'Sure,' Olivia and Sean say at the same time.

'Come on, lovey, off your mum...' Sean gently lifts Olivia to let me wriggle out. 'Apparently, she has only first-degree burns on her left hand, so she'll have that one back in a couple of weeks. The right is a bit more serious, but they don't think she'll need skin grafts.'

Sean assists me to my feet and slips crutches under my armpits. I feel surprisingly energised by the love that surrounds me. He hovers protectively as I negotiate the steps to the front door, and I ease myself onto the sofa in the big living room with a sigh of relief.

'I'm sorry to put you out all over again, just when you thought you'd got rid of us,' I say to Noel with a grimace.

'Well, it wasn't me that wanted you to go in the first place,' he reminds me. 'So, you're back, and I'm not sorry, though, sure, it wasn't me who put you through that for the privilege of your company.'

I grin. 'I hope not.'

'And don't worry. Jane is happy out, minding Olivia. She's going to stay in the house as long as we need her, at least until Olivia can eat and dress herself. Thank goodness your hands weren't burned.'

My hands are sore, scratched and red, but I suspect that will disappear soon enough. The burns on my stomach and legs, thanks to Olivia, are minimal. 'What a real treasure she is,' I murmur to no one in particular, but I know she's heard, as a secret little smile tickles the corners of her lips.

'Okay, so,' Sean says. 'I'm off home to change, then I'll go out to collect your mother and grandmother from the bus.'

'They're not coming for a week yet!'

Noel says, 'Sean phoned your mother and told her what had happened. They started out the next day, as soon as they could get a ferry booking. They're in Ireland already and on their way south.'

Sean adds, walking to the door, 'The Cork bus will arrive in Skibbereen at about four. I don't want to keep them waiting. See you in an hour or so, if the bus is on time.'

'Are they booked into the hotel?'

'They are,' Noel says, 'but I told Sean to bring them here, of course. We're not short of rooms.'

'Poor Jane,' I comment.

'Heh! She loves the bustle. The more the merrier!'

Sure enough, as we're waiting, Jane fusses over Olivia and me, asking every few minutes if there's anything we need.

I feel like a child waiting for Christmas. I didn't see Mum or Grandma so often while I was married, but being here, in Ireland, the distance makes their absence so much more poignant. I'd been wondering how and when I'd see them again. I don't know why I assumed it was me who would have to go to England. When Mum wrote to say they were going to come over, she said Grandma seemed a bit nostalgic about seeing where she was born. I know now, though, that it's not just the pull of her old home compelling her to visit but the thought of seeing her one-time lover. I cross my fingers that the meeting won't be one huge disaster.

33

GRACE

Noel's waiting with me in the lounge as the car turns up. We hear the bustle of their arrival, the front door opening, then the living room door bursts open, and Mum dives at me, giving me a big hug. 'Oh, darling!' she says, on her knees, crying. Then she pulls Olivia into an embrace with her other arm. Her tears are infectious, and I have to wipe my eyes.

I glimpse Grandma hovering in the doorway, as tall and sturdy as the girl Noel must recall from all those years ago.

When Mum releases us, Grandma leans down and gives me a soft kiss on the forehead. 'What a welcome home,' she says. 'For me, I mean. All this fuss and botheration. To nearly lose my granddaughter and my great-granddaughter in a fire. Well! It's going to take me a month of Sundays to get over it.' But she doesn't sound stressed. She sounds excited. 'And finding out that Noel is alive, after all. Well, that was a shock, I can tell you. Connor told me Noel had died in America, and that's where the money came from to buy the house.'

Noel is staring at her as she rises, and I see her as he must: her face lined with age, her eyes as blue and bright as ever. 'It was a gift,' he said, frowning, 'not a legacy.'

There's no hesitancy in her voice as she remarks, 'Well, well, Noel. It is you, after all. I didn't think it could be. I mean, I thought you were passed from this life. Connor told me, a long time ago, that you died in America. I had no reason to think he'd lie about that.'

Noel crosses the room in long strides and takes her hands in his. 'Caitlin,' he says, in a long, drawn-out sigh. 'This is difficult, and so very, very strange. Connor told me you'd died in childbirth. That's why I went to America. I didn't know what to do with myself. I thought I wanted to die.'

'Ah,' she says sadly. 'That makes it all clear, doesn't it?'

'He loved you so much.'

She grimaces but agrees. 'Yes, he did. He was a good husband, a good father and an exceptional grandfather. He said, once, he'd do anything to keep me, and it seems he meant it.'

Mum and I are staring at them, entranced. Then Grandma sighs and says, to the room in general, 'Well, this seems like an auspicious moment for revelations,' then almost to herself, 'I might as well get it over with.'

'Get what over with?' Mum asks, concerned.

Grandma's eyes are on Noel. 'I ran off to England with Connor because I was already pregnant.'

There's a long pause, while I'm thinking, *Well, there's nothing strange in that*, until she adds, 'It was your child, Noel. That's why I needed to marry quickly and leave, what with you already married. Connor saved me – and our child – from the nuns and their everlasting damnation.'

There's a stunned silence in the room, then Mum says, 'Dad wasn't my father?'

'He was your father in every way that mattered, love,' Grandma reprimands, turning to her. 'He loved you. He just wasn't your biological father. Noel is.'

'Oh, goodness,' Mum says, looking from one to the other.

Noel finally finds his voice, and is half laughing, half crying, as he says, 'Caitlin! You always enjoyed being the centre of attention, and you haven't changed a jot! I thought you were dead these fifty years, and you waltz in, as beautiful as ever, and tell me I have a family! Oh Lord.'

'I would have told you sooner, if I'd known you were alive,' she says, her amusement betraying the vibrant girl she must have been when Noel was madly in love with her all those years ago. Then I look at his face, and realise he's still in love with her, after all.

'Sure, it will take some getting used to,' she says. 'Of course, I loved Connor and miss him. He was a fantastic father and a loyal husband, but he always knew he was my second choice. I suppose that's why he lied. He always hoped I'd have his children, too, give you some siblings, Anne, but it never happened. Now' – Grandma's face opens into a beaming smile as she catches our eyes, one by one – 'Anne needs time with Grace and Olivia. They must have a lot to catch up on, and Noel and I have rather a lot to discuss, too.'

'Sure, sure,' Noel says, more flustered than I've ever seen him.

'I don't understand,' Olivia says plaintively.

I give a hysterical hiccup. 'It turns out that Uncle Noel is Grandma's father, which means he's my grandfather and your great-grandfather. We're all his family.'

She thinks about this for a moment. 'Does that mean we can stay and live here in the nice house?'

I can't contain my laughter. 'Olivia, we're going to live in our own house, once it's been rebuilt. After that, we'll see what happens.'

'Shall we take a turn around the garden?' Noel says to Grandma.

She reaches for his proffered hand and allows him to lead her from the room. To say they have a lot to catch up on is an understatement! Two whole lifetimes, in fact. But they're only in their early seventies, or thereabouts, and still have quite a few years ahead of them; ten, twenty, even more, if they're lucky. They deserve a bit of luck, I think. But, in a way, I'm glad Noel didn't find out about Caitlin before Grandpa Connor died. Connor will always be my grandfather, in everything except genes.

Sean has been standing in the doorway giving us space to meet and greet, but his face has dropped in surprise at the revelation. He stands aside, bemused, as Noel leads Caitlin past him, then comes to sit on the arm of the sofa I'm reclining on, my plastered leg taking up the rest of the space.

'So,' he says, ticking things off finger by finger, 'let me get this right. Your gran is Noel's one-time lover, your mother is his daughter, you're his granddaughter and he doesn't have any other heirs? Right. Now I get it. Darn.'

I frown. 'Darn?'

'You're going to be rich. Everyone is going to believe I knew that, and that I'm some kind of gold digger.'

I chuckle. 'He might leave everything to a dog shelter, yet. Inheritance is a privilege, not a right.'

'But still. Now, you are going to marry me, aren't you? Despite having such important connections?'

I burst out laughing. 'I'm already married, don't forget.'

'Well, the sooner we deal with that, the better.'

He stands and turns to Mum. 'Hello, I'm Sean, just in case you've forgotten. I'm going to marry your daughter. I do hope that's all right?'

'Oh, goodness,' Mum says. 'This is a bit of a soap opera. I suddenly find that my father isn't my father, and now I'm going to acquire a new son-in-law whether I like it or not.' She places a theatrical hand on her breast. 'I need time to recover from the shock.'

She doesn't look shocked, though; she looks amused. I guess the shock will cut in later.

Supper is a strange affair. We're all there, including Sean, the old and new families laughing and joking, like relatives at a wedding who haven't seen each other for decades. I glance around from time to time, watching these animated faces, wondering how it's all going to pan out. Noel tells Mum and Grandma that they're to stay with him, in Roone House, and that Jane has already made beds up for them – they accept it with equanimity, just another strange thing in a strange day. He asks Sean, would he mind running a message to the hotel to say he'll pay the bill?

Sean tips his imaginary cap and says, 'Yes, your lordship; right away, sir.'

Noel grins. I suspect Sean's lack of respect is a novelty for him.

'So,' Sean adds, 'I'll be leaving you to it for tonight. Mother will be wondering where I am.' He pauses at the doorway. 'Don't worry, I won't be running my mouth off.'

'Oh, whatever,' Noel says. 'Let the vine do its work. Caitlin O'Driscoll is finally going to marry me. It's best everyone knows.'

34

GRACE

It's strange to be waking up in Noel's house again, recalling the events of the last couple of days. Yet once I'm up and about, it feels as though things were always meant to be this way. It's as though fate has conspired to bring us all together, in the end.

Over breakfast, Grandma tells us that Noel's going to take her back to England to collect her things and put her affairs in order. They'll pay a last visit to Connor's grave and tell him they bear him no ill will, that they realise he did what he did for love. Then she'll return forever to live out her life in her native Ireland, in Roone Bay, the place she was born. But how she has been elevated, she says, from a cottage with no running water or anything else, to live in style in Roone Manor, which had been a ruin in her day... It was all grand, so it was.

Grandma has always been a dynamic and active lady, one who'd dominated her late husband in a quiet but immutable fashion. But I see a new stillness about her now, as though, for the first time in years, the need to rush through life has evaporated.

Mum hasn't decided what to do; it's all too new and confusing, but I suspect she'll come over to Ireland, too, in the end.

After all, if her mother and daughter and granddaughter are here, not to mention a father she had no idea existed before a day ago, she'll have no relatives left in England. But she needs to make that decision for herself. Uprooting herself, leaving her home, her friends, and starting off in a new country is a big deal. But the money from her house will buy her a nice, warm, modern home over here; she doesn't need to be dependent upon anyone else.

Noel takes Grandma and Mum out for a drive, to show them the town, the quay, the old graveyard and the house where Grandpa was born – a wreck once more – from behind the warmth of the car windows. I can imagine them exclaiming over the burned timbers, shuddering over the near tragedy.

I'm standing at the front door on crutches when Sean arrives with his cousin, the guard, in an official vehicle. Noel is following close behind, escorting his new-found true love and his new-found daughter back into the house.

The guard looks far too young to be a guard, I think, as he unwinds a tall frame from the driver's seat, looking like a schoolboy in a uniform that's too big for him. He has a shock of red hair, which sticks out every which way from under his flat cap. As Noel calls a greeting and instructs him to come on in, he removes the cap, puts it under his arm like a soldier and gives a strange little bow. Awed, no doubt, by being in the presence of the legendary Noel O'Donovan.

Sean says, 'Grace, do you remember Colm? He visited you in the hospital after the fire.'

'Of course,' I say and shake his hand awkwardly.

'I'm sorry for your troubles,' Colm says, squeezing my hand gently before letting go. 'You look better than last time I saw you.'

Noel invites them to share lunch with us. Apparently, the guard has news to share.

When we're all seated, and Jane has smothered the table in

far too much food, he begins, and gradually his shyness recedes. 'On the night of the fire, there was a witness,' he says, adding with a faint smile, 'Andrew was out on the poitín and stumbling home, so I don't think he'd come to much in court. He said he saw a big silver Rolls-Royce with an English number plate driving quietly down your road. He doesn't know what time it was, but it would have been in the early hours of the morning.'

I gasp. *Was it Graham, after all?*

'Wait,' Sean warns.

The guard looks directly at me. 'Your husband, Graham Adams, was in Northern Ireland, so he was picked up over the border and questioned. On the night of the fire, he'd been in an evening meeting with a business acquaintance, in a hotel. They can both be accounted for, by unbiased witnesses. He physically couldn't have been here.'

'But what about the silver Rolls?'

'Well, once we knew your husband couldn't have been the perpetrator, Sean here told us about Arthur, so we asked the English police to look into him for us.'

Sean casts me a sympathetic glance and takes up the story. 'It seems that a boy with Arthur's description hired a silver Rolls-Royce for a week, apparently for a wedding. The vehicle was then traced to a ferry booking to Ireland two days before the fire.'

'Arthur did it?' I whisper.

'I had my doubts about that boy,' Noel comments, evincing satisfaction in being proved right.

'But *murder*?' Mum says, stunned.

'God save us,' Grandma says, crossing herself. 'And there was me and your mum believing his sad story about wanting to see his little sister so much. And it was us sent the murdering little shite here!'

I choke on a laugh. I've never heard her use language like that before.

Sean barely hides his grin, and Colm continues. 'But the worst of it is, it seems he was trying to lay the blame on his own father, otherwise why wait until his father was in Ireland and hire a silver Rolls-Royce? Lucky for your husband, his meeting in Belfast was delayed, and he had to stay longer than he intended. When we looked deeper into Arthur's background, we found that his mother had died in suspicious circumstances in Spain. He and his father were questioned at the time, and the Spanish police were concerned about Arthur's involvement, but there wasn't enough evidence to convict him.'

'I thought it was Graham who was under suspicion in Spain?' I query.

Colm shakes his head. 'Graham was questioned, but Arthur was with his mother at the time. Apparently, they were on jet skis at a coastal holiday resort. The story was that she fell off, and he ran her down by accident. There were no witnesses. You know what it's like at the seaside. Everyone doing their own thing. No one saw what happened. Despite horrific injuries, she might have been rescued, but by the time the boy came in, screaming for help, she'd drowned.'

'Jesus,' Sean muttered.

So, the suspicion had been on Arthur, not Graham? Had Arthur subtly pointed the finger at his father by leaving me those newspaper cuttings to find, knowing I didn't understand Spanish?

'The English police have brought him in, and they're gathering evidence to charge him with attempted murder,' Colm added.

'But why?' I say in wonder.

'Inheritance,' Noel states. 'Graham ended up with his late wife's fortune, and it seems Arthur thought it should have been his. With his father out of the way, he could take charge of the business and the money, and with you and Olivia gone, he would be the sole heir, eventually. If he'd killed Graham while you were alive, you would have inherited a large part of Graham's fortune. But if you were dead, and Graham in prison for your murder, he pretty much had control of everything.'

The guard was nodding. 'That's the conclusion we came to.'

'I wasn't going to ask Graham for anything at all.'

'No, when my colleagues interrogated Graham in Northern Ireland, he confirmed that. He also told us he'd given most of his ex-wife's legacy to the man she'd been living with, because he thought that was what she would have wanted. Maybe if he suspected Arthur of murdering his mother, it was a kind of recompense to her lover, and one in the eye for his son at the same time.'

'Arthur didn't know he'd given the money away,' I comment.

It was a philanthropic gesture I wouldn't have expected, either.

'So, your Graham has some redeeming features, after all,' Sean says, glancing at me with a twisted smile. 'But I still don't think you should go back to him.'

'I thought Arthur liked us; me and Olivia?' I'm still struggling to believe he would try to murder us.

'He was devious enough to pretend to like you if it suited him,' Noel reminds me.

'Yes, but he must have been living that pretence since Olivia was born.'

'Biding his time,' Colm says.

'Yes, but murder!'

'Well, he's in custody now, and I suspect he'll go down for it. There are some legal hurdles, as the attempted murder was done here, in Ireland, and it's the English police who have him in custody, but they're pretty sure everything adds up. We're putting feelers out to see if anyone down here saw the car. Plus, he was in Ireland for two days, so he must have stayed somewhere. I think a jury will convict him on circumstantial evidence alone.'

When the subdued lunch is over, Sean and Colm make their farewells. Colm turns to me and adds, 'Oh, by the way, your husband said he'd fund the rebuild of your house, as it was Arthur who destroyed it. He's going to forward some money to your bank account over here.'

He knows I have a bank account? I shake my head. And I thought I was being so clever, using my maiden name. He probably knew about the account in England, too, where my allowance had been adding up. I doubt he'd suspected I'd been planning to leave him, though; his narcissistic tendencies would never have allowed for that possibility.

Later, when Sean and Colm have gone, Olivia is in bed, and Mum and Grandma have retired, I sit a while in the lounge, pretending to read, trying to unwind. It's been a strange day. I close my eyes, exhausted, and when I open them again, I find Noel in the big wing-back chair beside me. 'I'm sorry to put you to all this inconvenience,' I say.

He puts his newspaper down. 'Oh, sure, it's the best time I've had in years! One day I was rattling around in this barn of a place with just the dogs for company, and the next I discover I have four generations of family. I've discovered Caitlin, who I thought had passed a long time ago. I met my daughter for the first time, and found out that you and Olivia are my family, after all. It's been surreal, to say the least.'

'That would be a nice conclusion to your memoir,' I say.

'Maybe. But when you told me Caitlin was alive, I was incredibly hurt. Her being faithful to Connor all that time, I understand, but I wondered why she hadn't looked me up after he died. I wondered if perhaps our love had been more real for me than for her. I was quite grateful to discover that she didn't know I was alive, either.' His mouth compresses slightly, and he shakes his head, 'What a mess! When I go to the good Lord above, I'm going to give that Connor a piece of my mind!' He chuckles at a private thought.

'What?' I say, smiling in response.

'It occurred to me to visit Connor, in Birmingham, after he told me that Caitlin had died, so we could get drunk together and grieve for her. It's just as well I didn't!'

We both bubble over with laughter, but in fact, if he'd turned up in Birmingham, it would have been disastrous for everyone. Caitlin's and Connor's marriage would have broken up, and no one would have ended up happy.

Suddenly I'm crying for real. I'm overwhelmed, spinning between a wild range of emotions. Olivia nearly died, I nearly died, Arthur tried to kill us, Grandma's discovered her childhood sweetheart and now I have a new family.

Noel understands. He leans over and strokes my hair. 'Just take your time, Grace, a stór; it will all come clear. There's no hurry. You know, when I first saw you, I was puzzled by the strange sense of familiarity I experienced, and had the peculiar thought that we might well have met somewhere before. I knew we hadn't, of course. But you do remind me so much of your grandmother, you know.'

'And maybe yourself, a little!' I hiccup on a laugh.

My tears finally dry into a sigh, and he adds, 'There's something still bothering you?'

'You know, I feel sorry for Graham, actually. We all got excited about discovering each other, but he's lost all his family in one fell swoop.'

'He still has Olivia.'

'Yes, we must make sure we consolidate that, for both of them. Who knows, she might one day find she wants to go back to Cheltenham, maybe even inherit the business, after all. And, you know, I want to feel sorry for Arthur, too, because of his harsh childhood.'

Noel grimaces. 'From what you've told me, I doubt his childhood was great. But he was prepared to kill you and Olivia, and frame his own father for your murder, just for money. There's no excusing that kind of evil.'

I hide a wide yawn behind my hand. 'I think it's time I took myself off to bed.'

'Can you do the stairs on your own?'

'I have the crutches – and the banister. I had to do stairs in the hospital before they'd let me out.'

'Sleep well, Granddaughter.'

I smile. 'You too, Grandfather.'

As I lie there, nursing my burns and cuts and broken leg, and lamenting the loss of my home, I really do count my blessings. My physical condition is more than adequately balanced by my mental state, which I can only describe, for the first time in years, as content. I have family I didn't know about. Grandma and Noel have rediscovered each other. Graham isn't a total monster, after all. I still don't like him very much, but if I hadn't married him, I wouldn't have Olivia, and maybe I wouldn't have come to Ireland and discovered Noel and Sean.

Life has a funny way of going about things.

A LETTER FROM DAISY

Thank you so much for reading *The Irish Key*. I would love it if you kept up to date with all my novels and any other significant news from Bookouture, so do make sure to sign up at the following link. Your email address will never be shared, and you can unsubscribe at any time.

www.bookouture.com/daisyoshea

While writing this story, I became very involved with Grace's disappointment in life. Her hope that life must hold something better is a trope I suspect many women can associate with. While I threw some fairly hefty stumbling blocks in her path, I was rooting for her the whole time, and I was pleased when her underlying strength of character won out in the end.

Creating a work of fiction is to take a blank page and splash emotion upon it, layer by layer, investing fictional characters with trials, tribulations and the inherent strengths that ultimately lead to fulfilment. I absolutely relish discovering new characters, finding out what made them that way and learning how they claw their way to happiness. One of the greatest joys in writing – and reading – lies in discovering that satisfactory conclusion.

One of my most gratifying experiences as an author is to know that readers enjoyed the novel and closed the last pages with a sigh of satisfaction. If you did, then I'm thrilled! I'd be delighted if you would leave a review to let other readers know how much you enjoyed the story. Be sure, though, to dwell on the characterisation, the writing style and your own emotional responses, and don't give away any critical plot points.

I've lived in West Cork for many years, and it's been the most fulfilling time of my life. The wild countryside, the rocky seashores, the call of the sea, the scarred history, the underlying myths and legends, and most of all, the inclusive warmth of the dauntless Irish people. There's a wisp of fey here that subtly underpins all our lives; the magic of Ireland that quietly infuses my stories.

I do hope you're looking forward to my next book as much as I'm enjoying writing it.

All the best, Daisy

www.ChrisLewando.com

facebook.com/DaisyOSheaAuthor
x.com/westcorkwriter

I'LL TAKE YOU HOME AGAIN, KATHLEEN

I'll take you home again, Kathleen
Across the ocean wild and wide
To where your heart has ever been
Since you were first my bonnie bride.
The roses all have left your cheek.
I've watched them fade away and die
Your voice is sad when e'er you speak
And tears bedim your loving eyes.

Oh! I will take you back, Kathleen
To where your heart will feel no pain
And when the fields are fresh and green
I'll take you to your home again!

To that dear home beyond the sea
My Kathleen shall again return.
And when thy old friends welcome thee
Thy loving heart will cease to yearn.
Where laughs the little silver stream
Beside your mother's humble cot
And brightest rays of sunshine gleam
There all your grief will be forgot.

— *THOMAS PAINE WESTENDORF*
(1848–1923)

AUTHOR'S NOTES

DISCLAIMER

Roone Bay isn't a real town, and any individual homes and hotels mentioned are fabrications. There are many families in the area with the surnames I've chosen to use, but any similarity to real persons, alive or dead, is entirely coincidental. All views in the work are those of the characters, not the author.

OVERVIEW OF IRELAND

Ireland is divided into the four provinces: Connacht, Leinster, Munster and Ulster. There are cities and towns, but the term 'village' isn't used. Within the provinces, there are thirty-two counties containing around 64,000 townlands: historic areas that once might have been clan boundaries, and which can be anything between approximately 100 to 500 acres. Roone Bay is set on the southern coast of Ireland, in the mythical townland of Tírbeg, somewhere between Bantry and Skibbereen.

PRONUNCIATION

a stór: *ash-tore* (my love)
a chara: *a (as in apple) kaara* (my love/close friend)
Caitlin:*Kat-leen*
Finola: *Finn-oh-lah*

Poitín: *Po (as in pot)-cheen* (the Irish distilled liquor)
Roisin: *Rocheen*
Sean: *Shawn*
Sinéad: *Shin-ade*
Tírbeg: *Teer-beg*

ACKNOWLEDGEMENTS

My thanks go first to my husband, Robin, who's believed in me in every way from the moment we met. A staunch supporter of my passion for writing, he's the first critic of my work, my best friend and also my 'til-death-us-do-part love. Thanks to my lovely mother, Alma Yea, one-time librarian, for encouraging me to read fiction when I was a child. Thanks to Susannah Hamilton for seeing something in my writing that persuaded her to offer me publication with Bookouture and to her whole team, who manage the process so efficiently. Thanks to Angela Snowden for being an absolutely nit-picky editor and suggesting modifications in the most sensitive manner possible, to LaDonna, who has a keen eye for continuity, and Anne Hayes, who added her pertinent and often amusing editorial views. And last, but certainly not least, thanks to all the readers who enjoy my fiction. Without you, my work would be pointless, so don't be afraid to reach out and provide me with that much-needed reassurance that my stories have been enjoyed.

PUBLISHING TEAM

Turning a manuscript into a book requires the efforts of many people. The publishing team at Bookouture would like to acknowledge everyone who contributed to this publication.

Commercial
Lauren Morrissette
Jil Thielen
Imogen Allport

Data and analysis
Mark Alder
Mohamed Bussuri

Cover design
Dissect Designs

Editorial
Susannah Hamilton
Nadia Michael

Copyeditor
Angela Snowden

Proofreader
Laura Kincaid

Printed in Great Britain
by Amazon